Tell Me a Story

Cover by Colleen Nye

Editing by Pam Bollier and Loraine Hudson

Formatting by Colleen Nye

© 2016, 2018 Randy D Pearson

Second Edition 2018

EdcoCaly Press

Olivet, MI

This is a work of fiction. All characters and situations appearing in this work are fictitious. Any resemblance to real persons, living or dead, or personal situations is purely coincidental.

Dedication

To Wendy –
I waited a lifetime to find you,
but you were worth the wait.

Chapter List & Short Story Page Reference

~ Chapter One ~

"Tell me a story!" My wife peers up at me from beneath the thick comforter, her smile radiant.

I hear these simple yet powerful words all the time. They pop up when we're on the town or in the car, but more often than not, she says this to me at bedtime. Sometimes I'm already in bed and halfway to sleep before she whispers the request to me. Other times, like today, I've barely walked through the bedroom door. Though I'm a bit weary from a long day, I just can't say no to my beautiful bride.

"Okay," I say as I climb into bed next to her, and place my right hand gently on her leg – or what I assume is her leg. It might be a cat. "Once upon a time, there was a beautiful princess. One day, while traveling through the forest, she ran across a large, green dragon."

Pursing her lips, she says, "If your next words are anything like, 'The dragon ate the princess. The end,' I'm gonna go sleep on the couch."

"Ouch!" She knows that's a seriously painful threat to me. It took the first year of our marriage to realize two important facts about her. One, she loves sleeping on the couch. It's like camping to her, only a lot more comfortable with fewer mosquitoes and crawly critters. I also learned that my wife falls asleep on the couch at least once a week while watching TV, reading a book, crocheting, snuggling a kitty, or playing a game on her phone. Once she's asleep, forget it. She's there for the duration. I had to train myself not to take it personally. Of course, she now knows that's one of my buttons. I give her my best smirk. "No sweetie, of course not. I would never let a dragon eat you."

"I should hope not. It's not very original," she says with a scowl. "That's what my kids always do during story time. I've been eaten by dragons, bears, llamas, and tigers. Even a sloth once devoured me in one of their stories." Man, story time at her daycare sounds far too painful!

I snuggle in close to my wife, and give her a squeeze. "I promise that no harm will ever come to you in one of my stories. I've spent my whole life searching for you. Now that I've found you, no sloth's gonna chow down on my wife."

Smiling, she replies, "I'm glad to hear that, because I'm far too comfy at the moment to head out to the couch." After giving me a smooch on my right cheek, she says, "Okay, continue with your story."

Honestly, I have no clue where I was going with that dragon story. She probably would've been eaten, truth be told. So, I decide to switch gears. "Nah, forget the dragon, I have a much better story for you."

~ The Morning After ~

Monte yawned loudly, various joints popping in unison while he stretched. As he lay there, listening to the rumbling of a lawn mower somewhere in the distance, something seemed amiss. That lawn mower sounded awfully loud.

He lifted his head and peered around. Astonishment jolted through him when he realized he had been sleeping on the front lawn.

"Morning," his neighbor yelled over the growl of his riding mower, a smug smile upon his pudgy, middle-aged face.

Yawning again, Monte sheepishly waved at him. As the 25-year-old pulled himself to his feet and trudged toward the house, he fumbled for his keys. He frowned when he realized they were not in his pocket. As he looked down, another realization hit him. He had no pants on.

Underwear, thank goodness, but no jeans. Thinking back, Monte felt fairly certain he left the house fully clothed. He rooted around the garden for the spare key, finding it under the fakest-looking fake rock in the garden.

After stumbling in the front door and toppling over the futon, Monte got up, ran a hand through his thick, curly blonde hair, and grabbed the telephone. He knew he went to a party with Jennie, Jason, and Ben. He started with Ben.

Benjamin Watkins neared the climax of a fantastic dream. Though he did not recognize the girl, she sure seemed smitten with him. Then this annoying ringing noise began blaring out of her mouth. It really killed the mood.

Once Ben woke up, he glared at the ringing telephone. His gaze hit the caller ID, saw the name, and smiled through the hangover he just realized he had. "Monte," he croaked past parched lips, "up so soon?"

"A man can only sleep so long on the lawn. So, Ben, any idea where my pants are?"

Ben, while slogging toward the kitchen replied, "Y'know, I was wondering that very same thing. I wasn't with you for a lot of the evening." The young man with the amazingly unkempt hair, black as a moonless night, stared for a moment at a dirty glass before filling it with tap water. After taking a swig, he added, "You were definitely in rare form last night, dude!"

Still exhausted, Monte flopped down on the futon. "Okay, let's start from the beginning."

"Right," Ben replied. "I was born in a horse stall in Wyoming. My parents –"

"Shut up," Monte yelled with a snicker. "Now then, you, me, Jen, and Jason went up to Carl's farm, right?"

3

"Yup. Huge party. Live bands, bonfire, a keg or two. A regular slice of Americana."

Monte paused, trying to piece things together. "Okay, so, we got to the party. I had a beer or two -"

"Dude," his friend interrupted, "try like five."

"I'm getting there. I remember the band, Triple Dog Dare. They rocked hard."

"Yeah they did. You did shots with them after their set."

"Shots?" Monte had to concentrate on that one, but with some effort, those events seeped from his brain. "Right, gelatin shots. Ew! I hate Jell-O shots. Why did you let me do 'em, Ben?"

Chuckling, he replied, "Like anyone can stop you from doing anything. Besides, at that point I wandered off. I ended up playing Hacky-Sack with a bunch of teenagers. A surreal evening, to be sure."

"So, when you last saw me, I had pants?"

Ben laughed loudly, even though it hurt his head immensely to do so. Once he regained his composure, he answered, "I'm reasonably confident you had pants on, yes. When I came back to the car, you had passed out on the hood, pants-less. So, I dunno, but when I wandered off, I believe Jen was still hanging with ya."

"All right, man," Monte said as he got up and moseyed toward the kitchen, "I'll try her next. But hey, thanks for getting me home okay."

Ben had no clue how anyone got home safely, but he did not mind taking the credit. "No prob, dude. Later." Dropping the phone onto the floor, he turned and flopped face first on the couch.

Jennie felt rather impressed with herself. At the biggest, wildest party of the year, she got home late but still woke up nice and early, feeling spectacular. The fact that she nursed a beer the whole evening filled her with pride. After all, someone had to be the driver and she knew it would not be any of the boys, especially Monte.

The ringing phone interrupted her train of thought, but she smiled when Monte said hello. "I was just thinking about you, Monte. How ya feelin' today?"

"Like a man without pants who slept in the yard."

The pretty redhead giggled. "That would make a good saying."

Under different circumstances, Monte Parsons might have been annoyed with the whole situation. However, one thing that Monte excelled at, other than drinking himself half-naked, was finding the humor in any situation, so he laughed. "So, Jen, I'm trying to piece together the events that led to my de-pantsing. I'm just praying that there was a dynamite blonde in the mix somewhere."

"You mean a woman, right?"

After they both stopped laughing, he replied, "Uh, yah. That'd be a lot easier for me to live with." After a momentary pause, he added, "Last I recall I was doing Jell-O shots with the band."

"Yup, I was there. You were really putting 'em down. And here I thought you hated Jell-O."

"I do. Vile stuff. Why'd ya let me do 'em?"

"Like anyone can stop you from doing anything."

Ooo, deja vu, he thought. "Okay, so what happened next?"

"Well, lessee," Jennie said while staring into her hallway mirror. Momentarily distracted by what appeared to be a gray hair, she furrowed her brow. At 28, she felt far too young to be dealing with old-lady stuff like this. She wrapped her finger around the offending strand and yanked it out. "You and a few others started playing badminton.

Someone brought eight rackets, so two teams of four battled it out. You were doing pretty well, diving like crazy, even at ones you didn't need to. But they eventually kicked you out."

"Why's that?"

"You kept accidently whacking people with the racket. When you hit the lead singer in the back of the head, you two nearly came to blows."

"Yikes. I'll hafta apologize to him. They play next weekend at the Riv."

"Good idea. But after that, I kinda lost you. I went to the bathroom and I think you headed toward the bonfire, but I met up with some other friends and didn't see you again until I found you zonked on the hood of the car."

"So," Monte asked with a grin, "you had nothing to do with my loss of trousers?"

She giggled heartily. "You only wish, Monte. No, if I had anything to do with that, believe me, you'd remember. Or I'd have to kill you. Oh," she added, "but Jason was at the bonfire. He met a woman and was hanging out with her by the fire. He didn't ride home with us, but he may know more."

"Thanks, Luv. Talk later."

"Bye." As Jennie disconnected, she noticed another gray hair. "That's it," she said to the mirror, "I'm going blonde!"

Oh my, what a wonderful morning, Jason thought. Waking slowly, he noticed a gorgeous brunette in bed next to him, and his smile widened. Still sleeping, she lay on her stomach, snoring softly. Even with the morning-after appearance of disheveled hair and streaked makeup, this woman looked fine.

6

Across the room, he heard a slight rumbling coming from his jeans. He recognized it as his cell phone, set on vibrate. Easing himself out of bed as gently as he could, Jason tiptoed his naked, chiseled body over to his pants and produced his phone. He whispered, "Hang on," and crept out of the bedroom, trousers in hand.

After slowly closing the door he said, "Hello" a little louder.

"Hey Jase, it's Monte."

"Monte," Jason said with a little more volume than he intended as he began hopping into his pants. "How's it hangin'?"

"A little to the left, my friend. Say, I need a little help piecing together the events of the evening."

"I'll bet you do, wild man, though let me ask you something first. Did you see the beautiful chick I was with last night?"

Monte had to really strain to recall the bonfire, but nothing specific came to mind. "No, sorry, dude."

"Darn," he uttered as he started pawing through the pile of unopened mail on the counter. "Oh, here we go. Her name is Cindy. Phew. That can be pretty embarrassing."

Monte had to laugh at that. "Oh Jason, always the playa. Anyway, about me? The story so far is that I ate too much alcoholic Jell-O, beat Triple Dog Dare's singer with a badminton racket, and staggered over to the bonfire."

"Oh oh oh! You don't remember what happened next? Hee hee!"

"What!? C'mon man, I gotta know where my pants are!"

Dropping down on Cindy's couch, Jason said, "Okay. The next band started playin'. They were fantastic. Really fast, loud stuff. You started dancing. Well, technically, you were walking toward me and Cindy and you tripped over a rock. You caught yourself with a rather awkward looking twist, but managed to stay on your feet. Well, that started you on the strangest, most intense dance routine anyone had ever seen. You were gyrating, twisting, flailing in every possible direction. Truth be told, you kinda looked like you were in the throes of a seizure. But all the people around the bonfire really got into it, clapping and cheering, which added fuel to your insane fire. You kept spinning and jumping until you lost your balance and, well, you just sorta tumbled into the fire."

"I what? I fell in the fire?"

At that point, the pretty girl slowly shuffled her way out of the bedroom, approaching Jason on her way to the bathroom. She put her hand gently atop Jason's head and ruffled his already messy hair. Holding up the phone, he said, "Hey Babe! I'm talking to Bonfire Man."

She smiled and yelled, "Hey Fireball! Great party, huh?"

"Wha?" For the first time since he woke up, Monte walked over to his full-length mirror and truly examined himself. His legs were a bit pink, but nothing obviously damaged. Though, he did notice what little leg hair he had left was curled and charred. "Holy crap!"

"Yeah. Funny thing. After you fell into the fire, at first no one moved. Awfully surreal. All of us drunk fools just sat there, watching your pants catch fire. Luckily, it was only your lower half dangling in there. That frizzy hair of yours would have gone up like hay. But finally, someone got up and dragged you out. They beat you down with a blanket then quickly peeled your pants off."

"Holy crap," Monte repeated.

"Man, you wear your pants too tight. It was a real struggle getting those things off. Well, what was left of them."

"Wow. So, where are they now?"

"I got 'em. I'll bring 'em by later today. I think your wallet is intact." As the brunette walked in front of Jason and stood there, open robe exposing curves and bare flesh, he uttered, "Dude, I gotta fly. See ya," and clicked off the phone. He stood up, put his arms out, and seductively whispered, "C'mere, Cindy."

Folding her arms and furrowing her brow, she replied, "I'm Melissa. Cindy's my roommate."

"Crap."

Later that day when Monte opened his front door, a grinning Jason greeted him. In his grasp he held a scorched pair of blue jeans. Both legs had holes as well as blackened, sooty sections. "Dude, that was one lollapalooza of a party, huh?"

"Apparently. Man, don't ever let me do Jell-O shots again! I mean it!"

~ Chapter Two ~

Looking over at my wife as I complete the story, I expect her to be fast asleep. I imagine a small spot of drool on the pillow. However, she instead looks up at me with the widest smile. "I love your funny stories!"

"Thanks, sweetie, but I thought you'd be in snoozeville by now."

She shook her head slowly. "How can I, with such silliness in the air?"

Leaning over, I give her a soft peck on her left cheek. "Well, how about a more serious story?"

~ Neighborhood Watch ~

Looking out my bay window, I shook my head and frowned. Overnight, the colossal oak trees that lined my street emptied their contents onto the ground and throughout the day, the wind flung those leaves all over my yard. I sighed as I trudged outside to grab my rake.

I had assembled the wayward leaves into a large pile and commenced the bagging process when Ralph leaned over my gate. As one of the leaders of the Neighborhood Watch program, he always took the time to converse with me. I certainly didn't mind, but I wished he'd stop asking me to join. Other than him, I didn't know anyone on our street.

"Howdy Bill," the pudgy man said with a wave and a smile. "The eternal cycle, eh?"

"Yeah, autumn's a messy season," I replied, leaning against my rake. "Whose bright idea was it to create plants that litter?"

He shrugged. "Certainly not mine. But, it is kinda neat to see what the wind'll bring into the yard."

"Just leaves and garbage, my friend."

"Not always!" Ralph grinned as he brandished a ten-dollar bill. "Not only did I find this, but I ended up with a paperback and a pair of panties."

"Must've been quite a gust, huh?" After a chuckle, I added, "Well, I best get back to it. Maybe the rest of the girl is in this pile."

"Trust me," he spoke as he walked away, "if you'd seen the size of these bloomers, you wouldn't be in such a hurry to uncover her."

I raked and bagged for another hour, until a good share of my upper body screamed in pain. Though I made good progress, the only non-tree items I discovered were junk food wrappers and cup lids. Just as I decided to stop for the day, my rake uncovered a white piece of paper with writing on it. I lit up a cigarette while snatching it off the ground. The handwriting had an obvious feminine touch. Pretty and neat, it had lots of loops and swoops. I almost crumpled it up, but then my curiosity kicked in.

The note had the feel of a carefully thought out poem, celebrating the beauty all around us. It spoke of trees *with leaves of majestic fire* and the *coming brilliant luminescence of the full autumn moon.* I assumed she wrote it yesterday, since the moon looked almost full last night. Grinning, I felt a bit naughty reading someone's personal thoughts. Then, the tone changed dramatically, and my smile faded.

Oh, dearest Albert, how I love you...how I loathe you. I gave you my all... my trust, my love, my heart, my very soul, and in return, you have given me your anger, your grief, your infidelity. You have injured

11

my soul; you have wounded my pride. Your betrayal has cut me to the quick. I can take no more. You can surely live without me, but I have come to realize I cannot live without you. You were my first, and you will be my last.

By the time you read this, I will be gone. By the light of the full autumn moon, I will be no more. My death will come quickly and painlessly.

Will your pain linger? Will you even notice? If you are as selfish as I truly believe you are, you will not even mourn my passing. My death is on your hands, but I fear you will only wash them, dry them, and be clean once more.

If this is the case, all I ask is that you think of me on occasion and smile. Remember the good, for we were truly happy once.

In death, I will be happy once more.

Daisy

As I read it, my mouth dropped open. She clearly went all out concocting this letter, even taking the time to draw a little flower above the *I* in her name.

I stood there, utterly dumbfounded. My initial reaction told me this had to be a hoax. Maybe Ralph planted it in my yard as a joke. I doubted it, though. We didn't know each other nearly well enough for a prank like this. Still, why would a completed suicide note be blowing in the wind? It made no sense.

Again, I contemplated tossing the letter, it being none of my business. I've never even met the girl, so why should I interfere?

But no, I knew it would haunt me all of my days. Besides, I love a good mystery.

I decided to take the note next door to Ralph's house. He or his wife Lauren would certainly know Albert and Daisy.

"Sorry, I don't know these people," said Ralph with sympathy in his voice, "and Lauren's in Buffalo, visiting her mom."

With a furrowed brow, I asked, "How could you not? Haven't you met everyone around here due to the Neighborhood Watch?"

"Lauren handles most of it, actually. I mostly talk to you." He stood quiet for a moment, staring at the note in his hand. "Man..." he said softly and trailed off in thought. After a while, he looked up at me. "You're not just messing with me, are ya?"

"Oddly enough," I replied, "I was hoping the same thing of you."

"What're we gonna do, Bill?" The genuine concern plastered across his mustached face gave me pause. I really thought Ralph would have the answers.

"Okay, let's think this through logically," I said as I started walking toward the door. "Follow me." Once outside, we stood on the sidewalk. "The wind had been blowing from the east, so it came from down there," I said, pointing. "There are, what, a dozen houses in that direction?"

"More like sixteen, but at least it gives us a place to..." He paused and then his brown eyes lit up. "Oh, I know! Let's ask Margaret! C'mon!" He started jogging down the street, but he slowed quickly. Apparently, Ralph really needed to jog more often. "Margaret's lived in the neighborhood all her life," he wheezed. "If anyone'll know this girl, she will."

We knocked on a door four houses to the west of mine. Moving westward did not feel like the best of plans, but as soon as the door opened, I felt a wave of hope flutter through me. Margaret had the appearance, to me at least, of the quintessential neighborhood gossip. It could have been her pear-shaped body and hanging jowls, or maybe the inquisitive wrinkling of her brow gave me optimism. Of course, it might simply have been the fact that her ears looked too big for her head. I smiled politely as Ralph introduced us. "Oh yeah," she said with a country-girl twang to her nasally voice, "I've seen you a few times."

13

"Doing yard work, probably. Say, we were wondering, do you know an Albert or Daisy on this street?"

She quickly nodded her head. "Oh sure, I know Albert Turkel pretty well. Only met his wife a couple of times." She moved her head closer to us and lowered her voice to a murmur. "She's kinda flaky. She's one of them artsy-fartsy types. Prone to emotion, from what I've heard. But, of course, so's Albert. Got a temper, that one does. I hear he punched a hole in a wall once. Also, he's always chatting up the ladies. He even hit on me once." That image made me shudder.

She returned her head to its original position and added, "So, why ya askin'?"

I hesitated and then looked over at Ralph. I didn't feel it prudent to be blabbing any more gossip to this lady, but before I even finished turning my head, he had already yanked the letter from my grasp, handing it to her.

Once she read it, she desperately wanted to tag along.

We now had a little convoy walking down the sidewalk with a purpose to our stride. I had to keep slowing down to accommodate the rest of my gang, however. Apparently, this neighborhood needed an exercise regimen.

When we reached the Turkel residence, three houses east of mine, I felt increased trepidation, but having a posse with me helped to assuage my uneasiness somewhat. I doubt I could have done this on my own. I let Margaret ring the bell, but no one came to the door. We all looked at each other, not knowing what to do next. "Should we bust in?" asked Ralph.

"Um, no, I don't…" I started.

"That would be stupid," Margaret loudly blurted. "Forget it! This is probably someone's idea of a joke. I mean really, who loses a suicide note?" She turned and walked away without saying another word to us.

14

I looked at Ralph and shrugged. "Maybe we can keep an eye out," I said quietly. "If one of us sees either of them come home -" I trailed off.

"Yeah, Bill, good idea." He looked at me for a long moment, before adding, "I hope everything's okay." Then, he turned and walked toward home.

"Me too," I whispered.

Sleep did not come, so I sat on my porch, staring up at the full moon. If I craned my neck, I could just barely see their deck from mine. Every so often, I stood up and walked to the street, peering at their driveway for a moment before strolling back. I had to wonder what the rest of my neighbors thought of my late-night pacing.

After a while of sitting on my deck, I must have dozed off. When I jolted awake at around one in the morning, I saw a faint light coming from their patio. I jumped off my porch and started marching, my heart punching my chest like a boxer working over a speed bag.

As I advanced, I could see a single candle flickering in the night. There sat a woman with long, blonde hair, her back to me. Hunched over their picnic table, she wore a full-length white robe.

Good Lord, what am I doing? Only lunatics would be out at this hour, skulking in the shadows. Her neighbors had not raked, so the rustling of leaves announced my approach. She turned sharply and shouted, "Who's there?"

"Oh, um, don't be startled," I stammered, "I'm Bill, your neighbor. Something of yours blew into my yard yesterday."

"Oh," she replied softly before turning her back again. As I crunched closer, I could see her hard at work. Her head hung down and her pen moved rapidly across a piece of paper. I reached the deck and said softly, "Um, Daisy? May I come up?"

She continued scribbling for a few moments then paused and turned slowly. "Okay," she said softly, then clearly as an afterthought asked, "How...how do you..." but she trailed off before completing her thought, her concentration back upon her work.

I eased up the stairs. Though difficult to see, the candle tossed enough light on her paper for me to notice similar loops and swoops on the page in front of her. I walked up beside her and set the letter next to her on the table. "This blew into my yard."

She stared at it for several seconds before looking up at me through glassy eyes. She flashed me a weak smile. "Oh. I wondered..." and said, very softly, "Now I can stop rewriting..." and laid her head on the table.

At that moment, her predicament became apparent to me. She did not even flinch as I placed my fingers on her neck. Her pulse felt very weak. I pulled out my cell phone and dialed 911.

After disconnecting I asked, "Is Albert home, Daisy?"

With considerable effort, she looked up at me. "No idea where... which woman he's... the bastard..."

As the sirens began wailing in the distance, I pulled up a lawn chair and sat down beside her. "Don't worry, Daisy," I whispered as I rested my hand upon her head, gently petting her like a puppy in a lap. "The Neighborhood Watch is here."

~ Chapter Three ~

While my dear wife's "Tell me a story" requests often come in the evening when we're getting ready for bed, it's certainly not just reserved for bedtime.

We are on the road, heading to Lansing, Michigan for a book-signing event at EVERYbody Reads. Scott, a jovial and charismatic man, owns this independent bookstore. I would love this fella just for being a fantastic human who likes cats, baseball, and supporting local authors. However, this man introduced me to the woman who became my wife, so my admiration for Scott is monumental and will be eternal. Looking over, I ask, "Any idea if Marcy, Sawyer, Maddie, or Kei will be there?" I do so enjoy visiting with his wife and children.

"Not a clue," my wife replies, "though I wouldn't be surprised."

With dozens of miles to go until we reach the Michigan Avenue shop, she reaches over and takes hold of my hand. "So, ya got a story for me today, honey?"

"You know I do! This first one's pretty short, so I'll have time for a couple."

~ Mockle is the New Cockle ~

"What brings you here today?" asked Doctor Gordon.

"Well," replied Lincoln Greene, "It's my heart. It doesn't feel right. Kinda heavy... and cold, I guess."

The doctor ran several tests, leaving the room to study the results.

When he returned, Lincoln looked over at him while unsuccessfully adjusting his revealing cotton gown and asked, "So whatdya think, Doc?"

He looked Lincoln in the eye for a moment. "I have an idea, but first let me ask you a couple of questions. How is your home life? Are your wife and kids treating you okay?"

"Well sure, Gwen and the twins are great."

Dr. Gordon nodded. "Okay. How about work?"

"It's going fine, I guess." Lincoln shrugged as he added, "About as good as a professional wrestler's life can be, anyway."

"Oh that's right. Which wrestler are you again?"

"I'm Haiku."

Furrowing his brow, the doctor said, "Wait. Isn't Haiku a Japanese wrestler?"

Lincoln shrugged again. "Eh. Under a mask, we're all Japanese."

"I see. Have you had any drama or trauma lately?"

This made a chuckle escape Lincoln's mouth. "Of course, it's wrestling. Well, there is one thing. A couple of weeks ago, Shinjuku hit me with the dreaded heart punch. It gave me some wicked heartburn for a few days."

"Okay, that explains it. That shot broke your heart. More specifically, he damaged your cockles."

Lincoln gave the doctor a puzzled expression. "He didn't hit me that low."

"No, your cockles. I assume you've heard the phrase, 'warming the cockles of your heart' am I right? Well, that heart punch shattered most of your cockle supply. You are running on reserves here."

"Gadzooks! Is it serious?"

"Without properly functioning cockles, nothing will seem wonderful or exciting. Humdrum will be your future. However, there is a solution. We can do a cockle transplant, using artificial ones. It's the latest in cockle rejuvenation. They are called Mockles."

"Mockles? Are they safe?"

"Certainly. They're all the rage in Hollywood. Everyone is getting them. I replaced Miley Cyrus's cockles last year and you see how she has been acting lately. After all, mockle is the new cockle."

After thinking it over for a moment, Lincoln replied, "Well all right then, let's do it!"

Six months later, as Doctor Gordon was flipping through channels, he stopped when he saw Haiku in the middle of a WWE interview segment. The doctor smiled at the level of passion his former patient put into his tirade. Turning to his wife, the doctor said, "Listen to the moxie in his voice. And it's all thanks to his new mockles."

Mrs. Gordon listened to the man rant for a few moments before saying, "He doesn't sound very Japanese to me."

"Well, I'm told everyone's Japanese under a mask."

After a pause, Mrs. Gordon turned to her husband and said, "And by the way, I think you over-mockled Miley Cyrus. Just sayin'."

~ Crazy Uncle Reggie ~

I didn't mean to chuckle when the lawyer said, "Being of sound mind." Feeling the crowd's glare caused my face to grow pink with embarrassment.

Shrinking in my seat, I squeaked out an apology. The majority of the group returned their attention to the tall, bearded man as he resumed reading the will. However, cousin Gaylord held my gaze, a stern sneer upon his thin lips. My vision fell to the floor and my mind wandered. The world may have known his father as Reginald Battaglia, millionaire industrial magnate, but to me, he would always be crazy Uncle Reggie.

When I think back, my uncle's reactions may not have been so nuts. However, most of my childhood memories, during my family's annual visits to his palatial estate, consisted of me picking things up and him snatching them away. I'll never forget the time he plucked a nude statue from my nearly-teenage grasp. As he admonished me to, "Never touch my David," he fondled it absent-mindedly, petting it like a kitten as he bored me with the story of how he acquired the tiny naked man. It also struck me funny that he always wore a suit and tie, no matter the temperature. It still brings a grin to my face, the memory of Uncle standing in the summer sun, sweating through all his layers as he watched Gaylord frolicking with me in their colossal backyard.

The fuzzy-faced lawyer droned on, but I had lost interest, since I doubted any of this affected me. Along with those annual Fourth of July weekend visits, my dad once made me spend a whole, miserable summer in Uncle's overgrown house when I was twelve. But since Uncle Reggie rarely said anything to me other than, "Don't touch that," today's will reading felt like a waste of my afternoon.

"To my nephew Claude Battaglia," the lawyer said, snapping me back, "I bequeath my entire library of books, and all which lies therein."

21

I gave the room a puzzled grin. Books, huh? Ah well, at least I wasn't saddled with that nasty painting of him, the one hanging in the foyer.

The next afternoon I went to the mansion, cardboard boxes in hand. Upon entering the library, my mouth dropped open like it did when I was a child. I remembered looking up at this bookshelf with such a sense of awe. However, the years, and the inches I'd grown, had done little to alter my perception. The shelf still towered several feet above me and ran the length of the south wall. How many thousands of books must there be? I snickered at the meager supply of boxes at my feet. I'd need, what, a hundred more?

After an hour of work, I had full boxes, but I laughed boisterously at how little of the collection had been removed.

As I yanked out a leather-bound Poe, behind it I noticed a large book lying on its side. I wrenched it from its hiding place, dislodging other books. Though I did not recognize the author's name, I liked the ornate cover and the raised, gold lettering. Inside, a crude, square area had been cut out of the pages. Wedged in the hole, I found a small chunk of wood. It popped out with a small squeak. The back side of the three-inch square had a smooth, polished finish while the front had an elaborate symbol deeply engraved in it.

The square found a home in my overcoat pocket while the book ended up in a box. If I got nothing else out of this collection, I figured, I at least now owned a hollowed-out book where I could hide my stash.

An insistent rapping on my apartment door jarred me awake the next morning. "I'm comin'!" I yelled, stumbling toward the door.

A short, impeccably dressed man stood in the hall, an impatient glare across his sharply angled face. What black hair he had left he slicked back in a look that went out of style, easily, twenty years ago. "Hello, Claude," he said, his nasally voice irritating my sleepy brain.

"Gaylord," I replied with a roll of my eyes. "Lookin' sharp as ever. So, what brings ya here? Let me guess, the will?"

As Gaylord entered my apartment, he smirked at the dirty laundry heaped in the living room. He absent-mindedly tugged at his tie as he stepped over the fragrant pile. "Frankly, I expected more from my father, being his only son." He sneered as he continued, his eyes locked on mine. "I'll get to the point, Claude. I want to buy the books. All of them."

I grinned and shook my head. "Man, things never change, do they, Gay?" I loved calling him by the shortened version of his name. It never ceased to crack me up how it made him bristle. "You never did like me coming to visit. You hated sharing your toys. And it still eats you up when I get something you don't, huh?"

Gaylord pushed the knot of his pinstripe tie even closer to his large Adam's apple. "The books have… sentimental value. They remind me of my childhood." I could believe it. With a name like Gaylord, I'm sure the kids at school teased him unmercifully. Those books were probably his only full-time playmates. "I'll give you five thousand dollars."

This woke me up. I nearly jumped at the offer, but I knew I could work him. "I dunno, man. I was looking forward to reading 'em myself. Besides, there are at least five thousand books. A buck a book, Gay?"

"All right, ten thousand. And stop calling me that!"

After staring at him for a few seconds, grinning at the amusement of it all, I said, "Sold. There are a few boxes here. The rest are still in the library."

It gave me tremendous delight watching him attempting to lift one of the boxes. After an audible snap from one of his vertebrae he said, "I'll have someone come for these."

23

At the end of the week, I returned to the estate. It already had a For Sale sign in the yard. The family certainly wasted little time.

When I walked into the library, I gasped. Every last book was gone. The massive, empty shelves amused me somewhat, so I yelled, "Hello," just to hear the echo.

My cell phone rang, the monotone version of Black Sabbath's *Fairies Wear Boots* reverberating heavily off the walls. An irate Gaylord greeted me. "You took it, you bastard! I want it back! It's part of the deal!"

"It's part of what deal?" I asked, puzzled.

"The key, man, I want the key! From the book!"

"The key, from…" I stuffed my hand into the pocket of my jacket and fingered the piece of wood I'd forgotten about until now. "Oh, you mean this wood square thingy? This is a key, huh?"

"What? Uh, no, I just –"

There, previously hidden behind some books, I noticed a raised design in the wall. It matched the indentation in my chunk of wood, so I snapped them together. "Hey, look at this!" I gave it a turn, and the shelf slid across the wall, to reveal a secret passage. "Gay old buddy, it is a key!"

"No, Claude, don't –"

Down the rickety, wooden stairs I went, breaking cobwebs with my hand. Once I reached the bottom, I understood everything. All around me, I found paintings, a gold coin collection, even that statue of David. I disconnected Gaylord and phoned the lawyer.

As it turned out, the wording of the will was irrefutable. …My entire library of books, and all which lies therein. Uncle Reggie wanted me to have the bulk of his wealth. Now that I think of it, he'd once said, "You're the only person in this family who doesn't seem to care about my money." Of course, I was twelve, but still.

In the end, I treated Gaylord right. I bought back the books for twenty grand. I bought the mansion as well, and put those books right back where they belonged. I especially liked the one book. I keep my stash in it.

~ Chapter Four ~

Book signing events can be a heady mix of interesting, exciting, boring, and terrifying. While it's certainly fun meeting and interacting with book lovers, and I am (at times) practically charming and witty, ultimately I have to fight the introvert in me who would really rather snatch a book off the shelf, go find a comfy chair, and escape into another world.

While sitting at my signing table, a man with a thin head of hair, a sharp nose, and a sober expression approaches. With no hint of emotion evident on his clean-shaven face, he asks, "So, do you still have the business?"

I cock my head to the side, like a dog examining a possible food source. Scrunching my brow, I ask, "Do I still have what business?"

"The video game business."

Oh! Okay, I get it. The problem with writing a fictional story, like my first novel, *Driving Crazy*, is that people just assume it's based on real events. "Sorry, but *Driving Crazy* is a work of fiction. I never had that business."

Though he tries to hide his disappointment, it's evident. "Oh, I see. Of course."

"Yeah, I prefer making stuff up. It's usually more entertaining than my real life, plus I don't have to remember what actually happened."

He smiles, but to me it looks forced. "Sure. Okay, thanks." With that, he turns and trudges away.

I almost feel bad now that I didn't live the life of Jaymond Naylor. I have to admit, I really appreciate the people who believe the magic. I know of a few readers who are convinced that I drove to Weed Patch, California to pick up a Crazy Climber game and had all sorts of bizarre events happen. One fella even said to my wife, "I can't believe you married him after all the stuff he did! Have you read this? Oh my goodness!"

I hate to spoil that, as does my wife, who replied, "Yeah, but it happened before I met him, so it's fine." God love her!

Most book signing events tend to have these lulls in the middle, where there's no one around to talk to but the other authors, or my wife and the bookstore owner. In this case, at this moment, I only have Scott and my sweetie for company. As she rests her warm hands on my shoulders, she whispers, "Do you need anything?"

I turn and smile at her. Still, I find it hard to believe I got so lucky in finding her! "No, I'm good, my dear. Thanks."

Pulling up a chair next to me, she rests her hand on my right knee. "Scott and I are bored. Tell us a story."

"Sure!" Looking over at my vegetarian wife and my vegan friend, I ask, "One question first. Are Pringles chips vegan?"

~ The Rogue Potato Chip ~

Sitting back in my recliner, I finished chewing the Pringles potato chip in my mouth. I swallowed the pulverized chip goo, washing it down with the last swallow of Seagrams Original Wild Berries wine cooler. I fancied those specific wine coolers, and I particularly enjoyed watching wrestling on TV while drinking them. Being in the final hour of a three-hour special, I had just polished off wine cooler number six. "Ah," I said to Dr. Demise, the muscular dude on my TV currently mangling another muscular dude, "nothing beats wresslin', wine coolers, and Pringles!" Then I added, "Yea, pile drive the sucka!" Since I assumed Dr. Demise wouldn't really care what I did in my spare time.

I reached for, and managed to grasp, the can of Sour Cream Pringles on the end table. It took two tries, since all those wine coolers had caused my surroundings to lose their sharpness. Tipping the can, I managed to get the last chip to drop against my palm, but it held firm inside the lip of the container. Shaking the can did not dislodge it, so I reached inside with my index and middle fingers and wiggled it loose, setting the canister back on the table.

Before devouring it, I examined the chip for a moment. It looked like any other Pringles Sour Cream potato chip. It may have had a few more of the little green flecks they call the sour cream flavor, but I couldn't be sure. Frankly, it held no relevance, so I brought it up to my lips.

I bit down but felt no crunching inside my mouth. This seemed odd, so I squinted at my fingers. When I noticed them to be devoid of my chip, I glanced down at my chest and there sat the chip, still intact.

Shrugging, I picked it up and gave another try at my mouth.

Once again, it somehow dislodged itself and this time, it tumbled down to the green-carpeted floor. "That was weird," I said to the TV, "huh Doc?"

Dr. Demise was too busy pummeling his opponent to notice or care, so I rolled over in my fully-extended recliner and attempted to pick up the chip. But alas, it wasn't there. I allowed my head to drop off the armrest so I could get a better look at the floor.

Fifteen seconds of hanging upside down gave me an annoying head rush, but I finally caught a glimpse of the Pringles chip under my chair. However, as my vision focused on the chip, it appeared to disappear under my recliner.

I was puzzled, and rather dizzy with my head dangling like that, so instead of trying to get up, I simply rolled off the arm of the chair. As I hit the ground, I shot a glance under the chair. "Ah ha! There ya are!

Tryin' ta geddaway, eh?" Giggling, I shoved my arm under the chair. I reached where I last witnessed the snack food, but I still couldn't feel anything that felt chip-like. Pulling my arm out to get an unobstructed view, I realized the potato chip had vanished!

This all felt a bit too bizarre for me to comprehend. Standing up, I went into the kitchen and got another wine cooler.

Upon returning, I sat back in my comfy chair and continued watching the program. The next match had started, meaning Dr. Demise had already won, or lost. Frankly, it didn't matter to me. After all, the guy didn't help me with my Pringles situation, so why should I care about his win-loss record? "Screw it! I'll huntcha down later, chip. Haiku's wresslin' now."

I got about a third of the way through the next wine cooler when I caught some movement out of the corner of my right eye. I spun around and to my surprise, there sat the chip on the floor under the end table. I stared at it for what seemed like ten minutes but was probably less than a minute before I got up, dropped to my knees, and shuffled over to the end table. As I bent down to grab it, I decided that under no circumstances would I take my eyes off that chip, even for a second. In doing so, I forgot all about the end table and consequently bashed my forehead squarely upon it. Screaming a derogatory word, I fell over.

After what seemed like less than a minute but was probably more like ten, I wobbled back to my knees. Though not altogether sure what had just happened, it certainly felt like I had been head-butted by Dr. Demise himself. More than likely, I'd wake next morning with a massive headache, wondering about my bruised, goose-egged forehead. It occurred to me that after a night of boozing it up, I would often wake the next morning with unexplained injuries, but unfortunately (or perhaps fortunately), I usually couldn't recall exactly how I sustained said damage. It tended to be a bit embarrassing, having to call my friends to ask them what I did the previous night.

At that moment, I realized I was on my knees, staring at the end table. Since the reason why didn't immediately come to me, I glanced around the room a bit. Then, I noticed the Pringles can lying on the tabletop. "Oh yeah! I'm hunting a rogue chip."

I looked under the end table, and not surprisingly at this point, the chip had vanished. "Huh," I said as I crawled under the table, being mindful to keep my head as low to the ground as possible. I had no desire to allow this piece of furniture to beat me up any further.

As I turned my head and glanced beneath the couch, I found it. It looked the way most Pringles do, curvy. In fact, at this angle it almost appeared to be grinning at me. Mocking or taunting me, as if to say, "Haha! You can't catch me, sucker!"

Well, I never back down from a challenge, especially from an inanimate object or an audacious piece of snack food, so I shoved my hand under the sofa. After a few moments of intense hand wiggling, I felt a sharp pain on my index finger. I yanked my hand out from under the couch, and shook it wildly in the air. After doing enough flailing to satisfy my pain, I looked at the finger. A single drop of blood had oozed from a tiny pinprick. I yelled, "The dang thing bit me!" before sticking the injured finger in my mouth. The taste of sour cream dust overwhelmed the minute amount of blood.

After wiping my wet finger on my sweatpants, I sneered, "Okay chip, ya wanna play rough, eh?" Grabbing the couch from underneath, I flung it upward. The heavy sofa flipped, rolled over, and smashed against the wall, chipping off a hunk of dry wall. There, among the dust bunnies, I spotted one rubber band, two pennies, and a thumbtack, but no chip. Staring at the thumbtack for a moment, I wondered if the chip had actually chomped on my finger, or instead used the tack as a tiny sword. Either way, I had to stop that evil chip before it had another chance to attack.

"Where is it?" I screamed, scanning the room. As it ducked under my ancient brown dehumidifier on the other side of the room, I said, "Ah-hah! There ya are, ya little sumbich!" It did move. I was sure of that now. However, the realization of a mobile, possibly sentient snack item did nothing to cause me pause. Nothing mattered to me at that point other than getting my hands on that Sour Cream Pringle.

The dehumidifier sat about a foot and a half tall, maybe a foot wide. It had barely enough clearance for a bust bunny, or a Pringle chip, to slide underneath.

Grabbing the appliance with both hands, I lifted it to about chest level. Even empty, the metal and plastic unit had quite a bit of weight to it, but being nearly full of water as it was, it took some effort to heave it across my apartment.

It crashed into the offending end table, shattering it and a lamp in the process. Stale water splattered everywhere. Pointing at the pieces of my former end table, I yelled, "And that's for the head-butt! Anyone else want a piece of me?" When none of my furniture responded, I turned back to glare at the former home of the dehumidifier.

After I removed its hiding place, the rogue potato chip took off down the hallway. It had amazing acceleration, especially for a piece of snack food. I gave chase for a few steps before diving at it, my outstretched fingers growing ever closer.

As it slid under my closed bedroom door, I cursed my lack of foresight for not leaving the door open. The impact of my skull against the wooden door reminded me of Haiku's classic wrestling move, where he dives off the top rope, using his head as a battering ram.

Though I don't remember doing it, I apparently took a small break from chip hunting to lie on the floor for a while. My first attempt at getting to my feet sent me sprawling back down, landing hard upon my butt.

Once I finally regained my footing and steadied myself, I staggered into the utility room and grabbed a hammer. I then tumbled back into the living room, grabbed and tipped my wine cooler, finishing it off in three mighty gulps, and set the bottle back down. "Now..." I spoke with a raspiness my voice had never displayed before, "you die, Mr. Pringle."

I bobbled into my bedroom, hammer held high above my head. Once again, the chip had clearly found a suitable hiding place, but I would not let that deter me.

Hurling the contents of my room out into the hallway, I was only vaguely aware that a lot of my stuff shattered when it hit the floor or the far wall. Every so often, I heard what I thought might've been my neighbor pounding on her side of the apartment wall. However, being on a seek-and-destroy mission, I pushed it from my mind. Nothing would stop me, especially not Mrs. Filgby, the old bat from apartment 2C.

When I yanked the nightstand from its resting spot, I finally saw the chip cowering in the corner. The curve of the Pringle angled downward now, frowning at me. I tossed the nightstand into the opposite corner, then walked over and slammed the bedroom door shut. That damn chip wasn't getting out alive. I got on all fours, and glared at it. "You," I whispered, "are doomed. Do you understand? Doomed. Pringles Dust!"

Releasing a particularly satisfying chortle, I slammed the hammer onto the floor. The chip dodged my blow and then took off, hugging the edge of the wall as it headed toward the closed door. I swung my weapon repeatedly, beating holes in the wall and floor and breaking off chunks of drywall as the chip continued to dodge my onslaught.

I finally had it trapped in the corner, with the exit on one side and the overturned nightstand on the other. As it trembled with fear, I raised the hammer high over my head.

While I glared at it, blood lust in my eyes, the chip turned over slowly, switching its expression from a frown to a smile.

I paused to examine the little green-flecked chip as it shivered in the corner. My anger rapidly seeped away as I stared at it. "Oh, you poor thing," I said softly as I set the hammer on the floor. "I'm sorry little fella. You were just trying to save yourself, huh? You didn't want to be eaten by a drunk fool, and who can blame you." I put my hand on the ground in front of it, and after a moment's hesitation, it slowly crawled into my palm.

I sat on the floor of my trashed apartment, carefully petting the chip in my hand, when I looked up and saw the superintendent of the building, a couple police officers, and Mrs. Filgby gawking at me. "Um, hi," I said slowly. "We... had a bit of a disagreement, but it's okay now. This potato chip is no longer rogue."

Of course, this amount of damage voided my lease, and they politely asked me to move. I was okay with that, primarily because the apartment didn't allow pets. Just what do Pringles eat, anyway?

~ Chapter Five ~

Glancing up at the clock, I realize it's time to end this book-signing event. As I'm packing the unsold books and the plastic book holders into my black storage box, Scott saunters over to me. "So my friend, did you have fun?"

My smile beams up at him. "I'm here with you and my wife, at the best bookstore on the planet. How can that not be fun?"

He turns his head sideways and does his best imitation of an eight year old being told he's adorable. "Aw, shucks!"

When my wife walks up beside me with an armful of books, I shake my head slowly. "Good thing I sold a few copies today."

"But honey," she says with an innocent upturn of her eyes, "these are on sale…ish."

"We can never have too many books," I reply with a shrug.

As she walks up to the register and plops the pile on the counter, she glances back at me. "What are we doing for dinner?"

"I dunno, my sweet baboo." I answer with a shrug. Then I look over at my bookstore-owning friend. "Yo Scott, any chance you and the family would be interested in joining us for dinner?"

"It would be our honor," he replies gleefully. "We can go next door. The Avenue has a nice selection of vegan-friendly entrees."

"Let's do it!"

After my wife pays for our new books, we all walk next door and have a seat. They take our beer and food orders, and we chat amongst ourselves for a moment. When there's a lull in the conversation, my wife turns to me and says, "Tell us a story."

"Hmmm…" I have to think about it for a moment. "Okay, I have one. Although I have to ask, do they serve lasagna here?"

~ Lasagna and Sex Therapy ~

My dreams always attacked with a vengeance. The images in my head, while vague, always brought a strong sense of panic and urgency. I grew accustomed to the nondescript objects raining from above, crashing all around me, as well as the screams emanating from newly formed piles of debris. However, this dream felt different. I had a new series of images protruding into my mind. A thick, acrid smoke caused my lungs to clog while the heat grew unbearable.

I awoke with a series of barking coughs. Directly above me, inches from my head, flames crackled and danced. Fire engulfed my home.

While crawling out of my cardboard box, I saw my left arm ablaze. Fortunately, I couldn't feel the flames yet as they swirled along the sleeve of my thick overcoat.

Once I cleared the box, I ran toward the river as fast as my legs would allow, while smacking at the fire with my other hand.

Even though the river could only give me a few inches of depth here, it sufficed. Falling to my knees, I plunged my burning limb into the murky water. I submerged my arm up to the shoulder, welcoming the hiss as the fire graciously subsided.

By the time I had refocused on the large appliance box that I called home, little remained unburned. I yanked off my charred overcoat, using it to grab at a remaining edge of cardboard. First, I tipped it away from my body, hoping to save some of my meager possessions by forcing them out and onto the ground. Then, after tossing the burning cardboard into the river, I jumped up and down repeatedly on my stuff, desperately trying to douse the lingering flames.

Once I had the fire extinguished, my adrenaline began to ebb. I sat cross-legged on the banks of the Red Oak River and examined my arm. Fortunately, due to the chill in the air, I wore three layers last night. The fire tore through my overcoat and sweater, but the tightly fitting long-sleeved shirt fortunately remained, though in patches. As I carefully peeled the sweater off my arm, I saw several red splotches on my skin. Before I could continue looking myself over, I heard harsh whispering behind me, alerting me to something I had hoped and strived to avoid. I turned to witness several of the locals who had congregated in the clearing, up the hill from me. Once they realized I had noticed them, the throng came bounding down as one.

I dealt with the choruses of, "Are you okay?" "What happened?" and the like. While I knew them as residents of this small community, I did not normally interact with them, so I answered concisely.

A woman pushed her way through the crowd and dashed up to me, gawking with wide eyes at my charred sleeve, worry splayed across her face. "Oh my! Are you hurt?" She wore a white lab coat with the name Irene stitched in cursive above the festive Redi-Medi Urgent Care Clinic logo.

Before I could formulate an answer, she placed her hands around my charred forearm, one on my wrist and the other just above the elbow. "It doesn't look too bad, thank goodness, but let's get you to the clinic." Barely awaiting a nod of my head, she began sprinting toward the clinic, and since she still had a solid grip on my arm, I had little choice but to tag along. Her brow deeply furrowed, she asked, "Does it hurt?"

Not until she mentioned it. "Maybe a little, yeah."

We entered the clinic, rushing past two other patients seated against the far wall. A heavy-set woman with her right leg in a cast seemed annoyed at my preferential treatment, but the short, elderly man with the angry red rash painted across his right cheek looked at me with sad, understanding eyes. I tossed the stout woman a shrug as Irene pulled me past.

As she carefully cut the remaining bit of sleeve off my ailing arm, I felt the need to say, "Um, you know I'm a bum, right? I have no way to pay for this."

She smiled sympathetically. "That's okay. It's on the house. We take care of our own here in Red Oak. Besides, it doesn't look bad at all. Only first degree burns in a few spots. They're all superficial and should heal quickly enough."

As she applied some white goop to my arm, I gave this lady the once-over. She wore her long, black hair up in a tightly spiraled bun, a long stick smoothly piercing it at a 45-degree angle. While pretty enough for a woman I assumed to be in her early 40s, I couldn't help but wonder what she looked like in her 20s. I'll bet she turned a lot of heads.

"Okay," she said with a broad smile, "you're all set. So, what are you going to do now?"

"I dunno. I'll have to see if anything survived, and go from there."

She had a strange look on her face, like she wanted to say something else, but instead, her body language softened and she simply said, "Okay, well, good luck. If it gets any worse, feel free to come back."

After thanking her for the assistance, I walked out of the clinic and into the harsh sunlight, squinting until my vision adjusted. Still feeling the eyes of the town upon me, I headed directly for the river's edge.

Sadly, almost nothing survived the blaze. I now owned a shirt with a missing sleeve and torso, a half-charred pair of jeans, one sock, and lots of ashes. The only other remaining item was the lower half of a paperback book I had recently found. "Man," I said aloud, "I was only halfway through. Now, I'll never know who done it."

How could this have happened? I don't smoke and we had no lightning last night. The only possible explanation was that one of the neighborhood kids must have lit my box on fire. But while I slept inside it? What kind of monster would do such a thing to another human being, especially one obviously down on his luck?

This line of thinking disturbed me too much, so I decided to concentrate on my next move. With a heavy sigh, I knew I needed to head back into town. I preferred staying away from the village until after nightfall, to limit my sightings. Sneaking into Red Oak under cover of darkness, I could root around the dumpster of the restaurant, the used clothing shop, or the grocery store. Generally, I could scavenge a meal or some duds while avoiding unnecessary harassment.

Today, I did not have that luxury. With autumn fast approaching, the nights became chillier. The clothes on my back would not suffice. Besides, all this excitement burned a lot of calories. As if on cue, my stomach rumbled its demands.

After taking a few steps, my left foot landed on something. Assuming a rock, I lifted my foot and saw a colorful item partially buried among the weeds. Dropping on all fours, I discovered a psychedelically colored disposable Bic lighter. I had to wonder if I found the device used to torch my box. Holding it by the top, I dropped it into the pocket of my dirty sweat pants. I had no idea what I would do with it. Perhaps I would go to the police. Of course, there was no proof this lighter burned my stuff. Besides, why would they care about some bum like me?

Returning to my more immediate concern, I stepped into town and headed straight for my favorite dumpster, behind Paul's Diner. I thought of this one as my favorite because it always seemed to have something fairly fresh and tasty waiting for me. A couple days ago, I happened upon a pizza box with three whole slices. Before that, I found a Styrofoam container with quite a bit of salad and even a small dollop of ranch dressing still enclosed in a small, plastic cup. Why, on several occasions, I even lucked into a candy bar, still in the wrapper. The stuff these people throw away!

I turned the corner and had the dumpster in my sights when I froze. The restaurant's side door flew open and out walked a tall, heavy-set man. He had a brown garbage bag in one hand and a Styrofoam container in the other, heading straight for the trash. Even from a distance, I could tell the man towered over me by at least a half foot and certainly appeared to eat much better than I did. His belly protruded past his belt in a graceful cascade. With the red and white striped shirt he wore, his gut reminded me of a giant beach ball. He flipped up the lid to the dumpster and heaved in the trash bag, but then he paused. After popping open the Styrofoam "to-go" box, he stared inside for a moment. He glanced around, so I ducked behind a large oak tree. Then, he reached in the container and pulled out what appeared to be a large sandwich. Opening his mouth, he took a huge bite out of it before setting it back inside. As he chewed, a smile grew across his pudgy face. He closed the container and gently set it inside the dumpster. Still smiling, he turned and walked back inside the restaurant.

I stood there for a couple minutes before creeping over, feeling a bit like a stray cat. While lifting the lid to the trash, I reached in and procured the Styrofoam box. Inside, I found the whole sub sandwich, less the one bite, along with a pickle spear and a handful of plain potato chips. Although I thought the whole thing peculiar, my hunger had no problems with this. Tossing the box under my arm, I shot back to the safety of my charred piece of earth.

As I sat on the ground, chewing away at one fantastic sandwich, I kept noticing my grubby hands clutching the food I shoveled into my mouth. Wondering how many germs, how much filth I had ingested, I decided I wanted to clean myself up. I set the remainder of the meal down and sprang to my feet to begin the journey back to Paul's Diner. Though I really did not like doing it, I had found Paul's the easiest place to sneak into, since the restrooms were in a hallway directly to the right of the entrance. I popped my head in the front door and after making certain no one saw me, I made a beeline to the bathroom.

Once in the men's room, I dashed over to the sink. As I bent down and thrust my hands into the warm stream of water, I couldn't help but notice my reflection in the oval mirror. The man who returned my gaze startled me. In fact, it shook me to my core. How long had it been since

I last saw myself? My mind's eye remembered a clean-cut, shiny-skinned man with bright, clear eyes. The straggly, shaggy mane I now wore had turned a greasy shade of brownish-black, reminiscent of used motor oil, but the large streaks of gray added a bit of contrast. My thick, unkempt beard had turned almost completely gray, except for blobs of what had to be ketchup from yesterday's meal, a partially eaten hamburger from the trash can near the fast food joint.

I began to chuckle softly at the food I wore on my face, until I locked eyes with those of the hairy, scary man in the mirror. More bloodshot than brown, they looked at me through droopy eyelids. Never before had I seen eyes so sad and lonely, and worse yet, they belonged to me. It disturbed me to the point of uncontrollable shivering, so I forced myself to concentrate on the running water, lathering up my hands several times until the water stopped running black with my filth.

Continuing with my plan, Operation Shiny Hobo, I squirted more soap into my cupped hands and lathered up my thick beard. The sweet caress of the warm water felt exceptional on my face. I began working on my hair next, continuing until no more soap sprayed from the dispenser.

The gooey, filthy mess plastered on the sink and surrounding walls embarrassed me, so I tried my best to wipe everything down, using up nearly all of the paper towels from the dispenser. Then I stuck my face in front of the hand dryer, hitting the button several times until my hair felt dry enough.

At least now I could almost stand being stared at by the unkempt man in the mirror. Still, I avoided his gaze like I owed him money.

After creeping out of the restaurant and back to my safe haven, I finished eating my sandwich with some peace of mind.

Once I had a full belly, I sat there staring at my charred pile of stuff. Losing all of it made me sad of course, but I found myself especially disappointed by losing the book. I continued gazing at the remaining fragment lying there in the grass, reading the title over and over, *The Clock on the Floor*, by Phillip Brammen, or actually just *on the Floor,* since that's all that remained. This delightful mystery was the first book that enthralled me, as far as I could remember. I found it at the edge of Jeffrey's Park, buried face down in the tall weeds. It kept me from getting too bored these past few weeks. It helped that I read slowly, so I had been able to savor the plotline. Now, of course, I wish I had read it quicker.

The more I looked at it, *on the Floor,* the sadder I got. Then, I remembered this town had a local public library. I figured they would have a copy.

I sprang to my feet and began the journey, but it did not take long before my insecurities began their nagging. I wondered if they would even loan a book to a bum like me. That thought made me pause, but I really wanted to know who shot old man Filibuster.

Creeping up to the Red Oak Community Library, I peered in a side window. After spotting the elderly librarian on the other side of the building with his back facing the door, I had hope that maybe, just maybe, I could get in and borrow the book without being seen.

I had barely made it in the front door when the librarian turned sharply, quickly confronting me. He stood rigidly, his thin, bony arms crossed. His face thickly creviced with wrinkles, he scowled as he furrowed his brow, giving his forehead the appearance of a Shar Pei puppy. "Get out. We don't give handouts here," he snapped.

Doing my best to disarm, I smiled broadly. "Oh, no sir, I am looking for a book."

"You need ID and an address to check anything out of this library. Do you have either of these?"

My smile dissolved. "No sir."

The cranky old man jabbed a long, skinny finger at the door. "That's what I thought. Now get out of here, you mangy vagrant!"

When several people in the library turned to look at me, I quickly dashed out the front door.

After sprinting for several blocks, I finally ran out of steam. Standing on the sidewalk with my back arched and hands resting just above my knees, I panted like a dog.

As my breathing returned to normal, I began to feel more at ease. Then, a couple of pre-teen boys saw me and squealed, laughing as they ran away. Their chorus of, "Hobo, Hobo!" penetrated me. I tried to imagine one of them, a colorful lighter in hand, applying flame to my home as I slept. A shiver shot through me.

Once I regained my composure, I caught a glimpse of myself, full-length, in the front window of Gus's Barber Shop. My stained, charred shirt and faded, ripped sweat pants helped to strengthen my embarrassment. "Man, I look like crap," I muttered softly.

Through the barbershop's picture window, I saw a thin, nearly bald man gesturing my direction while talking to a couple other guys inside. I felt that uneasiness welling up again and I turned to walk away when the man flung the door open, waved at me and proclaimed, "Congratulations, you're my one thousandth customer! You win a free shave and a haircut!" Before I could protest, he draped his arm around me and ushered me inside the shop.

The two men in the small, rectangular building stared at me as I entered. A tall beanpole of a man seated in a row of chairs against the opposing wall crumpled his newspaper into his lap, while a fat, ugly guy stood next to him.

Then the thin, shiny-headed barber walked past me and scooped up his electric clippers, sporting a wide smile. He pounded his free hand against the barber's chair and said, "Have a seat right here and let ol' Gus take care of ya."

I smiled politely and replied, "Okay, thanks."

"So, ya feeling okay after the fire?"

Oh, of course these guys had heard all about it, too. I must have been the talk of the town. It certainly explained why people were being so kind to me. I answered, "Yeah, I guess. I'm alive, at least."

"Irene fixed you up at her clinic, did she? Good woman, that Irene." After a brief pause, he asked "So, any idea what happened today? How did your box catch fire? Were you smoking?"

"No, I don't smoke. I didn't do this to myself. I hate to say it, but I think it was one of the neighborhood kids."

"No, I can't believe that," said the tall guy, "The boys around here are decent people, with good, small town morals."

"They torment me, sometimes." My voice softened. "They throw rocks, call me names. Occasionally, I catch some of them rooting through my stuff. But I never imagined they could resort to this. I could've been killed."

Resting both arms on the table and cradling his wide chin in his hands, the fat man sighed. "I'll talk to some of the parents. We'll figure this out."

Not that it mattered, really, but I thanked him for his concern. I inhaled deeply, pausing for a moment before pushing it out with an audible sigh.

As Gus finished whacking at my snarled mass of hair, I gave myself a quick once-over in the mirror. "Looks great. Hard to believe I actually had skin under all that hair. Um, you sure you don't need some money for this? I don't have anything now, but…"

"What? Oh no. No worries. It's on the house."

Offering a sincere smile, I gave Gus my thanks and walked outside. After all this excitement, I felt the urge to be alone, so I went back to my home, or what remained of it.

Lounging by the river's edge, I thoroughly enjoyed the feeling of the sun upon my freshly-shaven face. Amazing, the difference a bit of hair can make. If I still had my beard, I'd be miserable. The tickling of the sweat drops as they oozed through my facial hair would be making me itch, like insects crawling upon my flesh.

Instead, the sun gently warmed me, dancing across my cheeks like a graceful ballerina. I lay there, eyes closed, feeling quite at peace, until I drifted off.

The sky tumbled around me, pieces crashing into the ground with metallic thuds. A grinding screech echoed from above as clouds twisted from their moorings and plummeted. Screams shot out from every direction, yells for help from people I could not see in the ever-widening dust storm. Then, a face emerged from the thick fog. It was that woman from the clinic, Irene. Standing over me, she had an accusatory look plastered across her face. Grabbing me by the neck and pulling me up to her face, she screamed, "How could you?"

I looked up just as a tree-sized baseball bat fell from somewhere above me, striking me across the right temple. I jolted awake with a yelp.

Sitting up, I gripped my head with both hands, squeezing until the pain eased. The lingering effects of the phantom blow still reverberated in my skull.

It took me a moment to realize I had company. The sight of Irene standing a few feet away caused me quite a fright.

"Sorry," she squeaked, "I didn't mean to startle you. I just thought you might need that dressing changed." Holding her arms up, she showed me a roll of gauze in one hand and some ointment in the other. Her smile looked genuine.

Pulling myself to my feet, I nodded my head slowly.

"Please," she gestured toward the ground, "sit. It'll be easier. We don't need to go to the clinic."

"Isn't it a bit soon for a dressing change?"

"Who's the professional here?" she asked with a nervous chuckle. As she unwound my wrapping, she added, "That must've been quite a dream."

"Yeah. They always are. How long were you standing there?"

"Long enough. The pain on your face…" Her voice trailed off. "You must have a terrible burden to bear."

Deflecting her question, I asked, "So, how's my arm looking?"

"Oh, fine, it looks fine. You'll be healed in a few days." She stood up and took a step back. Smiling a thin-lipped smile, she said softly, "I was wondering… would you be interested in coming home with me? For dinner, I mean. I made lasagna last night and I have too much left over. I'll never eat it all."

As I sat there, I couldn't help feeling a bit sorry for her. This thin wisp of a woman couldn't camouflage her sadness or her frailty. It bled through her ill-fitting blouse as well as the oversized skirt that tickled the tops of her ankles. While certainly pretty enough, the worries of life had invaded her face, evident not only in the beginnings of wrinkles, but the overall sorrow that adhered to her skin like poorly applied makeup.

I almost said yes when something occurred to me, something I wish I would have remembered before this. "Well, I do appreciate that, really, but I'm rapidly losing daylight and I need to find a new box and some clothing. What I'm wearing is all I have left and I bet it'll get cold tonight."

"Oh! Wait a sec. I can help you with the clothing. I have a closet full of my husband's old things. You can have as many as you'd like."

"Your husband? Won't he mind?"

Her vision momentarily drooped to the ground. "No. He's not around these days." When her eyes locked on mine again, the sadness burned off like morning fog. "So, whatdya say, a free meal and all the clothes you can carry?"

45

I had mixed feelings about this woman. She seemed trustworthy enough and had been very kind to me, but she seemed a bit too needy. However, a phrase came to mind at that moment: Beggars can't be choosers. I was a beggar, after all. "Okay, sure, thank you very much. It's awfully kind of you."

She perked up considerably as she spun on her heels. "It's all just going to waste, otherwise. It's this way, on the other side of Main Street." She reached for my hand to guide me, but thought better of it. "Come on," she said with a sweeping gesture. After a small pause, she added, "By the way, you sure look a lot better without all that hair."

"Yeah," I replied with a shake of my head, "I feel five pounds lighter."

As we walked, I engaged her in conversation. If I could find out some things about her before I entered her house, all the better. "So, Irene, how long have you lived in Red Oak?"

She stared at me for a moment before answering. "All my life, like most people here. The house has been in my family for generations. So, how long have you been living by the river's edge?"

"I don't know, really. All my life, I guess," I answered with a shrug.

"Are people treating you well?"

"For the most part, yes," I said with a cheeky grin. "This is such a quaint town. I mean, sure, there are a few people who yell and scream, and the children can be awfully cruel, but I'm continually shocked. It's like this place has adopted me as the village hobo. I caught the fat guy from the restaurant putting food in the trash, presumably for me. And it's not just him. I've managed to find clothes in remarkably good shape behind the consignment store. It's like I'm their pet or something!"

"As long as they don't try to scratch behind your ear, huh?" Irene asked with a boisterous chuckle.

I joined in the laugh. "Even that wouldn't be *so* bad, y'know? Just no flea collars."

"Or a bell around your neck." She pointed toward a charming two-story green house with a beautiful widow's walk around the chimney. "Here we are!"

I followed her up the porch steps and waited while she opened the door. Her house was elegantly decorated, with lots of antique-looking furniture, flowery wallpaper, and feminine knick-knacks. "Beautiful place."

She spoke a simple, "Thanks" without turning to look at me. As she walked toward the kitchen, she shouted, "Why don't you go upstairs and see if there's any clothes you like. It's the last door on the left, the master bedroom. Oh, and if you want, you can use the shower in the adjoining bathroom to clean up."

From the edge of the stairs, I yelled back, "Thanks, I'll do that. I'm sure I'm far too gamy for indoor activities." I heard her giggle as I trudged up the plush carpeted stairs.

I found the master bedroom easily enough. Even though closets flanked either side of the bed, I opened the doors on the right without hesitation.

This woman obviously assumed her hubby would be returning someday. Either that or she had serious pack-rat tendencies. I had never seen so many clothes in one place, so tightly packed I had to use both hands and a lot of wiggling to remove a pair of blue jeans and a white button-down shirt.

Holding the clothes up to my body at the full-length mirror, it appeared they would fit me well enough. I tossed them onto the bed and trudged into the bathroom.

The shower felt fantastic against my dirty, oily skin. Amazing, the difference between being caught, fully clothed, in a cold rain and standing naked in a hot shower. I could have spent all day lathering and smiling, but I knew a hot meal awaited, so I tried not to dawdle.

Once dressed, I lingered momentarily in front of the mirror. Examining myself in my new clothes, my fresh, collared shirt, and nearly brand-new jeans, I couldn't believe how different from yesterday I looked. My hand caressed my clean-shaven cheeks and I smiled at myself. My eyes, in stark contrast from earlier, looked much brighter and livelier. These peepers did not scare me.

Irene quietly pushed the door open and breathed, "Wow."

Her voice made me jump. "Huh? Oh, jeez, you're always startling me."

"Sorry. Dinner's ready when you are. You look good."

I grinned at her. "Yeah, apparently I clean up well. Thanks again for these clothes."

As she handed me a plastic shopping bag, she replied, "You're welcome. Here, you can put your old clothes in this. I'll go set the table."

She pivoted and left the room while I scooped up my nasty old clothes. As I snatched the sweat pants by a leg, the lighter tumbled out, its tie-dye colors clashing with the brown carpet. Bending over, I picked it up and tucked it in my new jeans.

During the meal, we chatted about all sorts of topics. I found her to be an easy person to talk with. I had not realized how much I missed simple conversation with another human being.

"Well," I said as we walked toward the living room, "that sure was a fantastic meal! Thank you."

"You're welcome," she replied with a huge smile. "Say, have you seen the latest Bruce Willis movie? It's been on HBO the past few weeks."

"Um... No. I never got around to getting cable in my cardboard box."

She giggled like a little girl. "Too funny! Well, it's on tonight. I hear it's every man's favorite new movie. Ya wanna watch it?"

I shrugged as I plopped onto her sofa. "If I do, I won't have enough time to locate a new box to sleep in before nightfall. So, Irene, the answer is yes, as long as you don't mind me sleeping on this couch tonight."

As she took a seat next to me, she nodded while tossing me a sly smile. It did not take long before I understood what that smile meant. Before the dust had settled on the first movie explosion, she leaned in and gave me a small, tender kiss. I guess the haircut and shower did more for my appearance than I thought. I returned the kiss with one of my own – long, lingering and passionate. We explored each other thoroughly. Being with Irene felt natural and comfortable. Before long, we found our way to the master bedroom.

When I awoke, for a fleeting moment I felt completely at ease, like I belonged right here. I rolled over and saw the back of Irene's head, disheveled black hair splayed against her white pillow, and I smiled. I also realized I had just slept a few hours without any horrible dreams, which hadn't happened in a long time.

Still, the moment passed. Even though a light rain fell, I felt a strong urge to leave. Being careful not to disturb her, I eased myself onto the floor and scooped up my clothes. I carried them down into the living room, where the streetlights streaming in through the rain-soaked windows pierced the darkness. Using that light, I began yanking the jeans over my hips.

While buttoning up my new shirt, my gaze landed upon a picture on the opposite wall. Framed perfectly inside a rectangle of light from the street, the photograph showed a man and a woman, smiling gleefully in front of a large oak tree. The woman I instantly recognized as Irene, taken many years ago. I smiled when I saw how young and giddy she looked in the photo. She really must have been in love with the man standing to her right.

"Do you like the picture?" Irene stood at the entrance of the room, her pink robe tied loosely around her waist.

My breath caught in my throat. "Jeez, woman. Give me a heart attack, why don't ya?"

"Sorry. The picture. Take a good look at it." She turned and flipped a switch, illuminating the room with blinding light.

After my eyes adjusted, I did as she requested. "You look so beautiful here. How long ago was this?"

"Oh, a decade or so. Now, look at the man. What do you think of him?"

As I stared, I asked, "This your husband?"

"Yes. John Millicutty."

Grinning as widely as Irene was, he seemed a happy fellow with his clean-shaven cheeks and short, brownish-black hair. I wondered if it ever bothered him, being a couple inches shorter than his woman. I had not noticed it before, but I also stood a couple inches shorter than Irene. Looking back at the man, I said, "I can't believe this guy was dumb enough to leave you."

"Extenuating circumstances." She sighed loudly before adding, "You still don't remember, do you? I really hoped the lasagna and sex therapy would help."

I spun to look into her eyes. "Lasagna and sex therapy?"

"Oh, where to start?" She asked as she picked up her purse and pulled out a pack of Kool cigarettes. Her hands shook slightly as she lit the cigarette with … with a vibrantly colorful lighter! "You see –"

"Irene?" I produced my lighter and held it at eye level. "I found this near the fire."

Her eyes widened and her mouth parted slightly. "No, I… Oh… John, I'm so sorry. I didn't mean…" She approached me, her hands outstretched. "You weren't supposed to get hurt. You were in the center of the box, so I thought… I thought you'd wake up before then. You

50

were always such a light sleeper. I didn't mean for you to get burned, John. Please believe me!"

Instinctively, as she moved closer to me, I inched toward the front door. "What the hell?! Why would you do this, you psycho? What've I ever done to you?"

"I just wanted to shock you into remembering. John, don't you get it?"

"Get what? And why do you keep calling me John?" I had to get away from this nut. I had backed almost to the door, so I spun and reached for the knob. "You're insane! You need help, lady."

"Why won't you remember? It's been over six months!"

As I yanked the door open and bolted down the steps into what had become a steady rain, she screamed, "Wait!"

Sprinting as fast as my body could stand, I ran down Main Street as the storm turned violent. "Crap!" I breathed as I suddenly recognized I had nowhere to go. Before I realized it, I found myself on the steps of the library.

Swirling wind smacked my face with leaves and rain as I yanked on the library door. It did not budge and I quickly realized they had closed for the night.

I plopped down onto the steps, panting heavily.

Sitting in the shadows of the Library's ornate overhang, I managed to find some shelter from the storm. I slumped down and fell into a restless sleep.

Gigantic metal trees loomed overhead, neatly in a row. Several people stood by my side, looking to me for guidance. Surrounded by large animals, the elephants and rhinos leapt and frolicked. Suddenly, a rhino staggered, slamming into one of the trees. It began to tip.

Cracking and popping sounds filled the air, quickly joined by screams of terror. The trees fell one into another like colossal dominoes, the metal forest becoming a torrent of artificial hail. Pieces crashed down around me as I pulled into a fetal position. A voice screamed out, "Help me John!" I looked around, but I couldn't see who called to me. The forest ...

I woke to someone repeatedly kicking the sole of my shoe. "You can't sleep here. Go away!"

"Wha? Oh, sorry." As I pulled myself to a seated position, I hugged myself tightly. Even though the morning sun poked through the scattering rain clouds, I could not stop shivering.

The librarian stared at me for a moment before he spoke again, clearly not recognizing me right away after my transformation. "Oh, it's you again. All cleaned up, huh?" The man smoothed his thin, gray hair, wiping his hand on the front of his beige slacks. After scrutinizing me for a few more seconds, his taut features softened slightly. "You look miserable. I may not like you, but I can't let anyone suffer like this. Come on in," he said with a loud sigh. Pulling out a large set of keys attached to a metal hoop, he fumbled through several keys before finding the one that opened the front door of the library.

Though I appreciated his attempt at hospitality, his hostility made me nervous. As I walked into the dry, quiet building, I felt compelled to ask, "Did you say you don't like me? What've I ever done to you?"

His forehead crinkled up and he gave me a harsh, disbelieving glare. "Seriously? This whole thing isn't some deranged act, to get out of your responsibilities?"

"Deranged act? What are you going on about?"

The old man shook his head slowly and walked over to the computer against the wall. "Come over here," he said with a sweeping arm gesture. He powered the machine up and after accessing the newspaper archives, I found myself reading a very miserable tale from April 1st, 2005. The headline read, *"April Fools Day Tragedy Claims Two."*

Two men were killed and one seriously injured yesterday when a series of steel trusses collapsed at a local area construction site.

Workers from the Johnson Construction Company were erecting the main supports for a building at 1543 Farhat Road when one of the trusses collapsed. This caused a chain reaction, which brought down all seven of the supports.

Abe Billman, 41 and Jesse Mason, 23, were killed after being buried under falling debris. Foreman John Millicutty, 39, is currently listed in critical condition. The other three members of the construction team escaped with minor injuries.

It took rescuers over 25 minutes to remove the heavy steel beams that trapped Billman and Mason. Billman was pronounced dead on arrival at Mercy Hospital in Menson, while Mason died on site.

"We believe a brace was improperly installed on the support truss," said Jason Johnson, owner of Johnson Construction, "and when that gave way, it caused a cascade failure. Everything came crashing down. I lost two good men today."

Millicutty was admitted to Mercy with severe head trauma. He has not regained consciousness.

I sat in the Library's hard, small-backed chair and stared at the article for a while. Underneath, the pictures told more of the story. A grainy, black-and-white photo of the accident scene showed a pile of debris, but the head shots of the victims mesmerized me the most. Abe Billman's picture showed me a man with a gap between his upper front teeth and a head with more bald spot than hair. I stared for several minutes at the shiny spot where the flash reflected off his head.

A young man in the prime of his life, Jesse Mason looked vibrant and rebellious, with wild hair and a cocky grin.

Then, I shifted over to John Millicutty. This guy kinda looked like the picture at Irene's, with a similar vibrancy to his eyes and the same chipper smile.

53

"Okay," I said to the librarian, "I don't get it. I see that something horrible happened to these men. But why show it to me?"

He looked at me like I sprouted a second nose. Again, he said, "Seriously? That's you, moron. You're John Millicutty."

"Excuse me? If that's true, then why, for God's sake, don't I remember any of it?"

"You need to keep reading." I accessed the next several days of newspaper archives.

It chronicled the coma that encompassed John Millicutty's brain for the next three days, as well as the amnesia he experienced upon awakening. One quote from the attending doctor said, "We expect his amnesia to be short term, but when coupled with the emotional loss he experienced, there's no telling how long it could last."

I looked over at the librarian. "Emotional loss?"

"The accident was your fault," he said matter-of-factually.

"What?"

"Or at least you blamed yourself. After all, you were the lead foreman. Of course, I blamed you, too."

"You... what?"

The old man shook his head slowly and scowled at me fiercely. "You don't even remember my name, do you? I'm Mac Mason. Jesse was my grandson. The authorities labeled it a freak accident, and I've come to accept that. But it's been difficult to get over the fact that your negligence killed my grandson."

I stared at the man blankly. "I... I don't –"

"Yeah, yeah, you don't remember. I know. It's either extremely convenient or a sad, sad situation. From what I understand, you didn't know my Jesse very well. But Abe... oh, his death must've really got to you. You and he were best of friends, inseparable as teenagers and just as close as adults. I know you guys went fishing a lot –"

"Okay," I cut him off, "So I spent a few days in a coma, woke up without memory of anything, and to this day, months later, I still have no memory of any of this? That makes no sense. What did the doctors do about it?"

"You didn't give them much of a chance. Keep reading." A couple days later, this article appeared: *Amnesia Patient Escapes Hospital.*

"Oh now, this is just stupid! It says here I simply walked out of the place in the middle of the night." After hearing a hush from someone on the other side of the library who I had not even noticed before this, I turned my rant into a whisper. "Seriously, this occurred days after the accident. Why don't I remember it, Mac?"

"Hey, you're asking me? No one completely understands the intricacies of the human brain. I certainly don't know why you snuck out of the hospital under cover of darkness, or why you don't remember. But this, John, is a fact. That man right there," he tapped the photo of John Millicutty, "is you. Your wife Irene searched for you, as did the rest of the town, but you disappeared rather thoroughly. No one even knew you were still around until a couple months ago, when Milner spotted you rummaging through the trash behind his Quik Stop. You've been the talk of Red Oak."

Looking over at the scowling old coot, I shrugged as I asked, "All right, so what do we do now?"

Mac hopped to his feet. "Frankly, I don't care what you do. I've come to grips with Jesse's death. It was an accident. Whether or not you're to blame for that accident, that's immaterial. At this point, it's up to you. Either you go apologize to Irene for abandoning her, or you crawl back under that rock. Makes no difference to me."

"Apologize? That whack-job set me on fire!"

Mac actually chuckled at me. "Wait, you're saying Irene did that? Oh, that's rich!"

"Rich? She could've killed me!"

"Well, now, you need to look at it from her point of view. You're in this horrible accident, then you wake up from a coma not knowing her. Then, you run away. You might as well've been killed in the accident. At least she would've had some closure. But instead, you slinked away to live in the woods."

"But I don't remember any of this!"

"And that's the worst part. She can't even be mad at you for abandoning her when she needed you the most. Maybe that's why she did it. Maybe she thought the fire might jar something loose. Hell, at least it got you motivated. Now," he added as he turned his back on me, "I have a job to perform here. Don't stay too long."

As it turned out, I did stay too long. I sat in that uncomfortable chair for hours, reading every article over and over, staring at the pictures, trying to burn them into my memory. Or force their release from the vault in my brain.

The sun hung low in the evening sky, hurling vibrant reds and oranges across the deepening blue of the horizon. Standing on Irene's porch, I beat loudly upon her door until she answered. When she did, I exclaimed with a deep scowl. "I need to know why you tried to kill me."

She turned pale. "I wasn't trying to kill you, John. You have to believe me. I… I was… Oh, I don't know, John. I guess I was trying to force you to come home. You live here. You're my husband."

"Yes, yes, I've been at the library, I read the articles. So how does flame-broiling me help?"

She walked past me and sat down on the porch swing. After burying her face in her hands for a moment, she looked up and with tears on her cheeks, she muttered, "I didn't plan to do it. I had heard rumors you were living down by the river, so I went to see for myself. I saw you sleeping there, and I guess I thought if I destroyed the box, you'd have to come home. I thought you'd wake up long before the flames got to you. I'm so sorry. It all happened so fast and I panicked."

I let her sit there for a while, sobbing into her hands. Eventually, I sat down next to her. "I doubt I can ever forgive you, y'know. But having read the articles about the accident, I sorta understand. I get your loneliness, your frustration."

She looked up at me with a face that looked like it had been caught in a rainstorm. "Did it help any? Do you remember who you are?"

I shook my head slowly. "But I wouldn't mind hearing about this man named John. Apparently, he's so great you'd fry a homeless man to get him back."

The two of us sat for hours in her living room, sipping lemonade and looking at pictures. "This one was taken a few years back, at Carlsbad. You were so handsome."

Looking at this photo, I fought to stifle a chuckle. The man, clad in beige Dockers and poop-brown loafers with a pink knit shirt nearly brought a tear to my eye. "Pink? Are you kidding? What, did you dress me?"

"I could lie and say you always loved pink, but no. You're right. You wore this outfit to please me."

"Wow. I must've really loved you."

The look she shot me caused instant regret of my wording. I looked into her teary blue eyes and asked, "So, how long after this did the accident happen?"

Blotting her eyes with a tissue, she replied, "Three, four years, maybe. There are a lot of memories in this book. Oh, here's my favorite wedding photo."

Irene sure looked radiant in that flowing white dress. Her smile lit up the whole picture, probably the whole room, and I told her so.

She smiled as a fresh tear tumbled down her cheek. "The reception was so much fun."

"Yeah it was! The look you gave me when I crammed that piece of wedding cake into your face. Priceless!"

It took a moment for the reality to set in. "John? You remembered that?"

"Oh my. I did, Irene. I did!"

We sat on that couch, in our tight embrace, for what felt like hours.

Frankly, I felt a bit guilty, pretending to remember like that. After all, didn't everyone smash cake at weddings? All I knew for sure was I did not want to be homeless through a cold, Michigan winter. I needed a roof over my head. Besides, I'd be a fool to pass up this sweet deal. I could certainly get used to Irene's lasagna and sex therapy.

~ Chapter Six ~

Overall, I've never been fond of yard work, though I have to admit I do kinda dig driving around my 1.5-acre yard on a riding mower.

If I had a better mower – one that didn't belch out plumes of smoke or suddenly not allow me to turn left – I would enjoy it more. Having to hold my breath as the wind changes direction, or mowing in concentric circles like I had to do at the end of last season, is not my idea of a good time.

Today, though, it's not so bad. My dear wife is on the side of the yard, moving rocks around to cordon off her flower section. This suits me fine, as it removes mowing space.

She waves me over, so I roll up beside her and shut off the engine. After a couple of dying coughs and a spasm of acrid smoke from the mower, it mercifully ceases to run. "I'm buying you a better mower next year," she says with a wave of her hands to help dissipate the black cloud.

I hope she does! However, I respond with, "Cool." Then I point at her right cheek. "Mosquito."

Slapping her skin, she misses the bloodsucker and it vanishes, like they do. "Grr!" Then she points at me, so I raise my hand to smack myself, but she says, "Don't you have a mosquito story?"

"You know I do, babe."

"Then tell me a story!"

~ No Picnic ~

Being a mosquito is no picnic, let me tell you. If we're not being swatted by a newspaper or shocked in a bug zapper, we have to be on guard against bats, birds, and dragonflies. Yesterday, I watched as Velma was devoured by a frog. A frog! Can you imagine anything more embarrassing?

Though I thrive in this heat, so do my myriad comrades. There's so much competition. Not that I need much blood for my offspring to survive. A few slurps from my built-in straw will suffice. But there are only so many humans around here, and most of my extended family is much stronger and faster than I am. While the others somehow use the wind current to glide from place to place – look at Raul doing loop-de-loops, the show-offee bastard! – I flutter and flap against this strong breeze, seemingly losing ground as fast as I gain it. However, I must continue my labor, as it's a labor of love, for my unborn children.

Fortunately, my clumsy tumbling has actually paid off, tossing me exactly where I need to be.

Sitting at a picnic table is a large human, his food spread out in front of him. Though he has obviously doused himself in some sort of bizarre-smelling chemical in a miserable attempt to confuse my senses, I can easily spot him. I mean, he's sitting right there!

Though this one seems easy pickings, I will have to be cautious. The human hand is a dangerous weapon, which has felled many of my kind. It only took one committed human to slaughter Daphne, Libby, Betty, and Javier. Oh Javier, he was one handsome skeeter! Legs like a rock star. Mmmm…

C'mon Veronica, focus! One well-timed slap and splat! I cannot die now. I must give birth to the next generation, and in order to do that, I must acquire what this guy has in his veins. Of course, I have no idea what the hell I'm doing. I've never actually sucked blood from a human before. I have a basic understanding. I've run simulations. Okay Veronica, let's do this!

I come in low, from under the table. Around his back side, I fly where the human's eyes cannot see. Zipping near his leg, I come up and over, and there – the perfect place to land and feed. I touch down quietly and stealthily, get my footing, and slowly but forcefully insert my proboscis.

Oh, the glorious nectar! Succulent, nourishing … a little thicker than I expected – it's sweet and surprisingly tangy. I look up when I hear my brothers and sisters laughing. "Hey Veronica, you're sucking on a ketchup packet, y'know!"

~ Chapter Seven ~

"My stories come from all sorts of different places," I tell my wife, "Many of them are prompt driven, either through my writing groups, like Writing at the Ledges, Everybody Writes, or Fiction 440. Some date back to the AOL weekly writing contest days of the early 2000s, while others were various contests I entered.

"However, some of these pieces come straight out of the fertile what-if section of my brain. A few actually came from watching a TV show or movie, and having my brain shut off the visuals to begin writing the story that interests me more."

"That's fascinating," my wife replies, "but that doesn't answer my question."

I crinkle my brow. "Sorry. What did you ask again?"

"What do you want for dinner?"

As my face flushes a light pink in embarrassment, I reply, "Oh. Um, food, I guess."

The glare she gives me is an ice-cutter to be sure, so I add, "Um, veggie burgers would be great."

"Mmm hmm."

She's still giving me the look. Though she's probably messing with me, I'd rather get her beautiful smile than this look, so I say, "How about a story while you make dinner?"

"So when did you die, Gabe?" asked Bill. Everyone looked at Gabe in anticipation.

Rubbing his smooth chin as he recollected, he replied, "It wasn't long after the election, so early 2009, I guess. January or February. I've kinda lost track. Wow, that means it's been over three years."

Fran, with a ghost of a smile said, "Time flies, huh?"

Everyone at the Dead People's Support Group nodded his or her head in unison.

"Uh-huh," answered Gabe. "So what about you, Fran? When did you kick the bucket?"

"Well, I was spending a year dead for tax purposes, but things got out of hand. I learned one important lesson. Make 100% sure you can trust the person watching your body."

As the members nodded their agreement with that statement, a beautiful, angry-looking young woman flew into the room. Gliding across the floor, she shot everyone a cross expression as she floated over to the empty chair next to Gabe. Gabe smiled up at her, but she did not look down at him. Gabe liked her haunting good looks, but he did not care for her negative spirit. It gave him the spooks.

"Good," said Bill, the moderator of the group, "I was hoping you'd decide to show up. Everyone, this is Raunay." Everyone muttered and moaned their hellos.

Exhaling loudly, she replied, "Not like this'll do any good. I'm dead. What's the point?"

"The point, Raunay, is that you are still here on this plane of existence. You all are, and none of you are going on to the next level until we figure out why you're still here."

"Next level? Sheesh," she hissed. "That makes it sound like we're trapped in a video game! What, am I supposed to defeat the dragon and save the princess before I get a free life?"

Bill replied with his smooth, calming voice, "If it helps you to think of this as a video game, then by all means do so."

"I was just making a point. I don't like video games!"

"I do," Gabe interjected, "especially Ghosts N Goblins. When you get hit in that game, you lose your armor, and you have to run around in your underwear. It's..." When he looked up and saw Raunay glaring down at him, he trailed off.

"Anyway," Bill said, trying to regain control, "Raunay, why don't you tell us how you died. It's always a good place to start."

"I was murdered." The room gasped as one.

"Calm dawn, everyone." After a short pause, Bill resumed. "Okay, let me read your bio to the group. Raunay McInerny, born in Holland in 1991, died April of this year of a single gunshot wound to the chest. The killer is still at large, but there is an interesting sentence in your police report. It says you reported that a man named Johnson Bradford shot you."

"Right! Exactly! I reported it. To the police! But because I'm a ghost, nothing I say is admissible in court. It's like I don't even exist!"

From the corner of the room, Fran interjected, "In the eyes of the law, you don't. None of us do. We're treated like images on film. We're... well, ghosts of our former selves. You –"

When the lights started flickering and chairs began to fly around the room, the group members instinctively floated to the ceiling for safety, even though such things could no longer hurt them. Bill, the only living creature in the room, ran to the corner, flipped a table over, and hid behind it. "Raunay! Stop this at once! Damaging public property will not help. If you wreck this old building, they won't let us meet here anymore."

As quickly as it began, Raunay's tantrum ended. The steel chairs clamored to the ground. "Why do we even have chairs, anyway? We can't freakin' sit in 'em!"

"Everyone needs to have their own personal space, and the chairs symbolize it. Now please, everyone come back down. I think we'll call it a night. I'll see you all Wednesday."

Raunay flew quickly out of the room, passing through Gabe. "Hey!" he yelled at her.

Pausing, she turned back to him, her anger tinged with incomprehension. "What?"

"You went right through me."

"So?"

"Well, it's rude. I would think you'd understand that. You're clearly upset over being treated as if you don't exist. How do you think it makes me feel to have you fly through me like I'm nothing?"

Her hostility ebbed as she examined Gabe. Even for a ghost, his features seemed ethereal, with his tired, sunken eyes and pursed lips. "You're right. I'm sorry. I didn't mean anything by it." After staring for a moment longer, she started chuckling. "Okay, I gotta say something about your wardrobe."

Now it was Gabe's turn to get angry. "I'd rather you didn't."

"No, no, I have to. You look ridiculous!"

Long ago, Gabe decided this was the worst part about being dead. "We weren't all fortunate enough to be killed at work, or at a fancy night club or something. I was at home, on laundry day. All I had was this faded, *Where's the Beef* t-shirt, my ex-girlfriend's Betty Boop sweat pants..."

"And what about the pink fuzzy slippers? Also the ex's?"

65

"My... feet... were... cold! It's not like we can change our clothes anymore."

"Right. Sorry." She spent the next few seconds trying not to laugh, but failing miserably. Gabe turned to leave when she said, "Wait, wait a minute Betty Boop!"

Spinning back to glare at her, he said through clenched teeth, "Gabe. My name is Gabe."

"Gabe, sorry. Sorry for all of it. I'm... I'm so new to this whole being dead thing. It's... unnerving."

"Believe me, I get that. It takes some getting used to. And truth be told, there are things you'll never get used to."

"Like what?"

Gesturing over to the window of Peterson's Fish Market, where people sat enjoying their meals, he replied, "Well, not eating is one. Sure it's convenient, but I really miss the taste of food. Like catfish, french fries, pizza..."

"Chocolate!" Raunay loudly blurted out. "I don't think I can make it much longer without chocolate."

Gabe shrugged. "You get used to it, somewhat. We can't smell either, so it's not like anything truly entices us anymore."

After a momentary pause, she said, "Where do you go? What do you do? I've... just been floating around the city... well, I was harassing the guy who killed me, but he got a restraining order against me. I can't hover within 500 feet of that bastard now!"

"I have a place. Come on, I'll show you," he said with a thin smile.

The two spirits floated down the road until they came upon a small, boarded up house. Looking at the condemned sticker on the plank of wood covering the front door, Raunay furrowed her brow. "Seriously? You live here?"

Nodding his head, Gabe replied, "Sure. It's not as bad as it seems. No one will bother us here."

They floated through the boarded up door and into the run-down house. With carpeting stained in some spots and ripped out in others, holes punched in the walls, and several missing light fixtures, it was apparent why the city condemned the place. "Again," Raunay said, "seriously? You don't really live here."

"This was my house. I spent most of my adult life here." After noticing the disgust on her face, he added, "It looked better back then, of course."

Hovering over the nasty floor for all of a minute, she blurted out, "There's no way I'm staying here! This is the most depressing place that ever existed! No wonder you're in therapy."

Gabe started to reply, but paused when the realization ignited inside of him. "Wow. You're right. This can't be helping me." After a moment of silence, he looked at her and said, "So, what do you think we should do?"

"I know what I want to do. I want to go back and continue haunting the bastard who killed me! That son of a bitch deserves every bit of torment I can offer him!"

"But you can't. Remember the restraining order."

When her eyes widened, Gabe felt an uneasy tingle. "But you," she exclaimed as her face lit up with optimism, "you can go haunt the guy for me!"

Gabe shook his head vehemently. "Oh geez no! That's not my thing. I've never done anything like that."

"For real? You've never messed with the living? Not even flickering the lights or moving a chair? Never done the disembodied 'oooooo' voice before? Oh, it's so much fun! You have to do this for me."

"No, no, I can't. It's –"

"It's what? So, you've spent the last three years haunting an abandoned house and going to support group meetings? Is that really how you enjoy living? Or deading? Or whatever we're supposed to call this?"

Gaping at the young woman with new found understanding, Gabe said through his down turned mouth, "I...don't really enjoy any of this. I just want it to end. It's not fair that I should die and just stay here. I don't even understand why I didn't go on to...whatever's next. Others have seen the swirling light from above, and have ascended from this horrible existence. But not me. I don't understand why. I hate this!" Tears ran down his face like the rain he could no longer feel.

Raunay let the dead man cry for a moment before she floated over and put her hands on him, one on the back of his head and the other on the small of his back. Falling into her arms, he sobbed heavily. "I...didn't realize ghosts could touch one another," she said softly.

Looking up with tear-stained eyes, he said, "Okay Raunay, I'll help you. I'll haunt this evil man for you. You're right. It has to be better than hanging out in this dump."

The two ghosts traveled across town until they reached a tall apartment building. "Johnson Bradford is on the 7th floor, room number 724. Right there," she said as she pointed up at his window.

Shaking nervously, Gabe asked, "So, um, what do I do exactly?"

"Go up there, move some stuff around, get in his face, just scare the crap out of him. Remind him that he's the reason why I'm dead."

"All right." Floating up to his window, Gabe peered in. A miserable-looking, unkempt young man sat at the kitchen table with a bottle of Jack Daniels in his outstretched hand. His white t-shirt had stains all over it, and his face had probably not felt the sting of a razor in several days.

"Okay, here it goes," Gabe uttered to himself as he flew through the window. "Ooooooo! I'm here to haunt you, Johnson Bradford!"

Johnson spun his head around to look at the ghost as it moved effortlessly through his outside window. "Oh God, not again! What do you want?"

"You killed Raunay Mac-a... something," Gabe paused, fighting the blush that attempted to overwhelm his face, before forcing himself to continue, "and I'm here to remind you of that. You suck, dude!"

Standing up, Johnson threw the nearly empty bottle of liquor at the ghost, which sailed through him and struck the window. Glass exploded outward, raining jagged shards down on the pavement below. Upon seeing this, Raunay smiled. "Way to go, Gabe!"

"Why did you kill Raunay, you dick?"

"I didn't mean to! It was an accident. I was just robbing her and... she rushed at me. The gun went off. I didn't mean to. Oh God, I can't take this anymore! I just can't!" Turning, he grabbed the phone and dialed 911. "Send the cops over to 1274 Bobla Avenue, apartment 724."

Oh crap, Gabe thought, he's getting a restraining order on me, too! I've never been in trouble with the law. This will be on my permanent record!

Johnson continued, "You must arrest me. I killed Raunay..." He turned to Gabe and asked, "What's her last name again?"

Gabe shrugged, so the man added, "I don't know her last name. But I'm Johnson Bradford. I killed her and you need to arrest me. I can't take the guilt any longer!"

After he hung up, he plopped down at the table. "Please tell her I'm sorry. I am truly sorry. So sorry."

"I will," Gabe said quietly. "You're doing the right thing here."

"I know. Now get outta here! I don't want to see another ghost as long as I live."

Floating back down to the sidewalk, Gabe gave Raunay a beaming smile. As the sirens rose in the distance, he said, "They're coming for him. He's going to confess to your murder."

The two ghosts hovered arm in arm as they watched the police lead the man off in handcuffs. As Johnson passed, he looked the dead woman in her eyes. "I'm so sorry I took your life away."

After the police car drove off, Raunay turned to Gabe and embraced him again. "Thank you! It's as if a giant weight has been lifted. I feel so light, so..."

Looking up, she saw what appeared to be a whirlpool of light in the sky above her, spinning tumultuously. "What is that?"

Smiling, Gabe replied, "It's your ride. You earned it, Raunay." He looked up at it for a moment. "Wow, that's an amazing sight. It looks nothing like what others told me about..." Then it dawned on him. "Wait! I can see it too! Is it my ride also?"

"I believe it is, Gabe. Apparently, you needed to do something good to earn your ticket."

The two ghosts levitated upward, allowing the vortex to pull them in.

~ Chapter Eight ~

Walking in the front door of The Creole in Lansing Michigan's historic Old Town, my wife wanders off to find us a table while I mosey up to the bar to get us a couple of beers. I see several of my Fiction 440 friends – Scott, Joan, Mike, Lucille, and Dan – seated throughout the lively venue.

While standing in line for our refreshments, I spot Aaron and Jeff engaged in conversation. I wave at them and they walk over.

"Hi Randy," says Aaron, one of the owners of the Creole, "are you reading tonight?"

I pat the pocket with my story in it. "You better believe it! I wouldn't miss one of these events for the world."

"Fantastic!" Jeff says before turning to chat with another patron, "We have a good crowd tonight."

Jeff and Aaron started Fiction 440 in 2010 with a simple concept. They give us a prompt, usually three unrelated words, or a phrase of some sort, and we have to invent a story using 440 words or less. We then get together at a bar or restaurant – usually a bar – and we read them to one another. We do no judging or critique. We just share our work, people laugh and/or applaud, and we go on to the next one.

Whether or not I've written a story, I always try to attend these fun-filled events. The level of talent that participates never ceases to amaze me.

71

Stepping up to the microphone, Aaron begins by saying, "Hello everyone! Welcome to Fiction 440. Today's prompt words are cornucopia, trumpet, and contender. Up first is Randy Pearson."

Aaron hands me the microphone, and I graciously accept it.

~ A Cornucopia of Crazy ~

I entered the bar, spotting my friend Alberto in the corner. "Hey bud, how's the divorce going?"

Tipping his beer back, he replied, "My ex has gone off the deep end. She's a cornucopia of crazy!"

"Really? What has Angie done? Did she key your car?"

"Dude, she keyed my house! She's been wreaking havoc at work, too."

I exhaled sharply. "Oh that's right. You work together. That can't be fun."

He sighed. "Not so much. She's been vandalizing my office. She removed the screws from my chair the other day, and yesterday, she TP'd my desk!"

"You should tell your boss."

"Angie *is* my boss!"

"Oh. Well, you're screwed, then. Are you sure you can't reconcile with her?"

Alberto stared at me as if I had just suggested he eat a plate of car parts. "Are you wacko? I mean, sure I still love her. But the craziness. When we were dating, I knew she was a bit ... extreme. Like when she beat up that Hooters waitress for giving me extra wings. At the time I loved her fire, her passion. Now I feel like a contender in a prize fight."

At that moment, I turned to the right, and noticed an angry-looking Hispanic woman sitting at the table next to us, her fiery eyes glued on Alberto. "Uh, buddy..."

When he saw her, he got up and sprinted away. However, since there were people at every turn, he ended up jumping onto the stage, headlong into the band. He elbowed the trumpet player, sending his instrument clanking onto the ground.

When I turned back, Angie sat in Alberto's vacated seat. Her smile sent a chill through me. "So Monte, is Al dating anyone?"

"N...not that I'm aware of. You, uh, you look nice today."

Her eyes softened. "Thanks. You're Al's best friend," she said. I wasn't, was I? Well, he once told me she frightened off all his other friends, so maybe I was, by default. She continued, "I don't understand why he's leaving me. Tell me why."

Yikes! I surely didn't want to be in the middle of this, but heck, maybe I could help. "He does still love you, but apparently, you've been way too possessive, jealous, and, uh..." I paused. I knew I couldn't say batshit crazy. How to word this... "Intense. I have no idea if you two have a chance, but I know if you don't stop being weird, you'll push him away completely."

With that she stood up, thanked me, drank the rest of Alberto's beer in one long swallow, and marched off. I put my head on the table and panted for a while.

73

~ Chapter Nine ~

After we arrive home from the Fiction 440 event, there are still a couple of hours to kill before bed time, so I pop in *Blazing Saddles* for us to watch. Snuggling with my wife on the couch, cats all around us (and in some cases on top of us), this is what I want my heaven to be like.

The time flies while watching such a classic, silly bit of Mel Brooks cinema. When the movie ends, I say, "Man, such a great movie," as I click off the TV.

Looking over at my wife, my face explodes into a smile. With eyes closed and a content smile, her face is aglow with peaceful bliss and silent serenity. "Honey?"

"Mmmm?" Her lids crack open, with barely enough space to see the outside world.

"Did you enjoy the movie?"

"Mmmm."

Oh yes, she's just about to enter dreamland. My chances of getting her to bed are slim at best. "You're going to fall asleep on the couch again, aren't you?"

With a sleepy grin, she replies, "Ooookay."

"No, not okay. You should get up and come to bed."

"Ooookay." In the early days of our marriage, this used to make me rather cross or hurt, as if I had done something wrong and this was my

74

punishment. However, I've come to realize that this has nothing to do with me. Once her brain begins to shut off, she's down for the count.

Reaching behind me, I pull the afghan off the back of the couch and carefully drape it over my wife. "Here ya go, sweetie."

She grabs it and snugs it up under her chin, giving a cat-like purr of contentment. "Tell me a story."

I chuckle softly. "You won't remember it."

Giving me a pouty frown, she replies, "Uh-huh!"

She gives me such joy. "Ooookay sweetie."

~ The Five-Year Itch ~

Usually, shaking the blues didn't take any more effort than this. Being far enough away from the highway in the southern-most corner of our three-acre yard, the roaring cacophony of traffic disappeared completely, nullified by the ambient sounds of nature. We had a bottle of Johan Klauss Liebfraumilch, Chloe's favorite white wine. I had packed a lovely picnic basket, complete with cheese squares, whole-wheat crackers, and those vile little cucumber sandwiches she so adored. I even made brownies to please my wife, a woman who cherished chocolate more than a cat loved tuna.

However, as we lounged on the grassy knoll, soaking up the afternoon sun, Chloe's occasional sighs continued to permeate the air. She had not been her normal, chipper self in quite some time. Rolling over onto my side, I slid my hand along the soft grass until my fingers gently tickled her left hand. I took her delicate hand in mine, brought it up to my face, and gave the back of her fingers a slow, lingering kiss. "So, how are you, sweetie?"

Her response consisted of, "Eh," more of a noise than a word.

I faked a smile, a pointless endeavor since her gaze fell elsewhere. Lying on her back, she stared up at the sky, but I doubt she even perceived that. I tried to draw her in with some idle conversation. "It's a gorgeous day, isn't it?" The afternoon blue sky practically glowed, punctuated with a series of small, puffy white clouds.

This time my query received no verbal response, only a slight shrugging of the shoulders. I inched closer to her, bringing her hand and mine up to my chest as I rolled onto my back. "Hey," I said, "look at that cloud! Looks like a face, doesn't it?" She didn't reply, so I continued, "Yeah, there's the nose, big and bulbous. There's the mouth, kinda like a yawn. The eyes are wide. Y'know," I said with a laugh, "it kinda looks like W.C. Fields."

She jerked her hand from mine, turning away from me. I could hear gentle sobbing. Sitting up, I looked over at her. "What?" I started, but trailed off as she leapt up, grabbed the wine bottle by the neck, and ran toward the house, the sobbing becoming more intense with each step. Standing, I contemplated giving chase, but instead sat back down. Reaching into my pocket, I procured my cell phone. Susan answered on the second ring. "Hey," I said, attempting nonchalance, "ya got a minute?"

"Anything for you," she said with her silky, seductive voice. "What's on your mind?"

I sighed softly. "It's Chloe. She's still so blue, so depressed. I've been trying everything, but nothing's working. You've known her for years. Any idea what's going on?"

She paused for a moment before saying, "Y'know, I think I do. You should come over here. It's best we talk in person."

"Umm," I stammered as I stared up at the house. I wondered which room my wife had barricaded herself into this time. Would it be the bedroom or the bathroom? Perhaps she'd mix it up and lock herself in the basement. "Okay Susan, whatever you think's best. I'm gonna go check on Chloe, then I'll be over."

Clicking off the connection, I slowly gathered up the picnic supplies. After carrying everything into the house and carefully putting it all away, I wandered through the house. When I noticed the bedroom door shut tight, I grabbed and turned the knob. She hadn't locked it, which surprised me.

Upon entering the room, I could practically feel the depression hanging in the air like a thick, acrid layer of smoke during a forest fire. I found her prone body on the bed, face buried deeply into her pillow. The abandoned wine bottle lolled recumbent on the bed, just beyond the tips of her sprawled fingers. A sizable trail of liquid had trickled out, soaking into the mattress, and on my side of the bed. "Dammit!" I exclaimed before pausing, to tone down the hostility in my voice. "C'mon Chloe, you've spilled wine on the bed."

In one quick motion, she thrust her hand outward, shoving the bottle off the bed. It clunked harmlessly onto the carpeting.

I sighed loudly, mostly for effect. "Honestly, honey, I've tried to be understanding, but you're just giving me nothing in return. For weeks now, this is all I get, sighing and crying. So, are you gonna tell me what's going on?"

When she started sobbing even heavier into her pillow, I knew I would not get an answer at this moment. "Okay, whatever. Look, I'm going out. I'll be back in a bit." I took her no response as a response and marched out of the room.

Susan answered the door with a wine glass in her hand, shoving it toward me without saying a word. I accepted it, taking a quick sip. "Oh, this is the same wine I'd bought for Chloe."

"I know," she replied. "Chloe and I were introduced to Liebfraumilch when we lived in Germany." I couldn't help but notice she had the top three buttons on her white blouse undone, betraying the otherwise business-like demeanor of the outfit she probably wore at the office today.

Taking another sip, I forced a smile. "So," I said as I sat down on the couch, "you're Chloe's best friend. Do you have any idea where this funk came from?"

She sat down next to me and briefly rested her hand on my back, patting it consolingly. "So, you two have been married for about four years, and dated for a year or so before getting hitched, right?"

"Yeah, that sounds about right."

"Yup," she said as she sat back, crossing her long, shapely legs, "the five year itch has struck again."

"The what now?"

Susan released a delicate sigh as she liberated her long, luxurious brunette hair from its bondage. Shaking her head playfully caused her locks to spill onto her shoulders. "I've known Chloe since high school. She's normally a very content woman, but every so often, she just loses control. She gets utterly bored with life. You've undoubtedly heard about our time in Europe, right?"

"Uh-huh," I uttered as I took a long swig of my wine. "That was just before we met."

"That was where she spent the five years before you. Before that, she spent five years in Colorado. Before that was college. Are you sensing the pattern?"

"Um, what, you think she's getting bored with me?"

Susan chuckled, which stung more than a little bit. "Not you exactly, Owen, just the lifestyle you represent. Being married, working in an office, the daily grind. All of it. Please don't take offense to this, but I told her not to marry you. I didn't want to see her put you through this. But she really thought this time she could overcome the urge for change, being older and presumably more mature. She assumed it was just a youth thing, and that you were the last major change she'd have to make."

"Oh my God," I whispered as I nearly dropped the glass. Reaching over, Susan put her hands on top of mine. Her hands were as soft as Chloe's. I looked up into her eyes, and her sympathetic smile calmed me somewhat. "I'm…I'm the reason she's depressed? Does she want out? Has she told you this?"

"No, Owen, not in so many words." She removed the glass from my trembling hands and carefully set it down. My eyes inadvertently settled on her cleavage as she bent over toward the table. She continued smiling as her hand settled on my knee. "In many ways, she's like a gypsy. She has always needed that freedom. Even if she didn't use it, she had to know she could flee at a moment's notice. She always needs an out." Susan stood up, bringing me up with her by taking my still-quivering hands in hers. The wine must have had more effect on me than I realized, as my knees buckled momentarily. Her hands moved up my arms, coming to rest on my shoulders. "She feels trapped, Owen. She loves you, and she doesn't want to leave you. But I'm afraid her instincts may be too strong."

As she pulled me in for a much-needed hug, I whispered, "What should I do, Susan? I love her so much. I don't want to lose her." Resting my head on her shoulder, I caught a whiff of Susan's hair. It smelled just like the lilacs in our garden.

She moved her head back slightly, putting the two of us practically nose to nose. Gazing into my eyes, she offered me a sad smile. "Go to her. It's all you can do." Then, for only a moment, she placed her lips gently against mine before releasing me and stepping back. "Go to her," she repeated. "Don't waste time here. Run straight home and be with her."

Walking out to my car, I felt my head spinning. For reasons I could not quite ascertain, I felt like I had done something wrong up there. Sure, I have always felt an attraction toward Susan, but my love, and certainly my loins, would never waiver. Chloe would always be my everything.

Needing time to think things through, I drove to our favorite coffee shop. Taking a table on the patio, I sat there for hours, getting wired on caffeine while staring at the same baby-blue sky and cotton-ball clouds that Chloe and I gazed up at earlier. W.C. Fields had long since vacated the scene, but plenty of other characters took his place.

I thought long and hard about what I should say. Though I liked it here in Michigan, with my job as a stockbroker, I could make a living practically anywhere. If she felt bored, perhaps we could sell the house and find a place elsewhere. We could try Seattle, or perhaps New Orleans. She really loved jazz. I had heard so many great things about San Diego. Why, we could even venture into another country! Thinking back, I tried to remember when she would talk about *what if*. It seemed like Mexico came up once or twice. Though she had already done Europe, perhaps she wanted to go back. After all, the sky would be just as blue in San Diego, Mexico, or Europe.

Before going home, I decided to make a quick stop at the florist. For some reason, I felt the compulsion to bring her some lilacs.

As I pulled in the driveway, the possibilities excited me. I shoved open the door and dashed into the bedroom. I felt a bit disappointed when I didn't find her still lying on the bed, but that certainly could be a good thing. Maybe she had snapped out of her funk a bit.

Then, I saw the note lying on my pillow. "Dearest Owen," it began, "I'm leaving. I can't take the depression anymore. Please understand that it's not you. Susan once told me I was a gypsy, a free spirit, and that I couldn't be satisfied with the simple life of a married office worker. I guess she's right. That is why we're leaving for Mexico today. I'm not taking any of our stuff, only what was mine when we came together. Please… you dear, sweet man, please forgive me. I'm sorry. Love, Chloe."

Plopping down heavily on the bed, I stared blankly at the note. It took a while for the realization to kick in, and a while longer to catch, "We are leaving today." We?! She didn't mean Susan, did she?

I sprinted back to my car and drove over to Susan's apartment as fast as my vehicle would travel. The note tacked on Susan's door read, "Sorry Owen, but I told you to run to her. I wish you'd heeded my advice. I did all I could. Don't worry, I'll take good care of her. Love, Susan."

I stumbled backward, my back crashing against the opposite wall. "I could have changed," I said softly.

~ Chapter Ten ~

I look over at my wife, and as I expected, she's sound asleep. Reaching over, I carefully remove her glasses. As they tickle past her ears, she opens her eyes and frowns. "What... What are you doing?"

"Removing your glasses so you don't roll over on them and bend them, my love."

"Huh." Her pout melts me. "You didn't tell me a story."

"Yes I did."

"No!"

"I did, but would you like me to tell you another one?"

"Ooookay." Now she's smiling. As she closes her eyes, she whispers, "I love you."

"And I love you! So, after this story will you come to bed?"

"Ooookay."

I chuckle softly. She won't, but that's fine. I sit down next to her on the couch, and she nestles up, laying her head on my shoulder.

"Y'know," Arthur said with an exhale of cigarette smoke, "I don't remember anyone ever coming up to us and saying, 'Hey, you guys are good.'"

Bob shook his head rapidly. "Oh now, to be fair, no one ever talks to the drummer." As he pivoted his head and waved his hand to flag down the cute young waitress for another beer, Bob noticed the pub door swinging open. Nigel sauntered in, still wearing the same old shabby patchwork leather jacket, followed by Frank, walking with a noticeable limp. Bob waved them over. "Lookin' good there, Nigel. Holy crap Frank, you've aged poorly. When did you go bald?"

Shrugging, Frank replied, "Eh, hard to say," as he reflexively reached up and ran a hand over his smooth skull. "You're one to talk about the ravages of time there, fat boy!"

"Hey, I've been on steroids for a while. Besides, ya shouldda seen me after I beat the cancer. Skinny as a rail, for a while, anyway."

Nigel plopped down next to Bob and patted his shoulder. "Yeah mate, I'd heard about that. Glad ya kicked it. All right, so we're all here. What's this all about?"

"Oh, you're gonna love this," said Arthur with a chuckle.

Beaming, Bob stood up and spread his arms out, as if to embrace his old friends from a distance. "I want to get Non-Rotten Lettuce back together." When they all laughed boisterously in concert, Bob added, "I'm serious, guys."

Frank, while continuing to stroke his smooth, hair-free head absentmindedly, replied, "You want to get the band back together? C'mon Bob, this is just your mid-life crisis kicking in, isn't it?"

"Perhaps. But really, I just want us to recapture our lost glory, have some fun, and while we're at it, make a few bucks."

Violently jamming the butt of his cigarette into the exceedingly full ashtray, Arthur said. "Uh, Bob, hate to break it to ya, but we never really had any glory, and I don't recall us making much money."

"Yeah," Nigel added as he waved at the blonde server, "but we did have fun. Remember that gig at the Roundabout?"

When the waitress sauntered over, Bob rested his hand gently on the small of her back. "Hey sweetie, take a good look at us. What would you say if I told you we're a recently reunited rock band?"

Once she stopped giggling, she replied, "Oh, you're serious? Sorry, I thought you meant like the video game Rock Band or something. So what's your band's name?"

Nigel, accentuating his British accent, belted out, "Hello, Cleveland! We're Non-Rotten Lettuce!"

The mention of the band's name sent the server into another round of convulsive laughter. "No really, what's your band called?"

With a dismissive hand, Bob answered, "Never mind. Just bring us another round."

As she dashed away, Arthur tapped another smoke from his pack of Gridlocks. "Oh yeah, that's exactly the response I would've hoped for. Perhaps we should rename ourselves Rotten Lettuce."

"Sorry mate, it's a nice thought and all, but I haven't been able to play a note on my guitar in years, ever since the arthritis kicked in." Nigel held up his right hand, balled it into a fist a couple times, and winced.

"Yeah, and I'm on too much medication." When the server brought their beers, Arthur held his up to his face, staring as the foam slowly dissipated from the narrow glass. "I shouldn't even be drinking this. I'll probably pay for it later." He took a sip and smiled.

Shaking his head slowly, Frank added, "And I broke my hip last year, remember? I can't stand for long periods."

Bob sighed loudly. "Okay, fine. We're all old farts now. We could work around it."

"My wife would kill me." The others all nodded their heads in silent agreement with Frank. "In fact," he added after he tipped his beer into his mouth, "I really need to go. Gotta pick up the grand kid from soccer practice at seven."

As Frank stood up, so did Nigel and Arthur. "Good seeing you all. Cheers, mates!"

Staying in his seat, Bob watched his college bandmates amble and limp out the door. "Crap," he whispered to no one, "I guess I shouldn't have quit my job."

"So," the blonde waitress said as she began clearing the table, "It's cool you old guys got a band. Where's your next gig?"

"In my dreams," he replied softly.

~ Chapter Eleven ~

This morning, we are on our way to Sunday church services. Our church is a good 20-minute drive. It might take less time if we took the expressway, but my wife generally prefers the back way into town. As we turn a corner and start down a hill, my wife yells, "Oh my!" and steps hard on the brakes.

We skid to a stop. I look over at her, and then out to the road, where I see a large brownish-green rock in the middle of the road. "Poor baby," my wife says, "We nearly hit her!"

When I see the rock move slightly, I take a harder look at it. "Oh, it's a turtle," I say.

Giving me a *Well, duh!* look, she opens up the car door and steps out. I open my own door and say, "What are you doing?"

"We can't leave her there. She's nearly invisible on this road. Someone's going to come barreling down the road and smash her!"

As if to prove the point, a red and rust-colored pickup truck hurries around the corner, and comes down the hill at top speed. It slows slightly as it drifts onto the left side of the road and rolls past us. The driver gives us a puzzled, agitated look.

Walking up to the big turtle, we both stare down at it. "Well hello darling," my wife coos softly.

Growing up in DeWitt, I used to catch hand-sized turtles (back when my hands were tiny), but this one, I must say, intimidates me somewhat. With a shell around 16 inches long and maybe 14 inches wide, this big girl is slowly traversing the two-lane road. Other than a few of the giant tortoises in zoos, I've never seen one anywhere near this big, and certainly not in the wild.

The turtle had nearly reached the centerline, but she still has a lot of work ahead of her to reach the safety of the grass on the other side of the 55 MPH country road. "Aren't you a pretty girl?" My wife says. "You're going to get squashed out here."

"So, why does the turtle cross the road?" I feel compelled to ask.

Shrugging, she replies, "Who knows. Maybe her babies are over there. Or food. It doesn't matter. We need to get her out of the road and get her to the other side. Do you want to do it?"

While I can't say I actually want to do it, it doesn't seem tough. "Sure. So what, do I just grab her?"

As another car comes over the hill, spots us, and slows down as the driver scoots around us, my wife replies, "Grab her firmly on either side of the shell. Be mindful of her legs, which can scratch you, and especially her head. A turtle this big could take your finger off."

Yikes! I didn't know turtles could do that! "Okay," I say tentatively, as I straddle the giant creature, reach down, get a firm grip on the shell, and hoist her up.

The moment she leaves Terra Firma, she looks up at me and hisses louder than any cat I've ever heard! "Holy crap! They hiss?"

"Yup! She's not at all happy with you."

As I walk her toward the grass, the turtle starts wriggling around, all four legs moving like she's trying to walk on the air. She weighs more than I expected, heavier than a bowling ball. She keeps whipping her head back and forth, alternating between biting at the air and hissing like a deranged cheetah. My heart is thumping as if I'm running a marathon!

Finally, I reach the grass, setting her down as gently as possible so she is facing the embankment. She throws another hiss my way as she turns to face me. We both back up, trying to put as much distance as

87

possible between us and the flipped-out turtle. "There ya go, little baby," says my wife to the turtle as we head toward our vehicle, "you're safe now."

The turtle takes one more step toward us, so we jump in the truck and roll away. "Wow," I say as she hands me a bottle of Purell, "that was invigorating!"

"Saving a life often is."

After a moment of silence, I ask, "When we talk about this, how big should the turtle be? Can I call it a tortoise?"

Smiling, she replies, "You can make it as big as you like. I don't plan to talk about it. It's just what people do when no one is looking."

"You know, I have a story that ties in with this theme."

"We have the time. Tell me a story!"

~ Once, When No One Was Looking ~

Standing out on Foster and Aubrey's balcony as Saturday night turned into Sunday morning, the chill in the air caused me to zip my jacket up a few more inches. I could tell my other three mates felt equally uncomfortable. As our other friends continued to enjoy the party inside, I muttered to myself, "Damn those non-smokers, anyway," before looking over at Misty. As I flicked my Zippo to light another Marlboro Red, I said to the group, "Do you remember the days when people were allowed to smoke indoors?"

"Hmmm," she replied, glancing up at the flakes of snow as they gently floated downward, "I'm sorry, I don't, Lou. Hasn't it been like this forever?" We all snickered. "What I also don't recall is when did Foster stop smoking?"

"Not long after he met Aubrey," Fred answered after downing the beer from his plastic cup.

After a short pause in the conversation, Misty shouted, "I know, let's play a game to pass the time."

"Okay," Stan responded, "how 'bout *Smoke the Ciggy!*" He started puffing wildly on his unfiltered Camel, smoke billowing from it like a horizontal chimneystack.

"No, ya goof. How about Once, When No One Was Looking?"

"Ugh," I said. "You know nothing good can come from this, right?"

Misty gave me a dirty glance, but filtered it though her sparkling smile. "No no, it'll be fun. I'll go first," she said with a glint of mischievousness in those alluring baby blue eyes of hers. "Once, when no one was looking, I shoplifted a purse."

"No way," yelled Stan with a loud chortle, "not prim n' proper Misty Bellows!"

Her lips curved slightly higher. "Way. I was like 16 or 17, I had no money on me, and I really wanted that purse. Um, this purse," she added as she lifted her old denim satchel.

The realization caused me to cough the smoke out of my lungs. "You stole that handbag?! You've had it for years. You hate that purse. You're always complaining about it."

Blushing slightly, she twirled the strap around her index finger. "Well, after a while I felt really guilty about it. I'm kinda punishing myself, using this bag until it falls apart."

"Well, two more threads pop on that thing and you'll get your wish. Okay, I'll go next. Once, when no one was looking…" I paused to exhale a heavy sigh. Not my proudest moment, this. "Okay, I was walking behind this old dude, and I saw him drop his wallet. You know me guys, I'm usually a decent fellow. But… well, not this time. I picked up the wallet, took the money in it, and tossed it back on the ground."

"Whoa," Fred breathed, "you evil bastard, you! How much did ya get?"

"Oh, like 30 bucks. Then," I continued, "after I ditched the wallet, I yelled to the guy to tell him he dropped it. He actually thanked me. When he went back for it, I sprinted away."

Misty looked deep into my eyes and asked, "You feel bad about it now, don't ya?"

"Like ten minutes after it happened, and still, to this day." Another sigh escaped my throat. "It's odd, and rather sad, the things we do on the spur of the moment when no one's watching us."

As I finished my story, the door to the porch flung open and a tall, dark haired man lurched outside. He caught the edge of one of the plastic chairs and stumbled enough to launch his cupful of beer off the top of the balcony. We heard a loud, "HEY!" moments after the splash.

"Sorry," the man slurred as he plopped into the chair. Pulling out a pack of Gridlock cigarettes, he lit up as he asked, "This is the smoking section, right?"

"Sure is," Fred responded. "Welcome to the banished!"

"Cool. My name's Clade," he said with a nod.

After we all introduced ourselves, Stan said, "Hey Clade, you're just in time. It's your turn."

To respond to his puzzled countenance, Misty said, "You start with, *once, when no one was looking*, and you tell everyone what the worst thing you ever did when no one was around."

The tall stranger stood up slowly, smoothed out his leather jacket, and said in a raspy voice, "Well, all right. Once, when no one was looking, I killed my wife and her boyfriend."

We all chuckled with varying degrees of enthusiasm. Stan started to speak, but the man talked over him. "She was cheating on me with some guy she knew from The Lone Cactus. She was a waitress there. I

90

found out about the affair and killed 'em both." He paused to take a long drag on his cheap cigarette. "This," he said with a sinister grin, "was the clever bit. I knew which way she drove home on the nights she would go to his place. She had to pass under a certain overpass. It was kinda off in the middle of nowhere, this overpass, so there was little traffic. I waited there with a chunk of concrete in hand. When they drove by, I timed it perfectly and put that rock right through their windshield! Woo wee," he yelped, "It was glorious! The car flipped over and rolled several times. They were dead before the car stopped!"

We were all stunned silent for a spell. "Wow," whispered Fred.

"Um, you win, dude," I said softly.

Once Clade comprehended the dazed looks on our faces, he must have sobered up a bit. He took his half-smoked cigarette and dropped it on the deck. As he ground it under his heel, he said quietly, "I believe I won another beer. Nice meeting you all." Before he left, he paused, staring intently at each of us in turn. I shivered involuntarily.

Once the door swung shut, Stan said, to no one in particular, "Let's never play this game again." Everyone silently nodded in agreement.

The rest of the party went well enough. I chatted up some blonde, who gave me what I assumed was a fake number, and I drank a few more beers. While heading for the door, I walked up to Foster to thank him for such a memorable evening. As I grasped his hand and began a hearty handshake, I felt compelled to ask, "Ya know that tall guy with the leather jacket, Clade I think he said. Do you know him?"

Foster shook his head. "He might have been friends with Sawyer. Or maybe Marshall. I dunno. But he asked a lot of questions about you four before he left."

"Really?" I did not like the sound of that.

On the Wednesday after the party, as I drove home from work, my cell phone started ringing. "Oh my God, Lou!" Misty shouted from the other end, "Did you hear what happened to Stan?"

I quickly whipped into the nearest parking lot. "No. What happened?"

"Oh God," she repeated and then paused for a moment. "They found him dead in his house. He fell down the basement stairs!"

Though stunned, I can't say I was completely surprised. "Are they calling this one a suicide, too?"

"No, Lou. They ruled it an accident. First, Fred kills himself and now this. Two of our best friends, dying one day apart. It makes no sense."

"Misty, you know what's going on. C'mon! Fred was so full of life, more than anyone I've ever met. For him to asphyxiate himself in his car, I just can't see it. There were no signs and he left no suicide note."

"That doesn't prove anything."

"The dude was a published author. Of course he would have left a note, and it would've been 10 pages, double spaced, with perfect grammar and spelling. And now, one day later, Stan accidentally tumbles down the stairs? I don't buy it."

The sound of her crying flowed with ease through the phone. Between sobs, she said, "What… what are you saying?"

"It's that guy from the party. It has to be!"

"What?! Are you insane? I barely remember the guy. Hell, I barely remember the night. Why would he care about what he said during a drunken evening with total strangers? It makes no sense!"

"Do psychopaths need a reason?" I asked, adding, "Where are you now? Are you home?"

"Yes," she replied faintly.

"Look, stay there and lock the doors. I'll come over in a little while. I have to go home first and then I'll be over."

"It's okay, you don't need –"

"You shouldn't be alone," I said, cutting her off. "Regardless of the reasons why, our friends are gone. I'll be over soon."

Not long after I arrived, Misty stood beside me, furrowing her brow. "What are you doing with my old desktop computer?"

I typed a few more commands and paused to take one last look before I replied. "I'm just getting ready. Just in case."

"Just in case? What are you –"

Insistent knocking on her front door interrupted the beautiful brunette. I decided to stay put as she answered it. I heard her say, "What? What are you – Oh my God!" I fought the temptation to vacate my seat, instead typing and clicking the mouse a few more times.

When I saw the terror on her face, I knew what was happening. Clade stood behind her, wearing a smug grin. He had on the same leather jacket from the weekend, but instead of a plastic cup with beer, his right hand held a pistol. "Well, howdy-do! Long time no see," he said with more than a tinge of arrogance.

I felt as terrified as poor, sweet Misty looked, but I was not about to let him see the fear welling up inside of me. Instead, I stood up and took several steps away from the computer. "Clade, dude," I said with an attempt at nonchalance, "why are you doing this? What did any of us do to you?"

He grinned softly through his several-day growth of facial hair. "You know too much."

"What!?" Misty screamed, "What do we know? We don't know a damned thing!"

"We only know what you told us," I added.

"Yeah," he said as his gaze fell downward, "me and my big, stupid mouth. I know better than to drink. I say the dumbest things." He shook his head slowly. Even through his bravado, I could see he was in over his head.

Misty started to yell something else, but I put my finger up to my mouth and forced a grin. She stopped immediately.

"So, you killed Stan Bishop and Fred Degner to keep your secret safe," I said clearly, but with a non-threatening tone to my voice. "Why did you have to do that, Clade?"

"I had to kill them. Don't you see that? You all know my secret. None of you can live."

"But none of us knew you. We wouldn't have done a thing. How could we have? We don't even know your last name."

"I still don't remember the night … it's all a blur to me," Misty added softly. "I don't want to die over a blur."

Glancing at Misty for a quick moment, he then shifted his steely gaze to me. He looked me dead in the eye, the gun leveled at my chest. "I can't take that chance. I killed my wife and her lover. There can be no witnesses."

"How did you find all of us, anyway?"

"I asked around at the party. You'd be amazed what drunk people will say."

"Oh," I said, growing louder, "you must think you're so clever! You killed our friends and made them both look like suicides and accidents. How're you planning on killing us?"

Reaching in his jacket pocket, Clade pulled out a bottle of sleeping pills. "You're both going to swallow these and you'll die peacefully in each other's arms."

"And if we refuse?" asked Misty. Sometimes, I loved that woman's bravado, forced though it may have been.

Clade showed us a sickening grin. "I'll shoot you both in the face, repeatedly, and leave you to die. I really don't need these to be suicides, but I'll -"

At that moment, the front door burst open and several uniformed police officers rushed through. In the momentary confusion, as Clade turned toward the commotion, I picked up a statuette from Misty's bookshelf and quickly smacked the gun from Clade's hand. The police ran in and tackled him to the ground.

As they were slapping on the cuffs, Clade looked up at me, clearly puzzled. I pointed toward the computer, positioned several feet away. "See that round thing on top of the monitor?" I asked. "That's a webcam. Ya gotta love technology! Luckily, our local police department has a couple of geeks on the payroll. I alerted them to some possible homicides and I linked our webcam to their server."

One of the officers said, as they pulled Clade to his feet, "Thanks for admitting to everything. Makes our job that much easier."

Misty turned to me, and to be totally honest, I wasn't sure what she would do at that moment. Her face displayed a cacophony of emotions. I braced for impact, but fortunately for me, she ran up and gave me a spine-popping hug. She then pulled back and yelled, "Why didn't you tell me?"

Though I needed her honest emotions to fool him, I figured it would be better to tell her, "There wasn't time. I'm sorry."

As she hugged me again, I whispered, "Once, when no one was looking," and when she pulled back to give me a quizzical glance, I placed my lips softly on hers. I could feel her smile on my lips.

~ Chapter Twelve ~

After church, we head over to the Denny's. The majority of the church crowd beat us there. "Oh man," I say, "We're going to be waiting for quite a while."

Smiling, my wife says, "Perfect. Plenty of time."

My brow furrows at her as I ask, "For what?"

"Tell me a story."

Boy, she cracks me up! "Okay sweetie. With the time we have to wait, I'll probably have time for two."

"All the better," she replies as she wraps her arm around mine and gives it a squeeze.

~ Wingman Blues ~

"C'mon," said Victor. "Ya gotta come with me! I can't go without my wingman!"

Octavio sighed. For one thing, Victor never needed a wingman. He'd score regardless. However, for Octavio, the bigger issue was his own psyche. It had only been three weeks since Cassie left him. He had no interest in standing around with a bunch of drunken people, pretending to be okay.

However, the gloomy expression on Victor's face proved difficult to decline. He even pouted, for God's sake! "Fine," Octavio said with a forced smile, "but I won't enjoy it."

"Sure ya will," Victor said with a slap to his friend's back.

It took Victor literally 20 seconds after arriving at the bar to spot a hottie and bolt, leaving Octavio to stand alone in the crowd, his misery growing. Surrounded by college students who were dressed to hook up with one another, he felt more isolated than ever.

Eh, screw it, he thought. Not only would he not play the mating game, he would go in completely the opposite direction.

He started by ordering an appletini, figuring that holding a neon green drink would deter the women.

However, one sip later and a vivacious brown-haired woman sauntered over. She said, "Curious choice."

"Shit," he breathed. Okay, plan B. "This? Oh, it's the only thing that won't irritate my bowels. I have this pulsating polyp see, and…" Even before he could finish the sentence, she crinkled her nose and took off.

Five minutes later, a lady in a low-cut red dress strolled up. When she asked him his profession, he replied, "Taxidermy. I like to take dead animals and put them in unique situations. Just yesterday, I did a scene from *Gone with the Wind* using a beaver as Scarlett. I have pics on my phone, if…" And she was history.

The next one, seeing the look on his face, asked, "Are you lost, little boy?"

Displaying his cheesiest grin, he replied, "Lust? Why yes, I am horny!" She groaned and fled.

He found he enjoyed messing with these vapid young women. Also, the appletini was unexpectedly enjoyable.

"What do you do for fun?" asked a pretty blonde girl wearing a Michigan State sweatshirt and baggy jeans. Her lack of slutty attire intrigued him.

He smirked and replied, "I watch a ton of cartoons. Danger Mouse is my favorite."

Grinning, she replied, "Crikey! I didn't think anyone knew about that old-school British cartoon. Who's your favorite character? Mine is Stiletto."

After spending an hour talking classic cartoons with her, Octavio realized for the first time in nearly a month that he wore a genuine smile. "Hey, can I buy you an appletini? These things are surprisingly good."

"Is it just me," asked Ed, "or is this a really tough corner?"

Sluggishly peering up from the soup can he used as a coin cup, Barney replied with a sigh, "It's not just here. The whole city's been cheap for months now." Then he slowly stood up, his old bones creaking like the floorboards of a condemned house. Before reaching his full height, Barney's legs buckled under the weight and he lost his balance, nearly tumbling back down. In the process, he dropped his cup onto the ground. Two quarters, three nickels, and a penny scattered into the snow. "Ah, crap!"

Setting his own can down, Ed crawled toward the spilled change. Barney growled and fell on top of the quarters. "Mine! Get away!"

"Jeez, Barn," Ed replied, "I was only gonna help."

"Like hell ya were! I earned this money. It's mine, ya bum!"

At that moment, a well-dressed man stepped off the sidewalk, heading toward the convenience store on the corner. He paused momentarily upon seeing the two men groping the snow for spare change. Shaking his head, he pulled out a five dollar bill and said, "If you two had jobs, you wouldn't need this," and tossed the bill at his feet.

Since it fluttered closer to Ed, he snatched it up. He wanted to yell at the man, "You have no idea how I got to be here, you stuck-up, ignorant prick!" but instead smiled half-heartedly and grumbled his thanks. Standing up, he said softly, "Keep your quarters, Barn. I have all the money I need now."

After scooping up his change, Barney shouted, "What, ya got enough for a bottle? I want some! You owe me, man!"

Ed, walking away at a steady pace, mumbled under his breath, "You don't want what I'm getting."

These days, Edward Monroe felt self-conscious when entering any sort of well-lit establishment. Even though the homeless of the neighborhood frequented this party store, he still felt all eyes upon him. Maybe the kid behind the counter thought the greasy, disheveled man would try to steal something. Perhaps he did not care one way or the other, but Ed prided himself on his honesty. After considering it a moment, he realized pride was not the correct word. Ed lost that a while back, but still, he was no thief.

Ed paused as he saw himself in the round, fun-house mirror designed to thwart shoplifting. Even this distorted view filled him with shame. In his youth, he was a handsome, clean-cut man. Now, he frowned at the haggard, unkempt, hairy loser staring back at him. His brown hair was now a greasy, mostly black fright wig, with streaks and blotches of gray. *When did I go gray?* he mused. A thick, scraggly mound of facial hair obscured his cheeks and chin. It grew wild over the tops of his cheekbones and under the curve of his throat, like a garden without a gardener. Under different circumstances, he might have been amused by the Halloween mask that dwarfed his countenance, but being on a mission, this image of himself sealed the deal in his mind.

Walking over to the medicine isle, Ed picked up a bottle of Unisom. He stared at the blue and white box for a long moment. *One will make you feel drowsy,* he thought, *two will help you to sleep. The whole bottle will put you to sleep.*

As he made his way toward the counter, a man wearing a full-length black duster came sprinting in to the store. The kid's Snoopy mask on his face gave him the appearance of a tall child. Looking around the store, he quickly pulled out a rifle from under the duster. He aimed it at the kid behind the counter and shouted, "I want all the money! Now!"

Ed and the four other store patrons all gasped as one and stopped in their tracks. Never fearing for his safety behind thick security plastic, the clerk actually laughed as he reached his hand under the desk. A loud click reverberated throughout the store as the front door electronically locked. Without uttering a word to the would-be robber, he calmly picked up the phone and dialed the police.

Already realizing his predicament, Snoopy panicked and pulled the trigger while aiming at the clerk. The bullet bounced off the plastic and ricocheted, coming to rest in a box of Ho-Hos. The other shoppers hit the tile floor, but not Ed. The homeless man raised his arms over his head and ran toward Snoopy, a primal scream reverberating throughout the store. *A gunshot will do the trick as well as a handful of pills,* Ed thought.

Even though Ed caught him off-guard, the robber still had time to react. Flipping the rifle around, he slammed the stock into the homeless man's gut, sending him staggering onto the floor. However, Ed got close enough to get his hand on the mask, pulling it off with a finger in the eyehole.

"Crap," yelled the thief. Turning the gun skyward, he put a bullet into the ceiling before adding, "I want all of you against the far wall, now!"

He turned to glare at each customer in turn. The elderly woman, visibly shaking, dropped the box of macaroni and cheese from her trembling hands and walked as quickly as her legs would take her. Next, he scowled at the businessman, the one who tossed the fiver at the bums, and aimed the gun at his head until he did as instructed. Yelling an obscenity-laced tirade at the teenage girl made her comply, but he did not need any additional words to make the middle-aged Asian man line up with the others. Finally, turning to Ed, the robber kicked him in the side until he slithered his ailing body against the far wall.

The man then turned his attention toward the clerk, who was still smiling as if he was watching an episode of *Cops* on television. "I want you to give me the money in the drawer and the safe, and I want you to unlock that door."

"Now why the hell would I do that?" snorted the clerk.

"Because," Snoopy turned and fired the gun again, this time just missing the Asian man's head by an inch, "if you don't, I'll kill them all."

101

"And why I should care?"

This stunned the gunman. So far, the robber had managed to remain calm, but he did not expect that response. "You... you don't want their deaths on your hands."

The kid shrugged his shoulders and smirked. "Whatever, dude."

At that point, the sirens became noticeable in the distance.

"The cops are here," the businessman said, "so you should stop this now."

"You really should, Peter." That came from Ed, still clutching his gut.

The gunman spun to gape at Ed. "Uh... Huh? How did you –?"

"We worked together once, Peter Jenks." Ed pulled himself to his feet, briefly leaning on the Asian man's shoulder for support. "You don't recognize me, do you?"

The flabbergasted criminal stared at the man long enough for the police to arrive. "Ed? Ed Monroe. Man." He added as an afterthought, "What happened to you?"

Before he could answer, a cop with a megaphone yelled, "We have the store surrounded. Put the gun down and come out now!"

"I can't," he screamed in response. "Moron over there locked the door!"

Hearing his cue, the clerk pushed the button and with a loud click, the door unlocked. However, before anyone could react, Peter aimed the rifle at Ed's head. "No one come in here or this man dies."

"Now Peter," the businessman started, "let's..."

With a sweeping motion, Peter brought the stock of his rifle around and clubbed the man solidly on the right cheek. The man in the suit went down hard. "I do NOT want to hear my name used again. Do you all understand?"

As everyone uttered agreement, the megaphone boomed again. "You must stop this now. Do not hurt anyone else."

Ignoring the police, he turned to glare at the clerk. "Lock the door, now."

Barry, who had celebrated his 21st birthday last week, was finally starting to feel scared. The kid with the shoulder length blonde hair had only been a Quick Stop employee for a few months. He figured the night shift would be perfect. Very few customers to annoy him, plenty of time to study or talk on the phone with his girlfriend and maybe, if he played his cards right, he could abscond a fifth of booze and get drunk for free. This was not part of the deal.

His manager informed him, in the unlikely event of a robbery, to give the robbers what they wanted and let them leave. Technically, he should not have done what he did, which to Barry seemed stupid. He had a cool button that automatically locked the doors and a bulletproof closet encasing him. A criminal could do nothing to him.

However, he did not plan on the emotions welling up within him. With the guilt bubbling to the surface, the seriousness of the situation finally sunk in. It went from *Cops* to real life in an instant. Barry stared, open mouthed, at the man with the rifle. He nodded slowly and with a click, the room was secure again.

"Good," Pete said. Now, he had some time to think. He realized, quite frankly, he was screwed. "I want you all to sit there quietly. I still have more than enough bullets to kill all of you, and I will if I have to." He walked to the back of the store, and stared into the beer coolers. Yanking one open, Pete pulled out a 40-ounce bottle of Colt 45. He always wondered what malt liquor tasted like, and this seemed as good a time as any. Sitting down, Pete slapped his back against the cold glass and took a heavy tug on the bottle.

Peter Jenks felt like crying. He thought losing his high-paying factory job was bad enough. With unemployment compensation used

103

up and no new jobs on the horizon, desperation overtook him. It seemed like a foolproof plan, coming to the seedy part of town where the bums, junkies, and hookers hung out. He would fly in, get the cash, and be gone before anyone knew anything. It hit Peter that he should have planned things a bit better. At least he should have come into this store once before robbing it. Releasing a slow, airy sigh, he took another long drink off the bottle, set it down, and buried his stubbly face into his hands.

The five hostages stayed quiet for several minutes, before the young girl with the low-cut dress whispered, "Hey, are you two okay?" She bent over far enough for both ailing men to catch a glimpse of an ornately inked rose tattoo just above her left breast.

Ed answered first. "Yeah, fine," he lied. When he went down, his weight landed on his left leg. It hurt worse than his gut did. The pain made it hard to breathe, but he was thankful the rifle hit the softness of his belly. At least he had no broken ribs. Turning to look at the businessman, Ed asked, "What about you, sir?"

"I'm not sure. I think he broke my jaw. It hurts like hell." After a pause, he added, "My name's Brandon, by the way."

"Pleasure to meet you, Brandon," Ed whispered sarcastically. "And thanks again for the money."

It took Brandon a moment, but then it dawned on him. "Oh, yeah. Right. Man, if I hadn't given it to you, you wouldn't even be in this mess."

"How's that for irony, huh?" Ed opened his right hand and was surprised to see that through the ordeal he still held the Unisom, clutching it tightly enough that his hand had turned white.

As the pink slowly returned to his hand, Brandon looked down and saw the pills. A puzzled look crept upon his swollen face. "You used the money to buy sleeping tablets? Wouldn't a 40-ouncer be more appropriate?"

"Man," Ed started out too loudly, and toned it down quickly. "Man, you know nothing about me." He paused and then decided to continue. "Two years ago, I looked like you. I had the suit, metaphorically speaking. I was head foreman at the Rufous Corporation. You remember Rufous?"

Brandon was acutely aware, but he only replied, "Car parts?"

"Yup. We supplied half the nation. It was a major employer in this city. When the economy went south, they kept laying off more and more people. Finally, the place went under. I was one of the last men standing."

"Sorry," said Brandon. "I hear the owner tried to keep the place alive as long as he could."

Ed snorted, but said, "Actually, I do believe that. I never met the man, but if he were anyone else, if the Ted Turners or Donald Trumps of the world owned it, it would have been closed long before that." Ed paused to sigh. "But it doesn't matter now. I was on unemployment until it ran out. I applied everywhere I could. I never even got a job interview. Lost my apartment, had to sell all my stuff just to survive. I've been living on the streets for months, throughout the summer. I don't want to know what winter's gonna be like outdoors. I just don't."

After a momentary pause, the girl butted in with, "Did ya try Burger King?"

Ed scowled at her, but replied calmly. "Of course. I needed any job I could find to avoid living on the streets. But these days, if you're not 18 or 68, you can't get a job in fast food. Apparently, 45 year old men don't get to ask if you want fries with that."

When the clerk chuckled, Peter became aware of the talking he had been ignoring while in deep thought. He stood up and yelled, "Shut up! Don't make me come over there!" Everyone snickered with nervous laughter, including the robber.

The Asian man leaned in close to Ed and whispered, "You know the guy! Go talk to him."

When everyone else nodded and gestured, Ed shrugged and slowly stood up. He could see through the glass door that the cop was putting the megaphone to his lips again, but when Ed put his index finger in the air, then both palms, the cop paused.

Pete jumped to his feet and started to yell for Ed to sit back down, but Ed's voice overpowered him. "I have a way out of this, Pe… sir. Can I come down there?"

After a momentary pause, Peter motioned him over. Ed labored his way toward the back, trying not to limp but failing miserably.

Standing in front of Pete, Ed winced as he shifted weight from his bad leg to his good. "Looks painful, Ed. Go ahead and sit." Ed plopped his sore body down against the freezer, grunting as he hit bottom. "So," continued the robber, "ya look awful. What happened to you?"

Ed smiled a joyless smile. "The same thing that happened to you. You were at Rufous South, right?"

Pete sneered at him. "Yeah. You were… East?"

"I was the head foreman, but stationed at East." Ed paused to breathe a heavy sigh. "All divisions went down around the same time. A lot of us hit the streets at once. Only so many jobs out there."

Peter suddenly felt very much like sitting, and did so. "We went different directions afterwards, huh?"

"Hey, if I had access to a gun, these roles might be reversed." They sat silent for a moment. Finally, Ed said softly, "Pete, I think I can get you out of this, but I'm going to need one thing in return."

"I doubt I'm getting much money outta this job."

Ed shook his head while saying, "No, not that. I want you to promise me that if we get out of this, you'll kill me."

It was a good thing Pete was sitting. That statement floored him. "Come again?"

Ed held up the bottle of sleeping tablets. "The summer on the streets was bad enough. My pride and dignity are completely gone. I had to do things to survive that I never would have thought possible." The man paused for a moment, putting his face in his palms. The memories overwhelmed him. He turned to face Pete and continued. "I ate out of trashcans. I drank rainwater out of the gutter. I slept on concrete, under the I-92 Bridge, when the cops didn't chase me off. You remember how hot it got in August, Pete? Imagine lying in the gutter, trying to soak up any ounce of sewer water that trickled by. I'd lie under peoples' air conditioners, for the odd drop of warm condensation. The summer was bad enough," he spoke softly, a small tear forming in his left eye. "I can't do winter outdoors. I won't."

Pete felt a shiver run the length of his body. "Damn. So you came in here to buy those pills to kill yourself." He felt sick to his stomach.

"Yes," he said flatly, then sighed heavily. "I'll be your hostage. We'll go outside, take a cop car, and drive to Mexico. It's not the best idea, sure, but it can work."

Picking up the beer bottle, Pete tipped it to the ceiling and drained the last of it into his throat. Then he sat staring at the bottle, watching the rivulets of foam slowly cascading back down to pool at the bottom. The desperate man imagined the bottom of the bottle as a gutter, with himself lying in the putrid water, rolling and wallowing like a pig coating itself with mud on a hot summer day.

He stared at Ed, trying to remember him as he was, back when they were both young and starting their new careers at the Rufous Corporation. Though they worked at different locations, Ed found himself at South from time to time. Pete recalled a time when a machine he was working on malfunctioned. The two men disassembled it, trying to fix the problem, when a lube line busted. It sprayed both men with oil, but Ed got the worst of it, coating him from collar to shoe. Pete exploded with anger, but Ed actually started laughing, telling Pete he could go home if he wanted, which he did. Later, Pete found out Ed stayed the rest of the day, in those greasy clothes. After fixing the machine, he went on about the daily business of running the shop.

He smiled at the memory, and was about to share, when the megaphone boomed once again. "We've waited long enough. If you do not come out now, we will come in."

Pete turned to Ed and said, "Okay. You got a deal."

Pushing the rifle in Ed's back, Pete led him to the front. He shouted to the others in the store, "Listen up. This is ending now. I'm taking my ol' buddy Ed here as a hostage. The two of us are walking out. I want you all to stay seated. If you do this, you will live and will have a great story to tell your families." He then turned to face the clerk. "Unlock it."

Barry did as instructed. The robber then motioned for the bum to push the door open and with the gun now leveled on the back of Ed's head, Pete yelled, "All right, cops. Here's what's happening. I'm taking this man and I'm taking one of your cars. The two of us are leaving. If you follow or try to stop us in any way, this man dies."

As the two men walked slowly out of the store, two things happened simultaneously. The first was a thought in Pete's head, realizing that in all the excitement, he never actually got any money from anyone. He turned to look back at the store, contemplating a quick retreat. Otherwise, he realized, this whole undertaking would be for nothing.

At the same time, Ed, whose leg still hurt badly, snagged a pothole in the blacktop of the parking lot. Losing his balance, he tumbled forward. Pete, who was just turning his head back, caught the heel of the falling bum and tumbled directly on top of the prone man. The rifle bounced from his hand and slid across the parking lot.

For a split second, no one moved. The scene was surreal enough that some of the cops chuckled. Then, the mad rush began. Peter tried desperately to crawl over Ed to get the rifle as the cops swarmed the robber.

Just like that, the ordeal ended.

In the aftermath, everyone considered Edward Monroe a hero. Even though he said he tripped, some people believed he did it on purpose.

While being congratulated, the man in the now-crumpled business suit came up to Ed and slapped him on the back. "Ed, I want to show my appreciation. And also, quite honestly, correct a horrible injustice."

"It's not necessary... Brandon, right?"

He smiled. "Yes, Brandon...but I didn't tell you my last name: Rufous."

"Excuse me?"

"I owned Rufous Manufacturing. I also currently own a couple of office buildings downtown and we need a new janitor. It's not a great job –"

Ed interrupted, "But it's a job. It sure beats..." He looked at his right hand, which still held the sleeping pills. "Jeez, I almost shoplifted these. I guess I won't be needing 'em." For the first time in ages, Ed smiled a genuine, happy smile.

~ Chapter Thirteen ~

Are we the only couple on the planet who get excited by going to Kmart? I wouldn't be surprised.

We both work full time jobs and have many friend, family, and church obligations, not to mention my wife's motherly duties. There is simply not much time for just the two of us. So, when the opportunity arises for us to go pick up some groceries together, it becomes Date Day for us. Even the most mundane activities are thrilling, when I know I can spend the day with the love of my life.

My sweetie pushes the cart down the aisle as I trail a couple of steps behind, lagging after I'd stopped to examine a bottle of flavored water. As I place the bottle into the cart, she gives me a disgusted look. "How can you drink that stuff?"

I grin and shrug. "I like it, what can I say? It's healthy, or at least it's not unhealthy. How can you not drink it?"

"Because it's not Dr Pepper."

I suppose we all need a favorite drink. Mine is usually boring old water, occasionally with a touch of flavoring in it, but normally just straight from the tap. It has always been my beverage of choice, partially due to my frugality, but mostly because it's better for me than those carbonated liquids that dot the landscape. "You should drink more water."

"Blech!" A disgusted look leaps onto her face. "Do you know what fish do in there?"

I give her a puzzled expression. "Swim?"

"Among other things too nasty to talk about. I'm not touching that stuff!"

"So you'd rather drink something that can dissolve nails?"

Nodding her head, she replies, "I'm not made of nails, so no problem."

I suppose I can't fault that logic, so I drop it. Besides, I doubt I'll ever actually win a discussion like this.

As we turn the corner to head up the next aisle, my eyes fall onto a plush stuffed kitty on the end cap. Knowing how much my wife loves cats, I reach for it. I barely get it into my hands before she asks, "What are you doing?"

Gazing at it for a moment, I smile and hold at her eye level. "Meow!"

"Oooh, that's cute! But you're not buying it for me."

Apparently, my motives are completely transparent to her, but I still feign ignorance. "You kiddin'? I'd never!" I set it back on the shelf, making a mental note to come back later when she's not around.

"Uh-huh," she says with a grin. "So, tell me a story."

"What, now?"

"You got something better to do?"

Shrugging, I reply, "I don't think I do! Just don't let me walk into an endcap or a customer."

"I think you're bluffin' dude," Bobby said to me as he tossed a fiver into the pot. "I'm gonna own you after this hand!"

He was right. I had crap for cards. My pair of fours wouldn't hold up under scrutiny, but hell, it's only money, right? Tossing a crisp ten-dollar-bill on the table, I said, "I raise. How 'bout you boys? You in?"

Frowning at his cards, Len shook his head slowly and slapped them on the table. "Nah. Ain't worth it." Shane followed suit, tossing his cards onto the pile with a look of disgust evident on his chubby face.

An expressionless Bobby stared at my eyes for a long moment, presumably trying to ascertain my level of sincerity. I always thought I had a decent poker face, but not until he folded his cards neatly together and set them on the table did I know for sure. "Forget it. It's yours."

"Wonderful!" As I reached my hands to collect the sizeable pile of cash, I heard a rapping on my apartment door. It caused me pause, because it didn't sound like a normal fist-on-the-door knock to me. I asked with a sly grin, "Hey Len, ya mind? I need to count my money."

Shrugging, Len stood up and trudged to the door. He looked out the peephole, inhaling sharply before turning back to me. "Uh, Ray, ya gotta see this!"

I pocketed my winnings, pulled myself up, and stepped over to the door. On the other side of my peephole stood a woman, whose head I couldn't see, wearing a sharp, tight-fitting pink dress. Her prominent feature was the axe held solidly in her right hand, handle-side up. She lifted it and using the handle-end, rapped forcefully upon my door. "Huh." I turned back to the crowd. "Now here's something ya don't see every day."

After I gave the other two a quick peek, I reached for the knob. Shane punched my shoulder. "What the hell?! You're *not* gonna open the door!"

"Well sure, why not? I mean really, she has an axe. If she wants to come in, she doesn't exactly need my approval." My door creaked as I slowly pulled it open. "Hello there. What can I do for you?"

The dark-haired beauty looked at me with no emotion. "I'm here to see Cory."

My other roommate had left a half-hour ago to pick up more beer. "Oh, I'm sorry. He's not home at the moment."

Her eyes, the darkest brown I had ever seen, pierced my calm exterior. Her gaze caused me to shiver slightly. "I need to wait for him," she said as she took a step forward. "It's important."

I stepped back on instinct, allowing her to enter my apartment. Looking around, my friends all wore shocked expressions as the stunningly attractive woman carrying a fireman's axe marched into our card game.

Shrugging, I said, "Cool. Okay, I'm Ray, that's Shane, Len, and Bobby. And you are?"

"Waiting for Cory. When will he be back?"

"Oh. Um, not sure, really. Not long, I think. He went for beer." I had to wonder why I told her the truth. Shane wondered, too. At least I assume that's why he whacked me in the shoulder again. "So I'd offer you a beer, but y'know."

Len blurted out, "So what's the deal with the axe, baby cakes? You gonna take a Cory souvenir home with you?"

"Geez, dude," Bobby whispered. "The hell's wrong with you?"

"What? Paula Bunyan over there's got a genuine conversation piece with her. Ain'tcha curious?"

113

I cracked the thinnest of smiles. "Paula Bunyan?"

"Yeah, that was lame. Would Lizzie Borden work any better?"

Before I could answer, the front door flew open. With a case of beer in one hand and another under his arm, Cory started to say, "The cavalry's here, boys! Get yer..." However, the sight of an axe-wielding woman caused him to cease speaking.

"Cory," she said levelly.

"Oh. Uh, hey... I wanna say... Margaret?"

She glowered at him for a moment before replying, "Judy."

Nodding feverishly, he said, "Right right, Judy. Of course. You're ... looking good. Nice blade."

"We need to talk. Privately."

The blood rushed from his face, turning my roommate a lighter shade of pale, as the old song goes. Setting the beer cases down on the floor, he pointed toward his bedroom. "Okay. We can talk in there. "

Shane, bless his heart, blurted out, "Hey, uh, can we hold your axe for you? Wouldn't want you to get carpal tunnel or anything."

Ignoring him, the lady in the tight pink dress turned and entered Cory's bedroom. I walked toward the door, but Cory held up a hand, shrugged, and whispered, "I got this, dude. But, y'know, if you hear what sounds like dismemberment occurring in here, call someone."

"Right," I replied as the door slowly creaked shut.

I turned back to my poker buddies. "So, whose deal is it? Len, I think it's yours."

Shane gaped at me with eyes wider than a typical Japanese artist draws an Anime babe. "Are you serious? We're just gonna freakin' play cards here?"

114

For his part, Bobby already had the side of his head pressed up against the door. He stood there, ear to door, for a few tense minutes. I decided to grab a beer while I waited for the card game to resume or a murder to occur.

When Bobby's eyes also grew to Anime size, I began to worry. But then a smile cracked his face. "It's okay," he said as a squeaking sound began to emanate from behind the door, "they're bangin'."

Being voyeuristic males, we all listened in for a moment. "Yup," Shane said, "them's sex noises. Unmistakable."

"Like you've ever had sex," I said with a grin. "Okay, so then, Len's deal? We..."

A knock on the apartment door stopped me in mid-sentence. Walking to the peephole, I looked and started chuckling. "I'm sensing a theme here."

Shane pushed me out of the way to take a gander. "The chick holding the crowbar is pretty hot, huh?"

"I like the other one better. What *is* that she's got? Is that what they call a morning star?"

"No," Bobby replied after taking his turn at the peephole, "a morning star is only a spiked metal ball attached to a stick. This one has a chain between them, so I think that makes it a mace or a flail."

"Cool," Len said with a large smile. "Well what are ya waitin' for? Let 'em in, already! It's not a party 'til the chicks and weapons arrive!"

Pulling the door open, I said, "Hello ladies! Who's up for a game of poker? Knives or better to open!"

115

Cole had been stuck at this bank for so long, he had lost track of time. He leaned and whispered to the lady next to him, "Hey, do ya think it's Wednesday yet?"

Turning her head and scowling, Bernice hissed, "Shhh!"

The man standing closest to him also spun around and glared. Adjusting his ski mask, he yelled, "If I have to tell you to shut up once more…" The robber saw no reason to finish the sentence, as the pistol he brandished said it all.

"But none of us have eaten since –"

Cole stopped talking when the gunman's shoe smashed into his stomach. However, Cole's comment got them thinking, so the bank robbers decided to order out. The leader of the group contacted the police who surrounded the building. Since the closest restaurant served Chinese food, within twenty minutes the nine hostages were feasting upon Cashew Chicken.

Cracking open his fortune cookie, Cole's mouth dropped when he read it. *You're next,* it read.

As he tightened his hand around the fortune, a megaphone from outside blared to life. "We've given you food, and your transportation will be here soon. Now, you must release some more of your hostages!"

Scanning the room, the leader's index finger slowly moved from person to person. He pointed at Bernice and said, "You." His finger then came to rest in front of the custodian, a frail-looking man with the name Sidney embroidered on his grey coveralls. "You."

Looking at his fortune again, Cole smiled. He leapt to his feet, but before he could utter a sound, the man who had kicked him earlier raised his handgun and shot him in the chest. "Not you," he said with a chuckle.

~ Chapter Fourteen ~

Walking into the bedroom, I find my wife concentrating on her cell phone. "Facebook or Candy Crush," I ask?

"Email," she replies, then sticks her tongue out at me.

She looks so adorable, in her red one-piece pajama outfit. It even has footies built in, each foot with a small fox's face embroidered on it. "You look warm," I say casually.

"Mmmm," is her reply. After pushing a few more buttons, she sets the phone on her right leg and looks up at me. "Tell me a story."

"Hmmm… Not sure if I have one handy."

Picking up her phone, she holds it high in the air. "Would you rather I do Candy Book Face Crush?"

Smiling, I reply, "No no, I got one."

~ A Job ~

Whenever Congressman Petrov told me he had a job for me, it usually meant I had to kill someone. I hoped that this time, it'd only be a scare, or a limb that needed breaking, but I couldn't pin my hopes on that.

Pulling into the parking garage, I saw a tall, heavy-set shadow lurking in the corner. I easily recognized the hunched-over silhouette, so I got out of my vehicle and walked briskly toward the figure.

"Morgan," he whispered, his whisky-soaked breath instantly assaulting me. "Here's the job I told you about." I had to work hard to suppress my gag reflex. He took a step forward and handed me a picture.

I turned so the full moon illuminated the photograph. "Oh," I uttered casually, "a woman, huh? What'd she do to ya?" I wouldn't describe her as pretty, but I had seen worse.

Even through the darkness, I could tell he wore a scowl. His raspy voice grew sharper. "It doesn't matter. Just take care of her."

I had to ask, "You mean permanently?"

He paused, but only for a second, before nodding. "I don't ever want to see this woman again. Are we clear?"

"Yes, sir."

"She lives alone." He moved closer, his halitosis making my knees buckle. Clapping me on the shoulder blade with his plump, meaty paw, he said, "I'll take care of ya, Morgan. When I make it to the top, you'll live the life. That I promise."

Great, a promise from a crooked politician. I'll hold my breath. Actually, I realized I was so I turned my head and exhaled sharply. After sucking in a fresh breath, I said, "I'll be in touch," and hopped into my car.

I watched his hulking shadow climb into his BMW and drive off. Turning on the dome light, I examined the picture. The chubby woman with the crooked smile wore her brassy, blonde hair past her shoulders. She looked to be barely twenty-one. Too young, in my opinion, to be fooling around with an old, married pervert like the Congressman. Flipping the photo over, I found her name, Mayra Simonson, and address written on the back. I slammed my car in gear and rolled into the night.

By the time I reached my destination, it was midnight. I parked two blocks away and casually strolled down the street until I found myself standing in front of her house. Though the surrounding houses were dark, her place had a single light aglow. "Let's get this over with," I whispered to myself.

Walking up the steps, I peered in the window next to the front door. I could see the ambient flicker of the television. Knocking on the door, I inhaled sharply and took a step back.

The door opened only a crack, straining against the security chain. An eyeball appeared in the gap. She said with obvious disdain, "What is it?"

"Forgive the lateness of the hour, ma'am," I said, using my professional Secret-Service voice. "I am from Congressman Petrov's office. Are you Miss Simonson?"

She nodded. "So, has Wally come to his senses?"

I paused, collecting my thoughts. Since he didn't give me much information, I had to wing it. "Yes he has. May I enter?"

Mayra looked me over, from my tightly cropped black hair, down my buttoned overcoat to my polished shoes. It always paid to dress the part, I found. After shutting the door, she fumbled with the chain and then opened it wider. As she stepped back, she said tentatively, "Sure, come in."

Right off the bat, I noticed the young woman looked a bit thinner and prettier than the picture indicated. She wore a plush pink robe, tightly knotted around her midriff, the flannel of her pajamas peeking out around it.

As she turned and started toward the living room, I slowly rested my hand on the doorknob, palming it locked. She offered me a beverage and went into the kitchen to get it. I seized the opportunity to scan the surroundings. A modest and obviously effeminate home, it had lots of knick-knacks, dainty glass figurines, and candles galore. I found no sign of a man's touch in this living room. Walking over to the sliding-glass door, I gave it a quick tug with my gloved hands, to test the lock.

Mayra returned, holding a glass of soda. I took the glass and quickly set it on the end table. "So," she said nervously as she sat down on the couch, "I was expecting Wally to do this himself. Why did he send you?"

I offered my best fake smile. "It's my job to clean up the Congressman's messes." With that, I reached in my overcoat and unholstered my pistol, aiming it at her chest.

Mayra quickly stood up, but plopped back down just as fast, her face turning pale. "Oh God," she whispered, "I never thought…" Her voice trailed off.

"Sorry, honey," I said as I stood, "You shouldn't have let the old man nail ya."

She looked up at me with a genuine look of surprise. "What!? You think I had sex with him? Ew! Is that what he told you?"

"I don't care what this is about. I'm sorry, really I am. But you've gotten yourself into this mess, whatever the mess is, and I'm here to tidy it up." My finger tightened on the trigger as I thought about how this scenario would play out. I probably should drive her out to the desert first. Then, I wouldn't have to mask the shot. Eh, no big deal. I'll volume up the TV before I kill her and then ransack the place a bit. Perhaps I'll grab a few things, some jewelry and cash, maybe that nice stereo of hers, to make it look like a robbery so the cops wouldn't dig too deeply.

I knew she'd beg. They all beg. However, she piqued my curiosity with the statement, "I'll split the money with you. Hell, you can have it all! Just please don't kill me!"

Slowly, I sat down opposite her. Sometimes, I enjoyed giving people that feeling of hope, a slim possibility that they might survive a visit from Morgan Cutler. "Tell me about the money."

She swallowed hard and released the breath she probably didn't realize she held. "I'm an intern. I volunteered during his reelection. I also designed his website, among other things."

"Right," I said firmly, losing interest by the second.

"I was working late one night when the congressman came into his office. He wasn't alone, if you know what I mean."

"Right," I said again, impatiently, "so you caught him having an affair and what, you were going to blackmail him? That's it? A few thousand is supposed to save your life?"

The woman turned even paler, which I didn't think was possible, but she persevered. "That's not all. This woman was Judge Dade. I heard them talking about bribes they both had taken, all sorts of incriminating stuff."

I stood up, shaking my head. "Great, the word of a nobody against a judge and a congressman. I'm guessing he wanted you dead for the sheer nuisance of it all."

When I brought the gun back up to her chest, she yelled, "There's more!" She shouted through rapid breaths, her skin so ashen I had no idea why she hadn't passed out yet. Her poor heart must've been thumping like that of a cornered rabbit. "His computer was still on, so I recorded them through the webcam. The phones go through the computer, so I got audio as well as video. I also rerouted the security cameras to my station and recorded footage of the two of them doing the nasty on the desk. I've got it all. We can blackmail them and get as much money as we need!"

This turn of events intrigued me. Sure, Wally Petrov had been pretty good to me, but this could be my way out of this lifestyle. Imagine, not having to kill anymore. I lowered the gun. "Tell ya what," I said casually, "if you can prove this, if I can see this footage myself, we may be able to make a deal."

She exhaled deeply and nodded her head. "I have it here, on my computer."

"Lead the way," I said, adding, "but if you try anything…"

"No, I understand," she uttered with a tremble in her voice. She stood on wobbly legs, using the couch to steady herself. As she shuffled over to the bedroom, she exclaimed, "Oh God, I'm roasting!" She untied her robe, tossing it on the bed. Even through the flannel pajamas, I could tell she had a nice body. That picture did her no justice at all.

Mayra sat down and started typing feverishly. Within a minute, some grainy, black and white footage appeared on the screen. It was Wally all right, wheezing and grimacing like a mating walrus. The judge, a comely lady in her mid-50s, didn't appear to be enjoying herself all that much, which gave me a chuckle. I found it difficult to believe that anyone actually enjoyed sex with that disgusting man. Then, after they finished their dirty deed, she keyed up the audio and we listened to two powerful politicians bragging about all sorts of indiscretions.

After witnessing the whole repulsive event, Mayra looked up at me. "That's pretty damning, isn't it?"

Smiling, I replied, "We really could blackmail both of them. They're both worth a lot of money and would do anything to bury this footage."

For the first time since I pulled out my weapon, Mayra had reason to be happy. She let a relieved sigh slip past her lips as she grinned. "How much do you think we could get?" she asked as she inched closer to me.

"Oh, I'm thinking a million each, easy." Once I holstered my weapon, I reached in my pocket to procure my cell phone. "Let me set up this deal right away…"

Mayra reached up and put her hand on my shoulder, whispering, "We can do that tomorrow." Then, she leaned in and kissed me softly.

The next evening, I contacted Petrov and said simply, "We need to talk. Meet me at midnight out at the Bangor construction site, outside of town."

"What's this all about, Morgan? Did you take care of my problem?"

"In a manner of speaking," I said firmly, "but bring your checkbook." I disconnected before he could utter another sound.

I turned to Mayra and said, "It's set."

The Congressman kept us waiting several minutes past midnight, but that didn't surprise me. The fat man had the propensity for tardiness. "Morgan," he started, and then he saw Mayra. "What the hell? What's she doing here?"

I grinned at him as I said, "There's been a slight change of plans."

With that statement out of my mouth, I pulled out my gun, turned sharply, and shot Mayra directly in the left temple. She crumpled to the ground, her glassy eyes staring up at the sky. The look of shocked betrayal frozen upon her face will forever haunt me.

I put the gun away and handed the DVD to Wally. "The only other copy is on her computer. After I bury her, I'll go and destroy it."

The fat man laughed boisterously as he slapped me on the back. "You had me going, Morgan. I thought a piece of tail and some easy money had swayed you."

"No, sir," I replied. "I know who my friends are."

He nodded and said, "I was going to save this for later, but under the circumstances, I want you to know something. The party has approached me. They want me to run for President. And when I win, you'll be my head of security."

I removed my glove and shook the hand of the devil. Even though his grip felt hot and sweaty, I shivered involuntarily.

~ Chapter Fifteen ~

"Goodness," she says, "that was kind of a sad, scary one."

I shake my head. "They can't all be light and funny."

Looking a little blue, she replies, "I know. But it's not the most conducive story for a good's night sleep."

Lying down next to her, I give her a long hug, and then a quick smooch. "I've got another story for you sweetie. One that's short and silly."

"Hey," she replies with a grin, "just like me!"

"Yup! And just like me, too."

"No wonder we're perfect together."

~ Trifecta of Regrets ~

"So, buddy, you got any regrets?"

I stared at Zanicus in disbelief. "You mean other than stealing the loaf of bread that got me arrested by the imperial guard and shackled to this dungeon wall?"

"Of course," my cell mate replied, "That's a given. Before that."

"Why would you ask me that? Do you have one?"

His laugh echoed against the slimy walls. "I do, but I asked you first."

"Well, I regret bragging at the bar about stealing that bread. Otherwise?" I sighed. "I regret never announcing my intentions to Gwendoline."

Zanicus tried to whistle, but the guard hadn't watered us in a while, so it came out as a loud puff of air. "You had a thing for Gwenny? Aiming high, huh?"

"Yup. She has the shiniest skin, and she always smells of lilacs. She would come to my blacksmith shop on Thursdays to have her weekly chastity belt buffing. I loved her something fierce, but I always found myself fumbling for the right words."

"Ever tell her you loved her?"

I sighed again. "No. Besides, I think she was betrothed to our guard, ironically enough." The memory overwhelmed me. Not wanting to find out what would happen if a severely dehydrated man cried, I said, "Okay, so your regret?"

At that moment, the guard slammed his key into the lock. I drooled instinctively. Apparently, I had enough moisture inside of me for that to happen. "We're finally getting fed!"

As the door squeaked open, Zanicus said, "My regret is about to be history. Look!"

Zanicus's right foot was no longer shackled!

"Quiet," The guard yelled as he clomped over to me, "or no food again today!" He dipped his spoon into the dirty bucket, brought up a glob of off-white gruel, and slapped it into my waiting mouth. It tasted as horrible as always, but I greedily accepted it. As I swallowed, I heard Zanicus say, "Hey guard, do you know who Gwendoline is?"

He stopped feeding me – *Hey, I wasn't done yet!* – and walked straight over to him. "She's my wife. What's it to you, scum?"

"Only this," he said before using his free foot to kick the guard squarely in the groin.

As he collapsed onto the cold dirt floor, I gasped loudly. He dropped our food! The bucket hit hard, splattering our only sustenance all over the dirt and himself.

Zanicus shouted triumphantly, "Yes! Direct hit to his sack!"

My mind finally got past the spilled food. "Oh hey, that's great! So what's next? How do we escape?"

"Next? No, that was it. It took forever to get that foot free. I saw my spot and I took it. Score! I've wanted to do that from day one!"

"Um, okay. You do realize when he gets up, he's most likely going to kill you. Right?"

Under the circumstances I suspect Zanicus would have shrugged, had that been possible. "Eh. I suppose. But it was totally worth it."

Therefore, to this guard I lost Gwendoline, my food, and probably my cellmate too. I wonder if that counts as three regrets.

~ Chapter Sixteen ~

Halloween at the Pearson household tends to be long and quiet, but that's what comes from living in the country. So, instead of sitting around waiting for no one to show up, we go to where the kids are.

Our family church gets many visitors, ranging in age from tiny kiddos to teenagers, and of course the adults who accompany them.

We get to Trinity Episcopal about an hour before the first kids are slated to arrive. My wife, with her clip-on ears and drawn-on whiskers, is the cutest kitty cat ever. As for me, I'm not a fan of Halloween, for some reason that I will probably never understand. When forced to dress up, I use my go-to 'costume' that consists entirely of me wearing my navy blue robe. Some years, I've told people I'm Hugh Hefner. During other Halloweens, I've been a mental patient, and once I was just a sleepy guy.

Most of the times, however, I grab a towel from the pantry and boom, I'm Arthur Dent, the lead character of my all-time favourite British novel, *The Hitchhiker's Guide to the Galaxy*. It's rare the person who gets the joke, but I hardly care. I get to be outside in public wearing my toasty-warm bathrobe. I've also found, while going to parties, a bottle of beer fits nicely in my robe's pocket. What's not to like?

After we get the chairs set up in the hall next to the front door, and fill a large bowl with candy, we're ready for the kids to arrive.

I look at my cell phone. "What time does Trick or Treating start?"

"At six," is my wife's reply.

"It's only 5:30, hon. We've got some time to waste."

128

She smirks at me. "Tell me a story!"

Grinning widely, I reply. "It just so happens that I have a story that is perfect for this occasion!"

~ Don't Mess with Tradition ~

I sighed when I heard the front door slam. Putting the bookmark in my science fiction magazine and closing it slowly, I sat on my bed and waited for the commotion to begin. My roommate Ezra could never simply enter the house and go about his business. For some reason, his life always had to involve me.

"Hey Dan," Ezra bellowed from somewhere beyond the other side of my closed door, "come out here a sec!"

Having an obnoxious persistence about him, I knew he'd only continue his caterwauling until I emerged. So I hauled myself out of bed, pushed my door open, and ambled into the living room.

His justification for my attention became immediately apparent. His hair, for starters, was dyed a bright purple. The majority of it shot upward in three large spikes, standing nearly six inches above his skull, while the remaining strands drooped haphazardly around his angular face. He had an awful lot of make-up on his face and neck, various shades of pink, baby blue, and purple. To me, it appeared as if a circus clown had attacked him. Clad mostly in leather, the vest and chaps offset the pink, neon tank top and cowboy boots quite hideously. He completed the ensemble with a clip-on hoop nose-ring and large, dangling earrings. He was certainly dressed to kill... or be killed. He looked at me through his badly applied mascara, smiled through his smeared lipstick, and spoke, in his usual manly tone, "I'm a punker! Cool, huh?"

Like he really needed to tell me this. This should've been the most humorous, ludicrous thing I had ever seen. Instead, every fiber of my being demanded that I run screaming from the house. Fighting the flight urge and with no expression on my face, I calmly replied, "I don't think the lipstick goes well with your chaps."

"It's the only color I liked," he said through a smile. "Besides, it tastes like strawberry."

This statement worried me. A lot. I almost released the words, *Excuse me, but I really have to leave now* when he said, "Do you think I'll win? I think I will."

With a furrowed brow I asked, "Win what, top freak of the campus award?"

"No," he laughed, "at the frat Halloween party, stupid!"

He must have seen the relief rush through me like a lake escaping its dam. I finally cracked a smile as I giggled, "Oh! Man, I thought you had gone completely mental!"

As I slapped my hand on my forehead, Ezra answered, "Nah, I know what I'm doing. But you obviously don't! You completely forgot about Halloween, didn't ya?"

"Yeah. Well, I've been busy."

"Haven't we all." Ezra glanced at the kitchen and then headed toward it as he talked. "I'm gonna be gone most of the night, so I guess it's up to you to hand out candy to the li'l gremlins."

I spun to stare at the back of his spiked head. "What?! Oh man, that's right! Kids. Crap! Do we have any candy?"

"Beats me," he shrugged, "I don't buy the groceries here. The question is did *you* buy any candy?"

Sometimes, I really hated that dude. "No, I never buy that garbage."

He shrugged and turned to leave. "Well, you'd best buy something. Don't want angry kids burning down our pine trees."

I gave him one of my best evil glares, but he wasn't paying attention anyway. Another wasted glare, I thought. "What, are they really all that crazy around here?"

"The children of Greene Street take Halloween pretty darned seriously. You remember those trees down by the end of the street? The charred ones?"

"Whoa! Kids did that?"

"Yeah," he nodded. "We've got vicious little scoundrels around here. They've destroyed yards, shaved pets, and even torched an entire white picket fence once, all because they didn't get good enough junk. Or so the rumors go."

Even though I really didn't believe Ezra, as he did tend to lean toward exaggeration, I felt apprehension creep into me. "Really?" I drawled.

He shrugged, grabbing at the doorknob. "I dunno. But I will say one thing. Go Trick-or-Treating around here. You'll get the best grub you've ever seen."

As he opened the door and yelled his good-byes, I interjected with, "Hey, how many kids we got around here?"

He shrugged again. "Dunno. Not many, really. Couple bags oughta do it. Well, catch ya later!"

I smiled, even though I didn't really feel happy enough to do so. "Sure. Have fun." I waved, but he didn't look back to see it as he yanked the door closed.

"Crap," I breathed to no one. I grabbed my keys and coat, and headed for the door, the car, and eventually the store. It was just past 5pm, so I still had time before the little monsters came out.

Entering the ThriftoMart, I came to the realization that I should've prepared for this sooner. Slim pickings, to be sure. I had to settle for a sack of suckers, but I managed to find a bag of Milk Duds as well. As a child, I used to hate the houses that gave out those tiny Dum-Dum suckers and wads of gum. At the end of the run, I'd be stuck with 35 suckers of varying sizes and textures; 23 gum configurations, be they balls, wads, or Bazooka Joe and his weird friends; and maybe, if lucky, about 10 miniature candy bars.

Oh well, I decided, I'm the adult now. I had every right to make them suffer just like I had to when I was their age. It's a rite of passage, after all. What do they expect for free anyway? Juvenile hoodlums wielding matches and electric razors wouldn't scare me off.

When I returned home, darkness had crept into the evening sky, so I knew I'd have to get ready for the little tykes. I dumped the Milk Duds and suckers into a ceramic bowl, and stared at it for a while. "Man, it looked like a lot more candy in the bags." So I jogged into the kitchen, and dumped everything into a smaller bowl. "There! That's better." I smiled as I sat the bowl next to the door and walked into the living room, flopping in front of the TV.

As I sat there ignoring the program in front of me, I thought back to my Trick-or-Treating days. One year in particular, I wore a Snoopy costume, complete with the thin, plastic mask. No one in the neighborhood recognized me and I loved that feeling of stealth. Another year, for some bizarre reason, I donned one of Mom's dresses and, complete with tennis-balls in the appropriate region, I went as a girl. Though I recollected all the laughter I received, I got some great candy that year.

At nearly 6pm, I heard the doorbell ring. Springing out of my seat, I rushed toward the door. I was actually beginning to look forward to this.

I flung the door open, looking down with a broad grin to greet the little ones. However, I quickly realized I had to look up to be witness to three gargantuan teens, tall and thick, dressed as football players with their helmets in hand.

"Gimme!" One of them said, and the other two grunted in unison.

I smirked as I pushed the bowl closer to them. One of the grunters grabbed a handful, while the other two picked a few Milk Duds boxes from among the suckers.

"This blows," the verbalist of the bunch said. The others grunted. They all turned and vacated, mumbling something about toilet paper.

I slammed the door, grumbling, "Well, that pretty much killed my enjoyment."

A few minutes later, the bell rang again. I stared down at four smaller children dressed as Iron man, the Incredible Hulk, a witch, and a homicidal maniac complete with a bloodstained hockey mask and plastic hatchet.

None of them said anything so I uttered, in a typical, *I am an adult and you are kids* tone of voice, "What do we say?"

The kid in the mask raised his hatchet and yelled, "Be hasty with your candy, sir!" The others laughed.

I shrugged my shoulders. Seemed reasonable enough to me. I handed the bowl out to them and again they mostly dug out the Milk Duds. They thanked me in an insincere tone as they left, which probably occurred only because their parents stood out front within earshot.

The same scenario continued for maybe a half hour, until all of the Milk Duds had vanished. Finally, when the children had no choice, the suckers started dwindling as well. When only eight suckers remained, I started handing them out one to a customer, which really irked them. I believe one little girl, dressed as a princess, even whispered a vile word under her breath. In retaliation I yelled, "Princesses don't use such language, y'know!"

Finally, when the doorbell rang at a bit after seven o'clock, I stood with my last sucker in hand. My sweat glands kicked in as I stared down at three small tykes standing at my door. I dropped the sucker into one of the bags, but what to give the other two? I quickly dashed toward my kitchen after yelping, "Hold on just a minute, you two!"

Flinging open the fridge, I cursed myself for procrastinating on my grocery shopping. I could hear them grumbling impatiently at the door, so I pulled open the fruit tray and grabbed a couple apples. Smiling as wide as my face would allow, I said, "Sorry, this is all I have."

As I dropped the fruit into their bags, I realized that one of these apples was actually a tomato. The boy, dressed as a Zorro-type character, saw this and looked up at me with wide, disbelieving eyes. The other kid, a gorilla, looked equally as perplexed with his apple. The gorilla said, in a deep, eerie tone, "No candy left? This is very bad."

Zorro muttered, "You shouldn't oughta mess with tradition, mister," and with that, they both spun and hopped off the porch.

Moments later, I heard a gooey sounding splat against the side of the house. I didn't even have to look to figure out where that tomato ended up. I made a mental note not to give out anything that could be used as ammo against me.

When the bell rang again, my heart began pounding like Neil Peart working a drum solo! What to give them? I dashed around, flinging open cupboards like a hungry old woman searching for her teeth. I heard the bell ring again and I knew I needed to find something right now. My vision landed upon a box of ChocoDucks cereal. Lunging at the box, I dashed for the door. I flung it open and there stood a Bart Simpson and an Indiana Jones. Indy snarled, "'Bout time!"

"Yea yea, sure," I mumbled as I poured about two seconds worth of cereal into both children's bags.

They looked stunned, believe me. Bart reached in his bag and pulled out a ChocoMarshmellow, and held it at arm's length between us. "Whazzis," he drawled, "some kind of joke?"

"Hey," I yelled, "ya want some milk with that, too? It can be arranged!"

Bart dropped the ChocoMarshmellow and I watched it descend to the porch. "Dude'll pay," he said to his partner.

Turning to Bart, Indy asked, "You got the eggs, right?" I didn't hear the answer as they walked off my porch and into my side yard.

The next hour brought a lot of anxiety. The bell rang too fast for me to think about my next move, so I constantly had to think on my feet – and my feet were pretty darned stupid, let me tell you. I handed the kids things like cough drops and antacid tablets stolen from the medicine cabinet at work, as well as ketchup and taco sauce packets collected over the years from various restaurants. Oh, it got worse. I gave them small bars of soap and bottles of shampoo from previous hotel stays, dusty packets of Ramen soup and cans of tuna fish from the top shelf, even packages of bologna and other crappy lunch meat that I saved for times of severe gastro-desperation. Why, I even gave a little boy a frozen burrito. Although, in my defense, he did have on a homemade Bandito outfit. He seemed grateful enough, but his father gave me one heckuva look.

While still digesting the father's perplexed glare, I thought I heard a noise coming from across the room. As I turned, I heard it again. It sounded like scratching. I cautiously crept down the hall toward the dining room. As I rounded the corner and caught a glimpse of the bay window, the doorbell rang, startling me.

Running into the kitchen, I grabbed a box of macaroni and cheese. I continued to hear the scratching noise, which worried me, but since I couldn't see anything on my cursory glimpse while touring the kitchen for goodies, I decided to deal with the problem at hand.

When I opened the door, no one stood there to view my friendly, albeit fake smile. Another good emotion wasted, I thought. Now, the scratching noise sounded an awful lot like an opening window, so I bolted toward the dining room.

Upon arrival, I saw a small window had indeed been pushed open. As I stood there, brandishing the box of macaroni and cheese like it was some medieval club, I had to release a quick chuckle at the absurdity of it all. Since the window hadn't been opened far enough for anyone to enter, I shrugged before shutting and locking it.

The doorbell rang once again. As I walked toward it, I heard a couple dull thuds against the window I had just shut. I turned, but from my vantage point in the hallway, I couldn't see the windows. Breathing a heavy sigh, I decided to deal with the door.

Again I stood alone at the front door, but at least this time the brats left a treat of their own, a burning lunch sack. Well, at least the pine trees are still intact, I thought, as I stomped on the bag. My first big strike caused a bunch of red stuff to spit out and onto my left shoe and pant leg. Kicking the bag, I shook my head slowly when out rolled a few packets of the ketchup and taco sauce I had handed out. "I'm gonna get you, Cartman and Harry Potter!" I screamed, directing it at the only two characters I could remember who received such treats from me. "And in my day, we used dog crap!"

As I slammed the door, cursing about the mess, I heard a couple more splats on the other side of the house. I hurried to the back and saw all the rear windows dripping with egg goo. Immediately after that, I heard more rustling on the front porch.

Anger now rushed through me. Grabbing a frying pan from the cupboard, I bolted toward the door. I flung it open and nearly plowed into the cutest pixie I had ever seen. This woman, probably in her early 20s, had a small child with her, dressed as a ballerina. They both let out screams, which sent me sprawling back inside, tumbling down and landing on my butt. The skillet skittered from my grasp and bounced into the wall, but I hardly noticed. This pixie costume looked fine on this woman, with her petite, shapely body and long, blonde hair. "Oh jeez," she said with a breezy tone, "you startled me! Sorry!"

"Um, yea, me too. Sorry, I mean."

"Twick or Tweet!" the little munchkin mumbled, with the biggest grin on her adorable little face.

The pixie giggled and then said, "She tries awfully hard, you know? Ya got something for her, for the effort?"

My smile faded. What to give this cute child? mac and cheese just didn't seem appropriate. Having no choice, I mumbled, "Uh, yea, um..." as I pulled out my wallet. I had nothing smaller than a $20, so I pulled it out and handed it to the child.

Both of their eyes got huge. "Wow!" the ballerina shouted.

"Wow!" the pixie echoed. "That's awfully generous of you!"

"Gee, twirn't nuthin. Say, you want anything?" I asked as I pointed the business end of my wallet toward her.

"Oh gee, uh, no thanks sir. But thanks," she quickly added. As they turned to leave, she said to her little partner, "What do you say to this nice man?"

She looked up at me, and gave me an even bigger, even cuter grin before exclaiming, "Wow! Money!"

The pixie laughed, "I mean, what else do you say?"

"Tank yew!"

"Chur welcum," I slurred back. "Bye," I said to both of them as they walked toward the street.

Standing there watching them leave, I actually felt some joy. The look on both of their faces might've just made this day worth it. I continued to grin, with the door open, until I heard the kid yell, "Look whut dat guy gave me! Money!" When I heard what sounded like twenty kids exclaiming their delight, my smile quickly failed. I knew I was in trouble when I not only heard but actually felt the trampling, like a thousand bulls stampeding toward my porch. I let out an involuntary scream as I slammed the door shut, to protect myself from the Running of the Children.

"Gah!" I exclaimed, imagining a zombie movie or the frantic scratching on the doors of a full fallout shelter after the nukes fell.

Hearing the horde chanting 'Trick or Treat' only made things worse. By the time I ran into the kitchen, grabbed the bag of in-the-shell

137

peanuts, and made it back to the door, I had nearly lost it. Part of me wanted to grab the frying pan and dive into the crowd, swinging maniacally. Instead, I flung the door open and yelled, "Treats!!! Yaaaaa!!" as I ripped open the bag and started whipping handfuls of peanuts at the throng of children outside my door. It felt kinda like trying to appease some intangible god in my mind, with the peanut sacrifice, but it came across more along the lines of an angry old coot feeding the pigeons with a vengeance. Clearly, I had lost complete control. Hearing all of the moans of disappointment and shouts of hatred only made me whiz the peanuts harder. I even nailed that Indiana Jones kid in the back of his little head as he turned to leave. As he bent over to pick up his fedora, I pegged him on his backside. When he spouted something about shaving cream, I knew I had made a tactical error, but I still smiled at my accurate toss.

Shutting the door, I felt a tiny bit better. Somehow, I managed to save myself a peanut. I popped it open and downed the two nuts as I walked back into the living room.

After a couple minutes, I thought I heard more rustling. However, this time it sounded like it came from the basement. At this point, I wasn't scared, only upset. I reaffirmed my grip on the frying pan, and flung open the basement door.

I took all of three steps before my ears picked up the sound of hundreds of peanuts bouncing off the house's aluminum siding. Furious, I let loose a primal scream as I turned and attempted to jump all three steps back up. I cleared the first two with ease, but the bottom of my left shoe caught the edge of the last step. I nearly regained my balance before bounding into and bouncing off the opposing wall, my weapon tumbling out of reach. I got up, cursed, and ran outside.

Once I arrived out there and looked around, my jaw dropped. I was flabbergasted. The little cretins had done an extremely thorough job. Most of the trees had toilet paper or other noticeably unnatural items hanging from them, and I found egg goo, tomato paste, or soap caking all the windows. Even the tiny basement windows had nasty words etched on them with soap. I found a couple wrappers from the soap bars I had given out, and sighed as I said to myself, "Another stupid treat, Dan!"

I felt a tap on my shoulder. My adrenaline still near maximum, I spun around like a jaguar on Mountain Dew. Ezra was rather lucky I no longer brandished that frying pan, because he would have been retrieving his pierced nose from across the yard. Giving me his very best shocked and startled expression, he screamed, "Geez Dan! What'd ya give the kids, suckers?"

"Yeah," I spoke softly and deliberately. "Suckers, Milk Duds, little bars of soap, tomatoes, packets of ketchup, money, lighter fluid, tuna fish, and frozen burritos. Just trying to be unique."

"Ran outta candy, huh?"

"Yup," I replied.

Ezra stared blankly at me for a spell, before he shook his head slowly and asked, "Um, dude, why didn't you simply turn off the porch light?"

If my brain had its own porch light, it would've popped on at that moment. I smacked my forehead and replied, "Lordy. That thought never entered my mind. It all happened so fast." I lowered my head.

After chuckling softly, Ezra sat down on the lawn. He just finished saying, "Dude, I'm not helping you clean this up, y'know," when he looked between his feet and noticed the ground was covered with in-the-shell peanuts. "What's up with this?" He extracted one from the grass and held it in front of me.

I dislodged it from his hand, cracked it, and ate one of the nuts. As I handed the other peanut to him, I said, "Oh yea. Forgot about these."

He sighed and then allowed his spiked head to fall back on the damp grass. As he hit, we both heard another peanut crack. Then we both started snickering under our breaths. "I don't suppose there'd be any full beer cans out here, would there?" Ezra asked.

"No, but I think I saw some pretzels over by the pine tree."

139

"The tree with the underwear and balloons hanging on it?"

"No, the one covered in shaving cream."

"Next to the one painted purple?"

"Yeah."

"Cool."

After a long pause, I said, "Ezra?"

"Yeah, Dan?"

"I really hate Halloween. What about you?"

"Nah," Ezra told me as he finished another peanut, "Halloween is cool. You just have to remember one important fact."

"Let me guess. Don't mess with tradition, right?"

"No," Ezra replied, "buy chocolate bars, stupid." He laughed, and eventually so did I.

~ Chapter Seventeen ~

Once the last of the festively dressed kiddos pick up their candy handouts from us, we fold up the folding chairs, putting them back where they belong. We shut and lock the door. My eyes gravitate to the bowl of remaining Halloween candy. "Goodness."

My wife asks, "What?"

Gesturing at the bowl, I say, "We massively overbought. We're gonna be eating candy for weeks."

She gives me a look of equal parts puzzlement and disdain. "Right! So what's the problem?"

"I don't need that much junk in my body." I place my hand on my belly.

"So don't eat it."

As if it was that simple. "You know I don't have any will power. Chocolate knows my weakness and torments me."

Grabbing the bowl with one hand, she strolls over to the trash container. She holds the bowl over top, tilting it toward the abyss. "Okay then, we throw it away."

My eyes pop open as large as they will go. "Wait now! Let's not get carried away here!"

"This is the easiest solution. Will power problem solved." No smile curls her lips. She's serious.

"Um… I can't waste food, either. Growing up, that was a sin in my family akin to your 'You can't move a sleeping cat' law."

She shakes her head slowly, though she keeps the bowl tipped at an angle dangerously unsafe for that candy. I fear for its life. "Uh-huh. How 'bout if we leave it here at the church, for Sunday coffee hour?"

I nod my approval. "That sounds fair to me."

Slowly, she corrects the angle of the bowl, walks over to the table in the main hall, and sets it down. I saunter up and snatch a fun-sized Snickers. My wife scolds, "What happened to not needing that junk, Hmmm?"

I shrug and offer her my best impish grin, but say nothing, so she adds, "All right, but now you have to tell me another story."

"Do I?"

"Yes. Telling stories burns calories. True story."

~ Spooked ~

"Oh Blake," Gina cooed while tossing her arms around her fiancé, "this place is just so perfect!" Kissing Blake on the lips, she added, "How did we get so lucky?"

"Um," he said while looking at the ground, "well, it'd been on the market for a while. They were… eager to sell."

Knowing her man all too well, she released her grip and pulled back a step. "Honey? What's up? What are you not telling me?" As he continued to avoid her gaze, she added, "Look at me, Blake!"

He knew that once his vision locked onto her stunningly beautiful hazel eyes, that would be it, but he did as instructed. "Okay," he sighed,

"I probably should've mentioned this. There's a small curse on this house."

"A… a small curse?" Gina reached up and shoved her auburn bangs away from her forehead. Spinning in a tight circle, she gave her new dwelling a quick once-over. "Hey, okay," she yelled at the top of her lungs, the sound reverberating off the empty walls of the unfurnished house, "if it's only a tiny curse, no problem! Like what are we talking? The blood that'll ooze from the walls will only be paper-cuts in size? The Native American burial ground underneath us only consists of one chief? What?"

Blake tried to smile, but his lips would not obey the command. "Well…" He wanted to sit down, but the movers had not brought their furniture yet. Turning to his right, he walked over to the grand staircase and plopped down on the second step. "Okay, maybe not a curse so much. More of a… haunting."

As her eyes widened, she replied, "Haunted? This house is haunted?"

"These stairs," he said, pointing his thumb over his shoulder, "well, as the story goes, fifteen or so years ago, the owner of this house tumbled down them and died. They say he still roams the place."

Gina ambled over and stood in front of her still-seated fiancé, putting the five-foot tall woman eye-to-eye with him. "So, what does he do? Is he dangerous?"

"Apparently, he won't let anyone live here. He's chased out all the other inhabitants."

She gave him her best *I should just slap you* glare. "And you thought, what a brilliant house for us to buy, a house whose former owner wants no new tenants? Why, oh why, haven't I married you yet?"

"Because you know the best is yet to come, baby," he said with a forced grin. "Please, I'm not that dumb. There's a clause in the contract. If we want out of this deal, we have up to 60 days, no questions asked."

143

Gina continued her stare down for a long moment before finally releasing a long, loud sigh. "Okay, fine. I hear the movers. Let's get this show started!"

The couple spent the first two weeks in their new house with only minor incidences, starting with creaking sounds on the floorboards. While in the dining room one morning, they both heard what sounded like footfalls above them. Heading upstairs, they saw nothing on which to blame the noise. However, the creaking moved toward and then down the stairs. As the footsteps moved past them, Gina and Blake shivered. Before they could reach the kitchen, they heard the shattering of glass. The broken shards of Blake's breakfast plate were spread along the baseboard of the far wall, a small gash in the wallpaper showing the impact point.

As Gina took a step into the dining room, she saw her plate fly off the table and strike the same spot on the wall. Shrieking, she turned and bolted from the room, bumping Blake on the shoulder as she exited.

Before Blake could follow her, both of their coffee mugs smashed into the same spot, one at a time. Though the food coupled with the broken drywall made quite a mess, neither of them had the desire to clean it up.

Switching to plastic dishware, they realized, made the most sense, as the apparition clearly liked flinging dishes at the walls.

After a few weeks of strange noises and broken glass, Gina neared her breaking point. One morning, she stood under a hot shower, trying to calm her frazzled nerves. She had just lathered up her hair when she heard the bathroom door creak open. "Honey, is that you?"

When no reply came, she began to panic. As the creaking of the floorboards inched closer, she tossed her head under the water to rinse the soap away rapidly so she could see. The floor directly next to the tub groaned as she finishing drying her eyes and reached for the shower curtain. Before she could yank it open, a loud crash emanated just outside the shower.

Gina screamed and backed into the corner of the tub, sobbing uncontrollably. Blake bounded into the steam-filled bathroom, and heard crunching under his shoe. Through the rolling fog, he could just make out the pieces of broken mirror. "I'm here," he yelled. "Careful, there's broken glass out here."

Shutting off the water, Gina pulled back the curtain and stood up. As Blake walked over the glass toward her, she donned the towel. Blake carried her trembling body into the hallway.

As he looked back, he could see, through the dissipating steam, a small chunk of missing wall.

After that incident, Gina packed her bags. "Good Lord Blake," she yelled as she threw a sweater into her suitcase, "I can't live this way! This is making me physically ill."

Blake's head drooped and he whispered, "I know. I understand." Then, he looked up and said with a bit more force, "You can stay with Mom until I get this sorted out."

Tossing him a wicked glare, she replied. "Whatdya mean, get it sorted out? What's to sort? You need to go to that realtor and revoke the deal today!"

"Honey…" He paused for a moment before adding, "I'm going to stay a bit longer. We have a couple weeks still."

Blake went to the library and researched the house and its former owner, reading dozens of old digitized copies of the local newspaper. Though it took him most of the day, he finally found some answers.

Arriving back at the house, Blake walked to the bottom of the stairs and yelled, "Sawyer Fellowes! Come down here. We have some things to discuss!"

Blake stood there for several minutes, calling for the ghost to appear. He felt foolish and was relieved Gina could not see this spectacle. "C'mon, Sawyer! You've been trying to get my attention, now you've got it!"

When nothing happened, Blake went into the kitchen and began fixing himself lunch. He had the sandwich on the plate and the soup steaming in the bowl when he heard the creaking coming from upstairs. "Finally," he whispered.

Waiting until the footfalls grew near, he said, "Sawyer Fellowes, at last we meet." When the steps reached the kitchen, he continued. "Look, I know how you died. You fell down these stairs and broke your neck. Your maid found you the next day.

"The newspaper wrote you off as a wacko recluse, afraid to leave this house. But I found something else that intrigued me. According to your maid, some unknown respiratory illness was making you sicker and sicker. Since your cause of death was obvious, no one did an autopsy. But I have to wonder, Sawyer, what made you fall? What disease did you have?"

Smiling a self-satisfied smile, Blake picked up his sandwich. The plate, still with a few potato chips on it, shot off the table and struck the far wall. Within seconds, the soup bowl as well as Blake's cup soared and smashed into the same spot on the wall. "And that's why we bought plastic, Sawyer my boy!" He said with a chuckle.

That comment must have angered the spirit, as every item in the kitchen, from the food in the fridge to the clock above the stove, shot across the room in a hailstorm of fury. Blake dropped to the floor as item after item flew overhead and exploded against the far wall.

After the melee subsided, Blake noticed the large, slimy black hole gouged in the wall. Amid the ketchup, salad dressing, and soup stains, he saw what appeared to be a large amount of a fuzzy greenish-black material. He reached up and ripped out another chunk of drywall. Never before had he seen so much mold.

The young couple had the drywall tested and the report came back. Toxic Black Mold infested most of the house. "Yup," the licensed contractor said with a southern drawl, "Good ol' Stachybotrys Chartarum. Ya live with this stuff long enough and it'll kill ya. Only recently have we begun to understand what this stuff'll do to your lungs. How'd ya find out about it?"

"The old owner stopped by and told us all about it," Blake said with a grin.

Gina and Blake snuggled on the couch, watching a movie. Gina turned and planted a big, sloppy kiss on Blake's cheek. Smiling, she asked, "Do ya realize what today is?"

"Hmmm," he said while rubbing his chin comically, "can't be our wedding anniversary. That's not for another couple months. Oh, have we been here for two years today?"

She tossed her legs over top of his lap and giggled, "Nope, that was last month. But you're close!"

He thought for a few seconds before his eyes lit up. "Oh, has it been two years since Sawyer left us?"

Before she could reply, they heard the stairs creak. Turning in unison, they found their cat trotting down the stairs. "Y'know," Blake said softly, "I really don't miss him."

~ Chapter Eighteen ~

Sometimes, my sweetheart comes with me to my Writing at the Ledges or my Everybody Writes monthly meetings. While she certainly enjoys hearing the poems and stories from the other members of my writing groups, I suspect her primary reason for coming along is to hear what I've concocted.

At this month's Everybody Writes meeting, the prompt is a picture of a Korean grocery store. Next to the store's name, printed in Korean, are the English words, "Very Suspicious Supermarket." That picture sent my brain into overdrive.

When my turn to read comes up, I look over at my wife. She's sitting off to the side, away from the members of the group. She doesn't do this to be anti-social, but because she doesn't want to interrupt or disturb. She is only here to listen.

Looking up from her crocheting, which she often brings to these meetings because she says it helps her to concentrate on the stories, she gives me a warm smile. This makes my heart skip a beat, like it does every time she smiles at me. I sure do love having her in my audience!

~ Very Suspicious Supermarket ~

Nathan looked over at Brad when he turned left instead of right. "Bonnie's party is on Jenison. Why are we going this way?"

Looking at his friend with a *duh* expression on his thin face, Brad replied, "We can't show up at the party without beer!"

"If you say so, but how're we gonna get any? I don't turn 21 'til August, and my brother won't buy us any. He's still pissed at us over the pork chop incident."

Brad used his right elbow to gesture in front of the car. "And that's why we're here!"

"In Korea Town?"

"Yeah, dude! Kevin told me we can get anything we want here, and they never card anyone! This is the answer to our problems."

Nathan looked out the passenger window, shaking his head slowly. "I dunno, man." After a few seconds of silence while watching the various buildings pass by, he added, "Which one of these is even a store? Everything's in Korean."

"There!" Pointing toward the only building in the area with at least some English on it, Brad said, "Yup, that's our place!"

When he read the name on the building, Nathan couldn't hold in his laughter. "Very Suspicious Supermarket? Oh my God, it's actually called Very Suspicious Supermarket!"

"I'm sure it's just their attempt at humor, or more likely it's their bad 'Engrish' translation of their store's name. The way I see it, they probably do suspicious things, like selling beer to minors. It'll be fine!"

Screeching to a halt in front of the store, the two young men hopped out of the car and walked up to the door. Nathan dragged his feet, so Brad turned to glare at him. "Dude, act cool! It'll work. Just let me do the talking."

Brad grabbed the handle on the glass door and pulled it open. Strolling in with a purpose to his stride, he tossed a smile at the elderly Korean man at the counter as he passed. Nathan trudged in slowly behind him with his head down, thrusting his hands into the pockets of his jacket.

149

"Hey! Hey you!" When the boys turned to look back at the man behind the counter, he added, "Why you here? What you want?"

Nathan stammered, "Wha... we..." before Brad elbowed him in the side.

"Hello sir," he said with a large, friendly smile, "We're just here to buy a few items. Snacks and refreshments."

Stalking out from behind the counter with surprising speed for a man who looked to the boys like a mummy recently unwrapped, he strode right up to Brad. Putting his face directly in front of Brad's, he glared at him for a long, uncomfortable moment. "Why you come here? Why not Kroger down town?"

"Oh... uh..." Brad started, as sweat began to bead on his forehead. For his part, Nathan had to tighten his insides so as not to soil himself. "We... uh, we heard you have great deals here. We're poor students." Quickly catching himself, he added, "College students. Senior college students." He inadvertently lowered his voice a couple of octaves and added, "Old, senior college students."

The ancient Korean man kept showing the boys the evil eye for a few more tense moments before saying, "Fine. You buy snacks and you go!"

"Okay, sir," Nathan blurted out as he turned and sprinted toward the back of the store.

Smiling a weak smile and shaking his head slightly at his friend's complete lack of grace under pressure, Brad replied, "We will. Thanks."

Upon reaching the back, Brad found Nathan with his head buried in a cooler, as if looking for the perfect six-pack. Brad grabbed him by the collar and yanked him out. "Dude, what the hell? Calm down! You'll get us busted."

"But he knows, man! He knows!"

"He doesn't know. We're fine, just play it cool, dude!"

The two young men wandered around the store, in search of a few bags of chips to go along with the beer. As they passed the other patrons in the store, each one stared intently at them as they passed. A tall, young, muscular Asian fellow glowered at the boys over the top of the newspaper that he held upside-down in his outstretched hands.

"Man," Nathan whispered, "this place is creeping me out!" He reached down to pick up a Snickers bar from the rack, but as he hoisted it, he noticed the wrapper felt too light. He held it between his fingers and squeezed. "There's nothing in this wrapper!" Quickly, he picked up a few more candy bars and none of them had any product inside of them. "What the hell?"

Grabbing his friend by the collar, Brad yanked him back to the coolers. "Let's not lose sight of what's important here. Let's just grab the beer and get going."

Opening and reaching into a cooler while still staring at Nathan, Brad's hand thumped loudly against something. He turned to look in the cooler, and realized the one he opened didn't actually have any beer... just a large piece of cardboard with pictures of beer on it. "Okay... I admit that that's weird. But look, the next one over is fine."

The two young men sidled over to the adjacent cooler, and each grabbed a six-pack of a beer called Secret Stash, turned and walked up to the counter.

Setting the beer on the counter, Brad elbowed Nathan, reminding him to get his money out quickly. The Korean man stared at the boys, then at the beer, then back up at the boys. Finally, the man said, "Why you buy this beer?"

Brad's brow crinkled. "What?"

"Why this beer you buy? Why not other beer?"

"Well, uh –"

"No!" The man interrupted, "You no buy this beer. This special beer." Pulling the six-packs off the counter and setting it behind him, the man added, "You go get Bud. King of beers. You like better." When the boys didn't immediately move, the old man yelled something in Korean. Moments later, the muscular Asian man approached from behind them, carrying two six-packs of Budweiser. He dropped them loudly onto the counter. "There. You like better. Now where money?"

Brad gave Nathan another nudge. "Oh right, of course!" Setting a twenty on the counter, Nathan said, "Here ya go."

After the man gave Nathan the change, the boys turned and marched quickly outside. As the door swung shut, they heard a loud click behind them. Instinctively, they spun around to see the old man locking the door behind them, scowling from his side of the glass.

Nathan and Brad, upon reaching the car, jumped in and quickly sped off. As they left the parking lot, they noticed several patrons from the store staring out the windows at them. "Well, okay," Brad said as the smile grew on his face, "that was weird, but we got the beer! Let's head to Bonnie's."

They drove about a half mile down the road when several black SUVs came hurtling around the corner, heading in the opposite direction. As the SUVs sped past, Brad's rusty Ford Taurus buffeted from the wind. "Wow! Wonder where they're headed in such a hurry?"

Brad surprised Nathan, and even himself, when he slammed on the brakes, popped the car in reverse, and started turning around. Nathan looked over at his friend. "What are you doing?"

"What the hell, man," Brad replied. "We got time. Let's check it out."

They barely started heading back when an explosion rang out from up the road. By the time they reached the Very Suspicious Supermarket, smoke rolled from the store and gunfire rang out. Men in black suits, crouching behinds their SUVs, shot their assault rifles at the market, while the Koreans shot their guns back at them through the freshly shattered windows.

Brad stamped on the gas and sped past the store.

After a moment of silence, Nathan uttered, "Well, you were right. They didn't card us. We'll totally have to remember that place."

~ Chapter Nineteen ~

I'm trudging through the house, clicking off lights. My wife is already in bed, hopefully not asleep yet, but I am mentally preparing for that possibility.

As I reach the living room, I see the top of my stepdaughter's head. She's sitting sideways on the couch, head down as she's putting the finishing touches on her art homework. She glances up and gives me a quick nod before resuming her work.

I stop for a moment to admire her drawing. She has created a spot-on rendition of the Eiffel Tower. "That's really good," I tell her.

She again looks up at me and offers me a smile that's a bit like a smirk, only without the arrogance. It's her way of saying thanks without using the words.

"Your mom's already in bed and I'm heading there myself. Which lights do you want me to leave on?"

Using her pencil, she points up at the closest light to her.

"Okay, cool." As I click off one of the other lights, I add, "Will you be up much longer?"

"Nope," she replies.

"All right, then. Good night!"

"Good night," she answers as she resumes fine-tuning her sketch.

As I walk into the bedroom, I smile at my wife. She looks all kinds of cozy as she's snuggled up in the bed, a thick comforter caressing her chin. "Hi sweetie," I say as I climb in next to her. "Your daughter is finishing up a drawing before going to bed. She's got some serious talent, y'know."

"Yes she does. She's a good kid." I nod my agreement with that statement.

I must admit, I had almost no experience with children coming into the relationship. Having none of my own, my limited exposure to kids ranged from my nieces and a nephew who are all adults now, to a few friends with kids as well as the offspring of the women I dated. None of these prepared me to take on the role of step dad.

However, I couldn't have asked for a better girl to become my step-daughter. This smart young woman has a fantastically offbeat sense of humor. How many teenagers enjoy British sitcoms and Doris Day movies? I also enjoy watching mother and daughter interact, ranging between silly and serious.

"What are you thinking about?" asks my wife.

"Huh? Oh, about being a step dad. I have no idea what I'm doing. Hopefully it doesn't show too badly."

She leans over and caresses my cheek with her soft, warm hand. "All you've ever had to do to be a good step dad is just be here for her."

I nuzzle her hand with my cheek. "I'll always be here for both of you." After a pause, I add, "Y'know, I have a story about a step dad. Would you like to hear it?"

"Tell me a story!"

Jacob Nayan sat in his pickup truck, his eyes rapidly scanning the side of the old dirt road. When his cell phone rang, he snatched it from the cup holder without a glance. He knew who was on the other end, so he answered by saying, "No, Maggie, I haven't found him yet."

"Oh Jacob," she wailed, "where can he be?"

"I told you not to fret, woman," he said, adding a slight chuckle to calm her. "I have a pretty good idea where the boy is. I'm sure we'll be home soon." He ended with, "Love ya," returning the phone to the cup holder.

As the 52-year-old man's truck approached the train tracks, he slowed, pulled off the road, and parked. After removing his binoculars from behind the passenger seat, he set his sights on the highway overpass a half mile down the tracks. Spotting a small figure sitting on the slant of the overpass, near the base of the concrete wall that separated him from the tracks, Jacob cracked a smile. He remembered sitting in that exact spot in his youth.

After tossing the binoculars back under the seat, Jacob began the short walk down the tracks.

The boy, preoccupied with a ratty, discolored tennis ball he bounced against the concrete wall, did not notice Jacob's approach. Jacob scrutinized him as he got closer, watching the boy's scruffy, dishwater blonde hair ruffling in the late-summer breeze. He sat silently, a distant look in his eyes. Oh, such troubles for a 12-year-old child, Jacob thought.

Jacob spoke loudly, adding a bit of bass to his voice. He wanted to startle the child. "Peter Williams," he boomed, "your mother's worried sick about you, boy."

A small yelp escaped Peter's throat as he leapt to his feet. Once the initial panic ebbed, he looked at Jacob with more than a little disdain. "Oh, it's you. How'd ya find me here?"

Sitting down beside him, Jacob replied, "I grew up in this town, remember? You ain't the first generation of kids to find this little haven, under the I-69 expressway. In fact..." Jacob stood up and walked up the 45-degree slant, to the top where the metal of the bridge connected with the concrete. Marching to the far edge of the bridge, he bent down and pushed some weeds out of the way. "Ah, yes, here it is." He paused, gesturing for the young man to come up.

Peter sighed, slouching his shoulders. "What? There's so much graffiti up there, there's no way yours is still there." He stood in his spot for a moment, arms akimbo, but curiosity got the best of him. He trudged up the ramp and kneeled down to see the one-inch high initials, carved into the concrete.

"I'm no dummy," Jacob said with a proud smirk. "It took me weeks, practically the whole summer. I wanted to leave my mark, but I knew if I wanted mine to withstand the test of time, I'd have to etch it, not just scribble it with a marker."

"Wow. When did you do this?"

"Well," Jacob said while fondling his thick, graying beard, "let's see. I was around your age -"

"So," the boy interrupted, "in the 1940s, then?"

Jacob shot him a dirty glare. "Boy, how old do you think I am? No, hold on, don't insult me again. It was in the late 70s. Me and my buddies used to come up here every day after school. We'd hang out until dinner, then come back if our folks would let us. Say," he said with a sweeping glance around the area, "where are the other kids? This time of evening was our prime time."

The young man looked up at his elder with a look as if to say, *what are you stupid?* "My friends don't come here, only the high school kids.

This is where they party after the sun goes down. I leave before they come. They're mean and stupid."

At that moment, Jacob noticed the piles of empty bottles that littered the landscape, and shook his head slowly. "So then, why do you come here?"

Releasing a sigh, he shrugged. "I dunno. To be alone, I guess."

After sitting in silence for a moment, Jacob said softly, "All right, let's get you on home."

Peter jumped up and yelled, "I'm not going home! You can't make me. You're not my dad."

Jacob stayed seated, even though the hard concrete began to make his butt ache. "No, Peter," he said calmly, "I'm not your father. I never made that claim, now did I?"

"No, but you're always bossing me around."

"Look, boy..." He paused, making sure the softness remained in his voice. "Pete, I know this is tough for you, but you need to understand. Your mother and I are in love. I asked her to marry me and she said yes. Understand that this is not a spur of the moment thing. We've thought this through. We feel we can withstand the test of time. She's been very lonely since your father left and moved to New York. You're a smart kid. You've seen the changes in her, right?" When Pete failed to respond beyond a slight shrug, he added, "When your dad left, wasn't she sad?"

The boy sighed softly. "Yeah. She cried a lot."

"And how has she been these past months?"

"Better, I guess."

"Okay, good. Look, it's important for you to understand that I'm not trying to replace your dad. I will be your mother's husband, not your Dad. Okay?"

"Yeah? Well, what about the other day?"

"I may not be your poppa, kid, but ya gotta obey your mom and me. If you don't, well, your mom gave me permission to whoop ya. As you found out, you ain't too old for that. But hey," he added, "let's just both promise not to make your mom's life hell, and we can be friends." When the kid shot him a glare, he wanted to ease the tension. Then, a thought struck him. "Say, before we leave, let's go check out the trestle. I haven't been there in years."

Peter's eyes morphed from slits of anger to wide open with trepidation. "Um, no. I can't."

"Why not?"

"I'm not supposed to. That's for the seniors. They'll kill me if they find me there."

"No fear," said Jacob, "I'm with ya. I'll kick all their butts. Tell ya what? We'll walk up to it and if there are teens there, we'll leave. But I wanna see if my mark is still on the bridge."

As the two of them walked on the train tracks, Peter asked, "Has the town changed much since you were a kid?"

Grinning wide, Jacob answered, "Oh my, yes. Maple River Valley was so much smaller then. Main Street was dirt until I hit my teenage years. They didn't put the stoplight in until after I graduated."

With a sarcastic smirk on his smooth face, Peter asked, "Did your folks let you borrow the horse and buggy?"

"Shut up, boy," he replied with a chuckle. "But when I was your age, maybe a little younger, I used to ride my bike around town, collecting rusted beer cans for my collection."

"Uh, you had a rusted beer can collection?"

"Well, they weren't all rusted. But ya gotta keep in mind that there were only three channels on our ol' black and white TV, and one of 'em,

159

ABC I think, didn't come in well. We had to find our own ways to entertain ourselves back then."

They continued their conversation until they reached the train trestle. The trestle stood nearly fifty feet above the deep, slow moving Maple River. The large, uncovered train bridge spanned the length of the river, over 200 feet from end to end. Jacob stood at the entrance, grinning like a child. "Man, so many memories here. We'd go out to the center and sit there, staring at the river and waiting for the next train."

"But what would you do if a train came?" Peter asked with worry evident on his face.

"Usually, we'd run back to safety. But occasionally, we'd play chicken. See who could stay on the tracks the longest. Then, the only choices were to jump in the river or crawl underneath and hang on to the supports. It was great fun. This one time –"

"You were nuts," Peter interrupted.

"You'll get no argument from me on that one." Jacob stood there for a moment before he took his first steps on the trestle. "Still am a bit crazy, I'd say."

"Uh, where are you goin'?"

"Told ya, I wanted to see if my initials are still out here. I wrote 'em in the exact center, on one of the supports." He paused, adding, "So, ya comin'?"

Peter stood there rigidly for a few seconds before a small, mischievous smile grew upon his face. He stepped tentatively out onto the tracks. "Wow, this feels weird. There's no rail to hold on to. Aren't you scared?"

Smiling broadly, Jacob strolled out using his thick, steady feet. "Nope. After all those years of roofing, I feel at home up here. But," he added as he glanced back over his shoulder, "if you feel at all unsteady, I'll slow down and you can hold my hand."

The pre-teen glared back at him. "I'm no sissy."

Jacob chuckled. "Never said ya were. But it's kinda like riding on the back of a motorcycle. Holding onto something makes ya feel more secure. If ya wanna use one of my belt loops to steady yourself, there's no shame in it."

Shaking his head, Peter replied, "I'm fine." Moments after saying that, he crouched down to regain his composure before continuing onward.

Trying not to laugh again, Jacob continued his steady gait until he reached the center. He sat down on the trestle, dangling his feet off the edge. He waited patiently until Peter joined him.

The two of them sat in silence for a while. Finally, Jacob said, "Man oh man, I forgot how great this view is. Isn't it incredible?"

"Yeah," Peter answered softly. With nature in full bloom, there were many shades of green from a dozen different types of trees. The river, moving at a moderate pace, splashed against the rocks and mud on the shore below. It carried leaves and the occasional bit of trash under them and off around the bend.

After a couple more minutes of silence, Jacob clapped his hands together, rubbing them while saying, "Okay, now to see if my mark is still there." With that, he spun his body around and secured his hand on the bridge.

Peter, with concern and shock splayed across his face, could only sit and watch as the grown-up who planned to marry his mom crawled down onto the angular steel supports. Up until now, the boy thought this whole thing was some sort of ruse. Never in a million years would he have expected this old guy to climb under the tracks. This impressed him.

When Pete heard Jacob laugh boisterously, he rolled onto his belly and tried to get a look for himself. "What? Is it still there?" From Pete's vantage point, he could see Jacob's legs, but little else.

"Sure is, kid!" Jacob exclaimed. "Don't know if you can see from up there, but I had to hang here, with my left arm cradling this support, for several minutes. I kinda messed up the B in Jacob, but I was starting to get tired. Say Pete, ya wanna climb down here and see? Or..." He paused, adding with a chuckle, "I brought a Sharpie."

With a devilish grin creeping upon his face, he said, "Well, okay, I guess. Is it safe?"

"Would an old man like me be dangling down here if it weren't?"

"Yeah," the boy responded, "you're crazy!"

Jacob chose to ignore the jab as he watched the boy slowly, carefully climbing his way down. As he reached Jacob's level, he advised him on to how to cradle his arm in the steel support. After Peter secured his grip, Jacob handed him the marker, watching with a grin as the boy wrote his initials on the same beam.

Once finished, Peter hung there, admiring his work with a wide grin. "Wow! I don't believe I did it! This is so neat!"

Jacob opened his mouth to respond when he heard the telltale sound of a train whistle off in the distance. "Okay, that noise signals the end of our adventure, Pete. Let's climb up."

Putting his hand on the edge of the platform, he felt the vibration. He pulled himself up to eye level and when he saw the train, his eyes grew. Lowering his body back down, he said slowly, "We're too late, Pete. I don't know how it got here so fast. I remember having a lot more time."

"Holy crap," Peter shouted over the ever-increasing noise, "What do we do?"

"Two choices, son. The best choice is to hold on as tight as you can. We'll have to ride this one out." The boy looked terrified, so Jacob tried to ease his mind. "Don't worry, Pete. I did this many times when I was your age. Just grip tight and stay as low as you can. We'll be fine."

At that moment, the train began rolling overhead. Clacking loudly, the whole trestle began to wobble and shake like a small earthquake. Still clearly terrified, Pete held on to the support beam with a death-grip. Then he yelled something, but the noise drowned him out, as a smile grew across his young face. This made Jacob laugh. He had a feeling Pete would enjoy this bit of rebelliousness.

However, Jacob's grip began to falter as the train continued with its journey. His elbow slipped out from his support and he had to grab at the beam with both hands. He held for a few seconds, but the vibration on the steel continued to loosen his grip. With one final wiggle of the trestle, the old man's fingers popped off the beam. He tried to exude a brave countenance, but he knew the panic would betray that. While falling, he saw Pete's mouth fly open in a scream easily lost in the thunderous clatter above.

As Jacob continued to plummet, face still looking upward, he wondered about the water below. Was it cold? Was it deep enough? It always used to be, but he was smaller and a lot skinnier then. Should I land feet first or –

He struck the surface before he finished his analysis, landing on his back with a loud, painful smack. The impact jarred his body and caused a quick flash of white light when the back of his head hit the water. He continued downward under the surface, wondering if he would hit the bottom of the river, and how hard.

After what seemed like minutes to Jacob, he reached bottom. Fortunately, he had slowed enough so that he barely touched the muddy floor. He quickly surfaced, looking upward to determine Peter's fate.

The boy, clearly relieved to see Jacob resurface, waited for the last train car to pass before releasing one hand to wave. "Are you all right?" He yelled.

"Yup," Jacob replied boisterously. "Climb up and off the trestle. I'll meet ya at the entrance." Then, he swam over to shore, having only minor trouble with the current. Climbing out and up the steep incline proved to be challenging, but after slipping down a couple of times and coating himself with slimy mud, he managed to extract himself from the water.

When Jacob caught up with Pete, the boy could not help himself. He pointed at his elder and let a loud laugh fly.

"I must look a mess, huh? Like the Creature from the Black Lagoon, or maybe the Swamp Thing?"

Pete shot him a puzzled look. "Who?"

With a chortle, Jacob replied, "We'll hafta rent those someday. So, ya ready to go home now?"

Nodding slowly, he answered, "Yeah, I guess. I had no idea you were this cool."

"Thanks. I guess we should make a stop at the store first. I don't think your mom would appreciate me coming home looking like this. Oh, and speaking of Mom," he added with a sly grin, "It's best we don't mention any of this to her. I doubt she'd understand."

~ Chapter Twenty ~

Lying next to one another in bed the next night, my wife sets her book down, reaches over, and places her hand on top of mine. "Do you know what I love about you so much?"

I shoot her a cocky grin. "Other than my rugged good looks?"

"Yes, besides that."

I mentally give her credit for not rolling her eyes. "I do, but why don't you tell me."

Offering me a warm smile, she says, "It's how you don't pretend to be something you're not."

This makes me regret the rugged good looks comment. I furrow my brow. "When did I not pretend to not be something I'm not... or something?"

"Do you remember our second date?"

I smirk half-heartedly. "Of course I do. But what exactly about it are you referring to?"

Smiling at the memory, she replies, "You invited me to your house for dinner. You made us microwave meals, and we watched Danger Mouse cartoons on DVD."

That description makes me cringe slightly. "Eech. Really?"

"Uh-huh! You were so proud that you'd bought a vegetarian Lean Cuisine for me."

"Wow. That's right! I picked up Fettuccine Alfredo for you, the one without the chicken chunks. Was that really our second date?"

Leaning over, she plants a kiss on my cheek. "It was. We sat on your couch watching episodes of a British cartoon on DVD while eating pasta out of plastic containers placed on TV trays. And I remember thinking, 'Wow, this guy is not the least bit phony. This is exactly who he is.' And I fell in love with you that day."

"Lucky me finding the one woman who doesn't mind me being me."

"Are you kidding? I adore you being you! Don't ever change."

After a long hug and a kiss, I roll back to my side of the bed. The smile will not leave my face for a while. "So, would you like a story? I have one where the guy is the complete opposite of me."

"All right!"

~ A Striking Blonde ~

I loved going to the bar with Joe. He called me his wingman, but I was usually just along for the beer… and the floorshow.

Leaning against the counter, Joe scanned the joint before nudging me with his shoulder. "Oh yeah, there we go!" Gesturing at a striking young blonde, he tossed me a wink and said, "I got the perfect one for her," and ambled toward her. I moved a little closer, to get within earshot. I sure didn't want to miss this pickup line.

As he sidled up, he set his beer next to her wineglass and said, "I hope you can help me out." When she looked at him, he continued. "You see, I have a lot of wrinkled clothes at home, and I don't have anyone to help. In fact, I have something right here you could help pull the wrinkles out of." Then he grinned and pointed at his crotch.

Her response was a slap across his right cheek, so intense it sounded like gunfire. The sharp report even lowered the decibel level of the bar by a couple notches, as people looked to see what had happened. Wow, I thought, that's gonna leave a mark.

Joe wandered back to me, his smile still intact. Gotta hand it to him. He took rejection, even violent ones, in stride. He then spotted a pretty redhead in a tight dress, turned to her and said, "Ya wanna play house? You be the screen door and I'll slam you all night long." She smacked him in the same spot. An audible whimper escaped his mouth before he jogged off.

Shaking my head, I turned back to my beer just as the striking blonde sauntered up to the bar to order another drink. Smiling, I opened my mouth to speak when she tossed a hand up. "I swear to God, if I hear one more cheesy pickup line..."

With eyes wide, I replied, "No ma'am, not me. I'm just here for the entertainment. Y'know, you possess an impressive right."

She cracked a smile. "You should see my left hook."

Flinching, I said, "I'd rather not."

Her smile faded as she spotted Joe coming our way. Joe's cheek did, in fact, have a remarkably pink handprint on it. "Oh God," she exclaimed, "not again! Okay, don't take this personally." She then grabbed me in a tight, passionate hug.

When Joe arrived, the blonde woman turned her head and said to him, "Your friend here said I had a beautiful body, so I held it against him."

Giving me a thumbs-up, Joe replied, "Nice one, buddy! That line never fails!"

~ Chapter Twenty-One ~

I am always honored when a bookstore allows me to come in and say hello to people. Often times, asking the storeowner if I can do a reading makes me more nervous than does the actual reading.

Walking into Haslett, Michigan's Blue Frog Books, Rob the owner greets me at the door with a smile and a cup of coffee.

I'm overjoyed at the number of people who showed up to see little old me! Flipping through my notebook, I scan each story until I find the perfect one to share with this crowd.

"Hi everyone! Instead of one of my usual short stories, I have a piece that I don't share very often. It's a deleted scene from my novel *Driving Crazy*. Though originally written as a stand-alone short story, I'd planned to insert it in the book at around page 39. During one of the edits, I decided it didn't exactly fit, so I removed it and added a different, smaller scene.

"This story gives a bit of insight into both of the main characters, Jaymond Naylor and Austin Ridenour."

Smirking, I add, "By the way, some of this story is taken from my real life adventures. Try to guess which bits are real."

~ Story Time: A *Driving Crazy* Adventure ~

Man, I hadn't been on a road trip in such a long time, I'd forgotten how utterly boring so much of it could be. We'd activated the quintessential road games. We tried Slug Bug for spell, but we stopped rather quickly because we both bruise easily. We also played the License Plate game, but that grew repetitive. So I started us on a game I invented a few years back on a trip to visit Mom in Florida. We both counted the number of Waffle Houses we saw, each of us keeping our own running tally. On my Florida trip, I counted over 115 Waffle Houses on I-75. In this version of the game, whoever spotted it first got to count it. We saw a lot of 'em, including some cities where they had Waffle Houses across from each other. At least that way, we both got a point.

However, that also became boring and tedious after a while, and I kept losing count. I had taken to making hash marks on my hand with a pen low on ink, which hurt more than a little.

Looking over at Austin, half-asleep at the wheel, I figured I'd better do something to revitalize us both. "Hey bud, I got something to pass the time. Tell me a story, something that happened in your life that I know nothing about, and I'll do the same."

He turned and looked at me with a queer expression plastered upon his face. "Jay, buddy, we've been friends forever. I highly doubt I got a story you haven't heard. Why, you got one?"

Grinning sheepishly, I replied, "In fact I do. This one took place back in the late 80s, 87 or 88. I was still attending college at LCC. By about this time, I had really grown sick of school. In the middle of my degree for computer programming, I came to realize how much I hated programming."

"Yeah, I remember how angry you'd get when the program wouldn't run right. You broke a lot of keyboards."

I chuckled softly at the memory. "True. But at that point, I still toiled forth. Actually, the only fun class I had that semester was Creative Writing. Being in my 'I need to be different' stage, I used to go to classes wearing an old, ratty, full-length brown jacket. This duster had three mismatched buttons and it hung really low, nearly scraping the ground. I had some heavy brown boots that could barely be seen sticking out under the duster. And to top off this ensemble, I donned a gray wide-brimmed hat, kinda like a cowboy hat, but more along the lines of what they wore back in the 50s. Just a cool hat, y'know?"

"Huh. You must've been quite a sight. Seems odd I never saw you in this getup."

"Eh, I only wore it to class, and occasionally to parties. In fact, I only went without it a couple of times, and it would cause quite the uproar. People got so used to me in that hat that they'd comment about how different I looked without it. It amused me, and I guess that's all that mattered." I paused for a second to smile at the memory. These days, I highly doubt I'd have the guts to be that different in public, but man, I had no fear at that age. I continued, "But one night after class, a pretty young woman named Claudia approached me as I packed up my stuff to leave. She had an exotic beauty, a mix of cultures that gave her dark, flawless skin to go with her long black hair. We had conversed a few times before, so I already knew all about her ex-Marine boyfriend and their on-again, off-again relationship. So when she invited me over to her place after class, I was intrigued, but understandably skeptical."

"Yeah, I would hope so," Austin said. "You were even skinnier and scrawnier back then."

"True. But she made sure I knew that the boyfriend would be there, as would a couple other of her friends. It was just a friendly get-together. So I decided to go.

"I followed her to her house, way out in the country. When we got there, she introduced me to the boyfriend Dennis. He was seated on the couch with one other couple. Dennis had only left the Marines a year before, so he still had the look and the attitude. He kept his hair tightly cropped and his muscles tightly packed. Still, he seemed friendly enough, shaking my hand with an overly firm grip. Once I wiggled free from his grasp, I said my hellos to the other couple, a clearly hippie-esque pair named Ernie and Lisa. They both wore tie-dye shirts and sported long hair, his brown hair touching his belt while her blonde locks ended in the middle of her back. Ernie looked a bit rough to me. He had a fair amount of stubble on his face, and had the appearance of a man who had not slept for several days. And Lisa looked, well, messed up. Actually, they both looked like they had been partying for quite some time. Dennis offered me a – Waffle House!"

"What?"

Pointing, I said, "There's a Waffle House up that hill."

"That's not fair, you distracted me!"

"Hey, I'm the one telling the story here, and I still saw it."

Austin snorted his disapproval. "Fine. You get the point."

"I know. Anyway, Dennis offered me a drink. They had apparently been pounding down Relska Vodka for hours before we arrived, and were well into their second fifth."

"Relska?" Austin shuddered involuntarily. "Oh lord, I remember that cheap, horrible Vodka. The hangovers we'd get on that stuff were legendary!"

"Oh yeah, that was to come. But for now, I didn't want to be antisocial and besides, it being a Friday, I didn't have class for a couple days. I could sleep it off. So, Dennis poured me a huge, strong glass of Relska and orange Kool-Aid of all things, and I drank it greedily.

"I started on my second glass, enjoying the conversation with Dennis and Claudia while we played cards at the kitchen table. Ernie and Lisa, well, they were kinda in their own world, sitting across the room on the couch arguing with one another. It seemed rather surreal to me, the military man being so calm and peaceful while the two colorfully clad, longhaired members of our little party screamed horrible insults at each other. And I do mean screamed. I tried my best to tone them out, but as they became more heated, it became harder to do so.

"Finally, when their yelling reached a crescendo, Dennis stood up and started walking over to them. I glanced at Claudia, and she had the tiniest of smiles on her face, so I figured this had to be a regular occurrence. The Friday Night Fight, I reckoned.

"It was at that moment when Hippie Lisa leaped from the couch, picked up a vase with some pretty wildflowers in it, and smashed it right into the side of Ernie's head. Flowers, glass, and blood flew all over the room as Ernie stumbled backwards and crashed into the entertainment center. He hit it with enough force that everything on it, books, glass figurines, and even the small, portable TV cascaded from it and clattered to the floor in all directions. The TV, when it fell, barely missed Ernie's head and landed squarely in his lap as he plopped down onto his butt."

"Good lord!" Austin screamed. "Sounds like a nightmare! What'd you do in all of this?"

"Whatdya think I did? Waffle House! I get that point." Austin glared at me, and I continued. "Anyway, I just sat there. I couldn't leave, since this was all happening right next to the door. Besides, I didn't want to look timid in front of Claudia, who, to her credit, didn't seem all that taken aback by the situation. She looked at me and shrugged, so I just kept on drinking and watching.

"So anyway, Lisa continued to pick up things from around her and throw them at Ernie, who used the TV to block the projectiles. Dennis, who stood there watching and actually laughing for a few more moments, finally walked up behind Lisa and put her in a Full Nelson headlock. You've seen it on wrestling shows before, I'm sure."

"Oh yeah, of course."

"Well, she was just thrashing around with all of her might, trying to break the military man's hold. Clearly, Dennis had put others in a Full Nelson before. Besides, he probably had at least 100 pounds of muscle on her, so she couldn't wiggle free. This gave Ernie a chance to get up, after setting the TV down on the floor next to him. He touched his face, noticed the blood trickling down his cheek, and got even angrier. He walked right up to her, put his nose an inch from hers, and yelled directly into her face, 'You stupid woman! You can deny it all you want, you can hurt me all you want, but I know you're cheating on me! Confess!'"

Austin let loose with a, "Whoa."

"It gets better. At that moment, she reared her head back and head-butted Ernie squarely on the bridge of the nose. Even from across the room, I could hear the sharp crack of his nose breaking. The man staggered backward, holding his nose with both hands, and again slammed into the entertainment center. The few remaining items showered onto the floor. He crumpled to the ground, sobbing softly. All the while Lisa, still thoroughly subdued by the ex-Marine, hung there laughing manically. Finally, she blurted out, 'Okay fine, ya dumb old fool. Yes, I've been cheating on you.' The whole room became very quiet. Ernie squinted up at her, still holding his bleeding nose, and quietly asked her who."

"Really?" Austin asked. "What'd she say?"

"Waffle House!"

"Dang it, Jay. Stop that!"

"I think I'm five ahead of ya. Anyway, at that moment, the big guy let her go. After shaking her arms a bit to get some feeling back in them, she tossed a thumb over her shoulder and casually replied, 'The guy over there in the hat. He's really good, too.' Then she turned and winked at me."

"Good lord!" After a quick pause, he asked, "Uh, you weren't, were you?"

"No, dude. I just met them, remember?"

"I thought so. Just checking."

"I'm no home wrecker. But anyway, after this little announcement, I jumped up quickly, but after two really strong Relska and Kool-aids, I plopped back down into my seat. Fortunately for me, the hippie wasn't fairing any better. Glaring at me through blackening eyes, he starting yelling for my head. Since he had a tight grip on his nose, still trying to get the bleeding under control, it came out all nasally-sounding. 'I'll kill you, you bastard! I'll kill you!' Which actually, under different circumstances, would've been hilarious."

"I see. So, not the peace-loving type of hippie, I take it?"

"Not so much, no. For my part, I was denying it left and right. 'Dude,' I told him, 'I just met you people today. She's clearly messing with you.' I looked at her and asked her why she would say such a thing. She just shrugged and laughed some more. The other two found the whole thing quite amusing, which just blew my mind.

"At that moment, Ernie managed to pull himself to his feet and began staggering toward me, arms outstretched. Well, he only had his right arm extended, since his left hand was busy pinching his nose shut. I finally managed to get to my feet but since he still stood between the front door and me, I dashed into the bathroom. I stood there for a minute, panicking and hyperventilating, listening to the mad man beating ferociously on the door."

"Sheesh! So what did you do next?"

"Once I overcame my panic, I looked around the bathroom. I kept picking up useless items as weapons, brandishing a toothbrush like a knife, then the hair dryer, holding it like a ray gun. Then I noticed the window. It looked too small, but I opened it nonetheless and started forcing my body though it. I got as far as my hips before I got stuck. It took a solid minute of wriggling and wiggling, not to mention praying, before I managed to get the rest of myself out of the house.

"Once I hit the snow-covered ground, I trudged around to the driveway, all ready to jump in my car and leave. Small problem, though. I left my coat, along with my keys, on the coatrack in the house."

"Uh-oh!"

"Yeah, uh-oh. Well, I stood shivering in the snow for a couple minutes, but I knew what I had to do. I went up to the front door and opened it as quietly as I could. Luckily, the coatrack sat right next to the door, so a quick escape had possibilities. Also fortunately, beating down the bathroom door completely preoccupied the Incredible Hippie, so he didn't notice me as I carefully pushed the door open. Everybody else did, and they all grinned at me.

"When I grabbed the coat, it didn't clear the coatrack, so it tumbled to the floor, clattering on the linoleum. Of course, that finally alerted him to my presence, and he turned and came at me. By then, I had a good enough head start, so I dashed into my car. I got it started as he flung himself onto my hood, banging on the windshield while yelling all sorts of horrible words at me. I reversed fast enough to toss him off my car, so I slammed it in gear and sped off."

Austin looked at me through bewildered eyes. "Dude, that's insane. Did anything ever come of all that?"

"The weird thing was, the next time I had class with Claudia, she said hello casually, but never brought up the situation. She didn't even grin or look at me funny. No outward appearance at all, so I decided not to say a word about it. Heck, maybe I imagined the whole thing, or it was a drunken hallucination. Who knows? However, she never brought it up, I never asked, and I never did get another invite. Not that I would've gone."

"Huh. That's a bizarre story, Jay. Waffle House. That's mine."

Chuckling softly, I replied, "Good for you. So, you got anything for me? A wild adventure?"

"Let me think on that." Austin sat silent for several minutes and two more Waffle Houses before he looked over at me and grinned. "Yeah, I do, as a matter of fact. Did I ever tell you about the time I stole a Big Boy from the restaurant parking lot?"

"No, I don't believe you have."

"Well, believe it or not, I used to hang out with a wild crowd. Well, wild for a bunch of DND nerds."

"Oh right, I forgot about your Dungeons and Dragons days. You were really into that for a while."

"Uh-huh. We'd get all liquored up and play for a few hours. Most times, we'd go our separate ways afterward. But occasionally, specifically when Silas Gibson would show up, we'd do all sorts of wild things."

I had to think about that name for a moment. "Silas Gibson... Yeah, I don't know him."

"Nah, you wouldn't. I met him through friends of friends. I suppose you'd call him the instigator of most of our weirder escapades. Seemed like every time he came to DND, I'd wake up the next day with a massive hangover and some weird items or injuries. One time, I woke to a big yellow YIELD sign leaning up against the door in my room. Another time, I awoke to find my hands all black and sore."

"What?"

He offered me a blurted chuckle. "Heh. Yeah. We'd go into the park sometimes and shoot bottle rockets at stuff, oncoming cars, each other, that sort of thing. Apparently, the more I drank, the more often I'd forget to let go of the bottle rocket and it'd blow up near my hand. It would leave a painful, sooty mark on my fingers."

"I see."

"Anyway, on this night we played well past midnight and polished off a fifth of, I dunno, something. Probably Relska. But we were definitely hammered. And Silas suddenly decided he had the munchies, so me, Silas, and Mel, remember Mel?"

Thinking a moment, I replied, "Uh, that the really tall guy?"

Austin shrugged. "Sure, let's go with that. We three cruised around for a while, not being terribly safe in Mel's beat-up old pickup truck. Basically, driving like drunken idiots, but we eventually ended up at the Big Boy in East Lansing. We got our grub on, annoying the crap outta the wait staff, until they kicked us out just before closing time. As we were leaving, Silas and Mel became fixated on the Big Boy statue-thing out in front of the place. It was one of the big ones, like six-feet tall and made of a fairly dense plastic, or something. Mel stood there, doing all sorts of unnatural things to it."

"Oh! That Mel! Sure, I could see that. He was a freak."

"Indeed. Silas asked him if he wanted it to take home. Of course, Mel didn't have to think about that one at all. So, they started unbolting the thing from the ground. I didn't want anything to do with it, so I went back to the truck and sat in the passenger seat. Apparently, I fell asleep, passed out, whatever."

"Sounds convenient."

"Well, you might think so, until I woke up the next morning, in Mel's barn, spooning Big Boy. They took all sorts of pictures and wouldn't let me live it down for months."

"So, you didn't actually help steal Big Boy."

Smirking, he replied, "Well, not technically I suppose, but I was an accomplice. I was complicit in the crime."

"That's funny. I always wondered what happened to that Big Boy. It took the restaurant months to replace it. So, what ever happened to the stolen Big Boy?"

"No clue. Mel stopped coming to DND not too long after that. I just hope the two of them had a good life together."

I had to laugh out loud. "I can picture the wedding announcement. Well, that was fun, Austin. I only have one more thing to say about that. Waffle House!"

"Grrr! I'll get the next one."

~ Chapter Twenty-Two ~

At our wedding reception, we had two pictures sitting on top of the piano in the Parish Hall of Trinity Episcopal Church. One was my wife's mother, and the other was my father Marvin. Unfortunately, both of these wonderful human beings passed before my wife and I met. Countless people have told me that her mom would've liked me. In fact, had Scott Harris (the owner of EVERYbody Reads) and she not been friends, my wife would never have met Scott. In turn, I wouldn't have met the love of my life, because I met her at the bookstore during a book signing. Therefore, when I tell people that her mother had a hand in us getting together, I fully believe it.

Conversely, I wish my wife could have met Marvin Pearson. My dad was an amazing man – kind, honest, happy, loving, smart, hard working.

However, I have helped her to know my father by telling her several stories he shared with me. A few months before he passed, he and I sat down in the living room, tape machine recording, so he could tell me about his life. Of particular interest to me was his recounting of World War II. This is my favorite adventure of his.

~ Loincloths and Bolo Knives ~

During World War II, Marvin Pearson held the Navy's lowest ranking, Petty Officer Third Class. Though possessing no culinary aptitude, the Navy saw fit to make him a cook on a ship stationed in the Philippines. At this time, they were anchored at a base in the city of Calicocohan. Of the Philippines' 7107 islands, Calicocohan sat near the tip of the northern-most island.

As the ship's cook, Petty Officer Pearson left a lot to be desired. He knew almost nothing about food preparation, relying heavily on canned food and hearsay. When he reported for duty, the Lieutenant informed him, "The commanding officer wants his steaks rare. Really rare. Drop it on the grill until it sizzles and get it on his plate pronto!" The commanding officer was a gruff Captain. Marv had never heard anyone say his name. However, due to a war wound that cost the Captain an eye, the men under his command had a nickname, which they called him behind his back: Latcheye.

One day, they received a special shipment of pork chops. Relying on the Captain's steak preference, Marv cooked his pork chop in exactly the same way: a quick hiss of the grill on both sides, and straight to the commanding officer.

The Captain took one bite and angrily spit it out. With his one good eye blazing, he bellowed, "Get Pearson out here now!" When Marv arrived, the yelling continued. "What's the big idea, serving me raw pork? What are ya doin', trying to kill me?"

Pearson looked his commanding officer in his good eye and said, "What's the problem, Mr. Latcheye?"

That should have cost Marv some brig time, but as it turned out, the Captain was being discharged in a few days and he did not want to bother with the paperwork.

A few days later, Marvin awoke to find himself too sick to get out of bed. He called for one of his bunkmates to help him. Upon seeing his face, the man yelled, "Oh my God, would you look at Pearson! He's all yellow!" He called several other soldiers to come gawk.

After they finished laughing at the yellow-skinned man, they drove him across the island to the hospital.

The doctors ran a series of tests, finding that not only had Marv contracted Jaundice, but he had also managed to come down with

Malaria. "You're lucky," the doctor told him. "Now we can treat them both."

Obviously, Marvin did not feel lucky. To make matters more unbearable, his doctor placed him on a strict diet of peaches and pears. "Eat your heart out, Pearson," said the doctor as he instructed the orderly to jam crates of fruit under his bunk. "You can have anything you like, as long as it's peaches or pears."

It took Petty Officer Pearson nearly six weeks to recuperate. While lying in that Philippine hospital bed, he passed the time by drawing pictures. His favorite subjects were the food items he desperately wanted to eat, like pork chops and steaks. He also sketched a cartoon of himself with the head of a peach.

When they finally released him from the hospital, his commanding officer sent a young corpsman to come pick him up and bring him back to Calicocohan.

This corpsman, however, had other ideas. "Say buddy," he said, "how 'bout we make a quick stop at the airstrip first? We'll take a ride up and come straight back. It'll be fun!"

My dad always was a bit of a rebel, like how he continually borrowed his commander's jeep simply because, as he put it, "he wasn't using it and I figured someone should," so he readily agreed to this quick diversion.

They found a small plane and chatted with the pilot. "Sure," he replied, "I have plenty of room. However, I don't have any spare parachutes."

Marv asked, "Well, you're not planning on crashing, are you?"

Of course he said no, so they hopped on.

The pilot flew them way down into the southern jungles, to a place called Indenowa, and landed on a small swath of land with barely enough clearance for the small plane to touch down. They wondered around the area for an hour or two, though there wasn't much to see. Finally, the corpsman asked, "So buddy, when are we taking off?"

The pilot looked at them funny. "Not until the morning. I'm here for the night."

He arranged sleeping quarters for the two men, with mattresses and blankets. However, the blankets came with a warning: "If someone tries to steal your blanket during the night, let them. The locals sneak into the huts at night and take what they want. If you put up a fight, they will just cut your throat and take the blanket anyway, so be sure to give it up. We got a lot of 'em."

During the night, Marv heard the padding of feet all around him, both in and out of his sleeping area. Fortunately, no one ever tried to take his blanket. Not that he intended to interfere, of course.

In the morning, they saw the pilot packing his plane. "Oh good," Marv said, "we're going back now."

"Well, not back, no. I have to fly to Zamboango now, down near Borneo." Heading nearly as far south as one could go and still be in the Philippine Islands, the men realized they were flying even further away from their base.

"Are there any other planes headed north?" the corpsman asked.

"Sorry mac, I've got the only plane around here and I got these trips to make."

When the trio arrived in Zamboango, they saw nothing but barefoot natives. Wearing only skimpy loincloths, their large Bolo knives hung menacingly from their hips.

Though somewhat alarmed by the savage look of the natives, Marv had other, more immediate needs to satisfy. Having run out of cigarettes, he decided to take a walk. Though it seemed unlikely, he thought perhaps he'd find a store up the makeshift dirt road.

However, the further away from the plane he walked, the more the natives took notice. As he marched past, they stared with an anxious intensity, their hands moving instinctively to rest upon the handles of their Bolo knives. All eyes followed the white man in military green, turning their heads to ensure an uninterrupted line of sight as he passed.

The deeper he went, the more he realized he probably should not have been there. At this point, he thought, *Whoops, I think I made a mistake. I can do without the smokes, but I don't think I can go back the way I came.*

He continued down the path, walking for several miles until he came upon a small, military-style shack. Knowing the guard shed would be his best chance for survival, he opened the door and walked inside.

Upon entering, a fellow military man who resided from Marv's home state of Michigan greeted him. "Oh my God, you walked here from the airstrip? Are you mad!? I wouldn't go back if I were you."

"Oh, I have no intention of that. Too many loincloths and Bolo knives out there for my taste."

"I'd say. You can stay here for the night and ride back with me when my relief shows up in the morning."

Petty Officer Pearson stayed all night in the little guard shed in the middle of nowhere, with a man from Flint, Michigan for company.

In the morning, he got a ride back to the airstrip, returning just as the pilot readied to take off. "Good Lord Pearson," the corpsman yelled, "Where have you been? We thought the savages got ya!"

After explaining his story to the two men, he said to the pilot, "Okay, so can we go back to base now?"

"Sorry fellas, but I'm off to Borneo next. However, there is a U.S. airfield there, so you boys can get back to Calicocohan that way."

Marvin and the corpsman took one final ride with the friendly pilot, arriving in Borneo at a very opportune time. There were two large troop transport planes readying for flight. However, after these two, no more planes would be available for days. They rushed up to the lead plane and started to board when a Private stopped them. "Where are your passes?"

At that point, they came to a realization. In this high-security, densely populated area, things would not be as simple. The clever-minded Pearson improvised. "Oh, they must be back in our duffel sacks."

"I'll need to see 'em to let ya fly." Since the man would not let them board, they walked away and watched that first plane take off.

With little time to spare, Marvin came up with another ploy. He turned to the corpsman and said, "Follow my lead," and ran up to the second plane as they were yanking the door shut. "Wait! That plane took our passes but left without us! He was supposed to wait!"

Though a bit skeptical, he ushered the two men onto the plane and they quickly departed Borneo.

Breathing a sigh of relief, Marv and the corpsman sat down on the last remaining seats. They stared out the window at the marvelous sights of the jungle they were finally leaving.

Looking out at the other plane, they watched as one of the engines started sputtering. Within moments, it took a nosedive and crashed into the ground. It exploded in a massive fireball. Marv said softly, "Wow. Glad we weren't on that one," stating the obvious.

When they arrived at the airstrip, the corpsman got off the plane first. As he turned to the right and took a couple of steps, the Military Police promptly swarmed him and arrested him for being AWOL for the last three days. When Marv saw this, he instead took a sharp left, walked over to the road, and stuck his thumb out. The first man who stopped his Jeep told Marv, "Hey, it just so happens I'm heading to Calicocohan," so he hopped in.

When he got back to base, Marv walked in during roll call. When he heard his name, he yelled, "Here."

The man stopped and looked over at him. "Where were you yesterday?"

Marv furrowed his brow and answered, "I was here."

"You didn't answer when I called your name."

"Yes I did. You must not have heard me."

After another pause, the commander shrugged his shoulders, said, "Oh, all right," and went on to the next name on the list.

Later on, Marv learned that everyone died in that plane crash. Only fate kept him off that doomed flight.

Gone from his base for a month and a half, AWOL for three days, and nearly killed, Petty Officer Marvin Pearson still made it back in time for roll call.

~ Chapter Twenty-Three ~

"I sure do love Saturdays," I say to my wife as I randomly flip through channels. I look at her for a few moments with a hint of a smile on my face.

Without returning my gaze, she says, "What?"

"Nothing. I just like looking at ya."

She utters that, "Pppppsh" noise she makes when she's disregarding or dismissing something. "Stop it," she says with no discernible emotion.

"No," I reply, adding my own, "pppppsh!"

"Pppppsh!"

"Pppppsh!"

"Well," I say as I lean in and give her a smooch, "this is getting us nowhere." After a momentary pause, I ask, "So sweetie, what's for dinner?"

Turning, she crinkles her brow at me. "I don't know. What are you making?"

Before we met, my food life consisted entirely of cereal for breakfast, sandwiches for lunch, and prepackaged microwave meals for dinner. In a pinch, I could make pancakes. "Oh," I say as I bolt up and off the couch, "how's about pancakes?"

"All right! And facon?"

"Well, of course facon," I say, referring to the vegetarian version of bacon we have in our freezer. No one in the history of the world has ever confused this stuff with actual bacon. However, as textured vegetable protein shaped to look like bacon goes, it's not bad.

As I dig around in the cupboard for my Perfect Pancake maker (one of those *As Seen on TV* items with two frying pans hooked together) she says, "Can you tell me a story while you're cooking?"

"Sure! As a matter of fact, I have two stories that are perfect for a man who can't cook, who's trying to impress his lady."

~ Cooking Up Excitement ~

Craig shot Simon a toothy grin. "But dude, you don't cook. You live via the microwave and Deluca's Pizza."

"Sure," Simon replied, "but this is a big deal. It's Sharon and my one-year anniversary."

"So why not take her someplace, y'know, nice?"

Simon glared at his friend with mock anger. "Cooking isn't all that hard. I just hate doing it. Besides, I found a cookbook at Volunteers of America. I'm gonna whip up something she'll never forget."

Shaking his head, Craig replied, "Okay man. Good luck."

Though the book apparently assumed a higher level of culinary skill than Simon possessed, he did his best to emulate a couple of the more intriguing recipes. However, he had to buy some ingredients that seemed rather peculiar to him. "Well, the book clearly knows best," he muttered to himself.

When the big day arrived, Simon could not contain his rapturous smile. Sharon opened the front door and right away said, "Um, what smells so ... unusual?"

Turning the corner of the kitchen with a champagne flute in each hand, Simon replied, "That would be dinner! It's something special. But first, here are the drinks. Oddly, the recipe called for these to be served in bottles, but I opted for a more traditional approach." Handing her a glass, he added, "To one year," and lightly clinked her flute with his.

"Oh, Simon," she cooed as she lifted the glass and took a drink.

She immediately spit it out, forming a small puddle on the hardwood floor. "Oh my God, what the hell is this?"

Simon furrowed his brow in disappointment. "It's a cocktail, sweetheart. I followed the instructions to the letter... well, mostly."

"Uck! It tastes like turpentine."

"Oh, like you know what turpentine tastes like," Simon said as he took a swig. He also spit it out as rapidly as he could. "Geez, you're right! Wow. I'll get us some wine. No more Molotov Cocktails for us."

Sharon's head shot around. "Molotov Cocktails? Where did you get this recipe?"

Walking into the kitchen, he grabbed the book from the table. "From this. It's a cookbook."

Eyes wide, she replied, "Yeah, the Anarchist Cookbook! This is how to make bombs and stuff, you moron!"

"Y'know, I did wonder why the recipe called for them to be served in a bottle, with a rag sticking out the top. I thought the rag was like a homemade straw or something."

With panic growing, Sharon leaned her body to look toward the kitchen. "So, uh, what's cooking in the oven?"

The ensuing explosion shook the entire neighborhood.

~ Cooking Up Excitement 2: Criminal Mastermind ~

The police had waited patiently to discuss with Simon the leveling of the 2400 block of Division Street. While his coma had only lasted a couple of days, his rehab took weeks.

In the interim, they spoke to Simon's roommate Craig, who was infuriated because he lost all his stuff in the explosion. They interviewed his former girlfriend Sharon, who had nothing nice to say about the man. She used the word idiot a lot.

Finally, the doctors said Simon had healed enough to answer some questions.

They sat the young man in a small white room, with a mirror covering the entirety of the far wall. He'd seen enough crime dramas to know what that was all about, so he waved at the mirror and said, "Hi Mom!"

Slamming his fist on the table, Detective Falters yelled, "This is no laughing matter! You're a terrorist who nearly destroyed a city block. I want to know why!"

Giving the detective a puzzled look, he said, "A terrorist? Because I inadvertently blew up my kitchen? And my girlfriend? How is Sharon, anyway? No one will tell me."

"Oh, she's healing up. Most of her hair has begun to grow back."

Simon winced. "Geez! I feel awful. It was just supposed to be a celebration."

"A celebration of what, your acceptance into the Taliban?"

"No, of course not. You kiddin' me? I couldn't grow a beard that long." When the officer did not even crack a smile, Simon added, "Kidding. No, it was our one-year anniversary."

Reaching behind him, Falters produced a charred, smoky-smelling book and dropped it on the table between them. "Can you explain this?"

"Well, yeah. It's a cookbook. Or at least I thought it was."

The Detective's eyes narrowed to slits. "Are you seriously trying to tell me you thought this was a normal cookbook?"

"Well, yeah."

"The Anarchist Cookbook?"

Simon's gaze fell to the floor. "Uh-huh. I made the recipe on page 92 as our entrée."

The detective glared at the man, then spun the book around and turned it to that page. After reading it, he stared wide-eyed at Simon. "This? An entrée?"

Simon nodded. "I thought it was some sort of fancy soufflé."

"Wow. You're either the biggest criminal mastermind, or…" Lifting the book, he flipped through the pages until he located a singed bookmark. "Okay, I found this page interesting." He sat it down on the table and rotated it back to Simon. "This section is all about how to make Molotov Cocktails. How'd they turn out for you?"

"Oh man, they tasted awful!"

Falters slowly closed the book. He stared at Simon for a long moment before saying, "Okay, you're free to go."

~ Chapter Twenty-Four ~

"Gadzooks," my wife says with eyes wide, "I hope those weren't based on a true story!"

"No, not at all," I reply as I place the first of my pancakes on a plate. It's a bit overly cooked, with a fair amount of black on it. Fortunately, my wife doesn't seem to mind eating burnt food, especially if someone else cooked it. "I wrote those for a Fiction 440 event, with the prompt of 'It's a cookbook.' Nearly everything I write is fiction. Occasionally, I'll try my hand at creative non-fiction. But, truth be told, my memory is so bad that I can't trust myself to actually remember events as they occurred."

Walking over to me, my wife rests her hand gently on the small of my back. "Yes, I'm very well aware of your memory." After a quick pause, she says, "What did we do on our third date?"

"Ooo, I know this one! We went to a place, did a thing, and ate some food. Right?"

She pats the top of my head as if she's petting a puppy, and then picks up the plate with the burnt pancake on it. "Sure, why not," she says as she walks over to the table.

Her response makes me grin. "Hey," I say, "I do have a true story that I actually remember. Well, it's mostly true, anyway. And I mostly remember it. Would you care to hear it?"

Taking a bite of pancake and swallowing she says, "Yes please," using a lilting British accent reminiscent of a UK children's cartoon featuring pigs. Then she adds, "So wait a second. Are you saying you don't remember going to a place and doing a thing on our third date?"

I quickly bounce my shoulders up and down. "I dunno. Was I there?"

I'm glad she's not a thrower, because even I feel my response deserved something to be tossed at me.

~ Valuable Life Lessons ~

I learned a valuable life lesson today. Well, technically, two lessons. Even with the best of intentions, never approach a woman in a parking lot, and wow does pepper spray sting.

The day started innocently enough. Normally, I wouldn't have been at the Farm and Farmer Supply Company at 3:30 on a Thursday afternoon, but my boss Brian cut me loose early, and I had some shopping to do.

Up until the day before yesterday, I had never set foot in this store. Shawn, my boss's boss at the warehousing company ODN, had sent me here on Tuesday to purchase some heavy winter gear. He did this to make the newly acquired outdoor portion of our jobs a bit more tolerable. As of early January, we were now responsible for managing the steelyard at the Delmer Corporation. On that first day, I had to stand outside for hours, slapping white barcode labels on large slabs of steel. It wouldn't have been a bad job, except for the 20 below zero wind chills numbing me to the bone. My outdoor wardrobe consisted of a flimsy jacket without a working zipper, and a pair of gloves with holes in two fingers.

After I spent the rest of the day whining about being so cold, Shawn decided the company could be magnanimous, footing the bill for warmer gear. Whiner gets the gig I guess, so off he sent me to purchase a couple of full-body suits for Brian and me, as well as two pairs of gloves and ski masks.

"Okay," I said with my best fake smile. "Do you give me a check, or what?"

Shawn smirked at me. "No, just use your credit card. You do have one, right?" When I nodded, he added, "Just bring me the receipt and we'll reimburse you."

I can't say I was thrilled with that scenario, but being new to the company, I agreed.

The problem with this situation didn't confront me until I arrived at the store. Standing in front of dozens of different sizes of Carhartt coveralls, my six-foot, 220-pound boss only armed me with the vague instruction to, "Get an extra-large." As a man who stood six inches shorter and 80 pounds lighter than Brian, I felt completely out of my element. After engaging the help of a big guy I found pushing a broom around the store, I confidently left with what I assumed to be the correct size. After all, he looked about the same size, and he told me, "This is what I'd wear."

The next day, I tried not the snicker as I watched Brian attempt to wriggle his 46-long body into a 42-regular Carhartt snowsuit. He got both legs and an arm into it, but after nearly dislocating a shoulder, he decided to stop trying. I assumed I'd find myself back at the store that evening, but Chris, one of the other supervisors, told me he'd be going by there in a couple hours, and would be happy to take the suit back and swap it out for something more appropriate. It sounded good to me, saving me the hassle.

A couple hours later, I received a phone call from Chris. He informed me they didn't have any Carhartts in the appropriate size. However, they had a store brand that was cheaper. This sounded reasonable to me, except they needed to have my Visa if I wanted the credit. Since he obviously didn't have my credit card, I ended up with a gift card valued at $22.64.

Therefore, this explains what I was doing at the Farm and Farmer at 3:30 on a Thursday afternoon. I was wandering around the place, trying to find stuff to use up the gift card. I had a couple of needs, like a snow shovel or an un-holey pair of gloves. Unfortunately, in the clearance glove bin, they only had extra-large men's and small women's sizes left. Sure, why not be nearly out of gloves. After all, mid-January in Michigan, during a stretch of below zero temperatures, was a perfect time to be completing their winter clearance sale. I tried on the remaining pairs of gloves. My hands swam in the extra larges, and lost circulation in the smalls, not to mention the embarrassment of being seen trying on gloves with a large, brightly-printed LADIES tag hanging off them, like a beacon professing my lack of manliness.

Okay, I figured, how about a snow shovel? My plastic one had seen better days. Nope, they only had three flat, metal ones left. I hated metal shovels, all heavy and noisy. The scraping metallic sound reverberated all throughout my neighborhood.

At that point, I knew I had to get clever. Wandering the store like a nomad searching for food, I found all sorts of weird possibilities. I stumbled upon a box of road flares. Shouldn't everyone have a flare or two in their glove box? I nearly snatched one up, until I saw their supply of flashlights. Though sparse, they had one of the old-school lantern-style torches, the style that used a large, square battery. I already had two flashlights, one in the kitchen junk drawer and one in my bedroom, but it seemed reasonable to have one in the trunk. It was an $8.00 item, so that left around $14.50 on the card.

Suddenly, for some reason, my mind flashed back to the original version of Wheel of Fortune. Back then, the winner of a round had to go shopping with the winnings, drifting through a cavalcade of mostly crap items, with the occasional trip thrown in. I imagined myself on the show, as the disembodied head looking at all that balderdash: "For $250, I'll take the Burgundy Goat's Head Lamp. For $400, give me the alabaster lion statue… oh, all right, I'll take the giant purple vase for $100, and the rest on a gift certificate." However, since my moolah was already on a gift certificate, my analogy didn't quite fit. Still, it made me chuckle out loud, which elicited a puzzled, creeped out glare from a woman I didn't notice until now, standing to my left looking at a big bag of horse-chow. As I offered her a smile and a shrug, I realized she looked somewhat familiar. I couldn't tell if I actually knew her, or if she just looked similar to someone else. I found I couldn't stop staring at her curly brown hair, with part of it matted to her skull while other sections jutted out at uneven angles. This haphazard mess had probably spent most of the day under a hat. Either that or she enjoyed playing with electrical outlets.

Oh well, I brushed it off and continued my search. I managed to find a couple other semi-useful items. Noticing the light bulb section, I remembered that the three-way bulb in the living room lamp had burned out. First, it lost the 50 and 150 watt simultaneously, which always filled me full of irk. The lamp always lost both of those choices together, leaving me with CLICK darkness, CLICK light, CLICK darkness, CLICK darkness, CLICK darkness, CLICK light, etc. Then a couple of days after that, the 100-watt filament burned out as well. I decided to purchase two of these bulbs at $2.29 each. The card was under $10 now, so I was making progress.

After that, I wandered around for several more minutes, not seeing much of any interest. As I turned the corner and into the plumbing aisle, I nearly plowed into the horse lady. I started thinking of her that way, due to the bits of what appeared to be straw on her jacket. That, and her angular face and slope nose did look a bit horse-like. *Man, where do I know her from? Does she work at the factory? No, I don't think so. Bowling? Nah. Writing group? Uh-uh.* Crap, this would continue to annoy me.

I just realized I'd been staring again, and I suspect I had an irritated look on my face, if her countenance offered me any indication. I turned my back and walked down the plumbing aisle. Hmmm... I guess I could buy a plunger. I don't necessarily need a plunger, but mine had seen better days. I'd owned it since before I bought the house. Do plungers go bad? Eh, I don't know. However, I decided on a better purchase when I laid eyes upon a sink clog remover from the Roto-Rooter people. *Opens up slow running drains*, it bragged. My bathroom sink had been perpetually slow for most of my 12 years there. After running water down it, it would make this GLUG GLUG sound repeatedly for around a minute. The Roto-Rooter was a bit expensive at $8.29, but I tossed it in my cart. After doing the math in my head, I figured I was pretty much there, within a dollar of my mark, so I decided to call it good.

As I pushed my cart up to the front, in the area where most stores have candy bars and gum in what retailers call the Impulse Area, I noticed a six-pack of men's crew socks. The socks currently on my feet had a hole in the heel, so I knew I needed those babies. I grabbed the bag, and said aloud, "Well, this is the first time I've ever impulse purchased socks." Horse woman, standing behind me in line, snorted. It could've been a laugh, or perhaps a whinny. Before I tossed it on the checkout counter, I noticed a word on the sock bag that caused me to laugh aloud. *Resealable*. Sure enough, there was a strip of off-brand Ziploc on this bag. I looked at the sales clerk and asked, "Why do all socks nowadays come in resealable bags? What possible purpose does this serve?" When she gave me a shrug, I continued, "I mean, do you suppose men store their used socks in these bags? Do a lot of people return socks, so the manufacturers felt the need to pop some Ziploc on the bags? And if that's the case," I say as I toss the other items from my cart onto the stationary counter, "is it possible these socks are used? Maybe someone tried one of these on, walked around for a couple hours, and put 'em back?" I should've stopped, but I was on a roll and would not be denied. "Or are we supposed to reuse these bags once the socks are depleted? Should I be putting my sandwiches in here? Come to think of it, I have a buddy who's using his sock bag to hold spare change."

I stopped speaking, finally, and realized I had several pairs of eyes upon me. The cashier shook her head slowly and held out her hand for payment, the bagger smirked at me and Horse Chick looked rather aggravated. I handed the cashier the gift card, and still owed a couple of bucks. After digging the cash out of my wallet, I carried my two bags of stuff out to my car.

Standing at my trunk, I had a conundrum related to the flashlight I had just purchased. I couldn't decide if I wanted to remove the battery from the sealed pack and put it in the flashlight before putting it in the trunk. Would having it installed, I wondered, drain the battery quicker? After a minute of thinking, I opted to consolidate the flashlight. If I needed it in a hurry, I rationalized, it'd be best to have it ready.

As I finished dropping the battery into the flashlight, the Horse lady vacated the building. Suddenly, it hit me. She works for the Post

Office! That's where I know her! I could now picture her in the blue and gray uniform, though I couldn't recall if she was a mail carrier, or if she worked at the Collins Road location I frequent.

I felt compelled to know so I approached her, flashlight in hand, yelling, "Hey lady, I figured you out!"

That's when the pepper spray hit my eyes. While rubbing snow from the parking lot all over my face, I began speculating about the legality of pepper spray in Michigan. In the end, I decided that mail carriers could probably have the stuff. I just hope she's not my home mail carrier, or at least has no idea who I am.

~ Chapter Twenty-Five ~

Looking at me with a sideways stare and a half-smile, my wife asks, "Did you really get pepper sprayed?"

I wonder if I should I go for the funny answer or the real one. I've become marginally better at resisting the urge to be a smart ass, or at least being able to discern the proper times for each. If I had had this skill set when I was 19 and working as a temp at the Coca-Cola bottling plant, I might have been invited back for a second day of work. Instead, when they opened the cooler and asked me what soft drink I wanted, my inherent goofy nature made me think, "Do you have a Pepsi?" would be hilarious.

The complete silence that greeted my comment made me instantly recognize my smart assery. People actually stopped working to gape at me. "Kidding," I said with an inane grin. "Coke would be great."

Too late. I'd already done peed in that pool. The next day, I would have to wait for the temporary agency to find me a new job.

Therefore, I look at my wife and I reply, "Nah. I've never been tasered, or sprayed, or anything like that. The story was real up to that point."

She walks over and rests her hand on my cheek. "Good. Otherwise, I'd have to go back in time and teach her a lesson. No one sprays my man," my wife says, before the gleam in her eye intensifies and she adds, "except me."

I barely have time to react to her grabbing the sprayer from the kitchen sink and aiming it at me. Holding up my hands in the universal sign for *please don't hurt me*, I say, "Will another story appease your itchy trigger finger?"

"Maybe. You gonna lie to me again?"

"I wouldn't be surprised."

The extremely cold water, as it hits my face and neck, alerts me to another failure in my goal not to be a wise guy.

~ This is How My Heart Was Broken ~

What do you mean you don't agree with me? Do you realize who you're dealing with? As the *Ren and Stimpy* cartoon played on my TV, I only half-watched it. I'd seen it a bunch of times and could practically recite it word for word, and besides, my attention was elsewhere. Out of the corner of my eye, I kept noticing Gloria Montgomery as she picked up and dusted my numerous knickknacks.

At first, I used to feel a bit weird sitting around while this short, skinny, chocolate-haired woman cleaned my house. Sure, it was her job and I paid her to do it, but having a stranger come into my domicile to touch all my stuff seemed overly opulent. However, she didn't charge all that much, and if she didn't do it, the dust would grow thick, as I was far too lazy to bother. And as a bonus, she was rather pleasant to look at.

After wiping off my alligator skull, she turned to look at me just as Ren boisterously called Stimpy, a *fat, bloated eediot*. She crinkled her nose and gave me an amused smirk. "Seems like you're always watching cartoons. Don't you ever watch anything normal?"

"There's no point while you're here. You're too much of a distraction. It's just easier to have something mindless on."

"Sure, I get that. But cartoons? What a waste of time."

Shrugging, I replied, "Well, it's either that or Masterpiece Theatre."

"Don't you mean professional wrestling?"

She knew me too well, darn her, so I decided to mess with her. "I'll have you know I actually meant Masterpiece Wrestling. They yell poetry at each other and hit one other with antique furniture. The big match today was Thespian Tony and Haiku vs. Shinjuku and Sir Abdullah the Pontificator."

Gloria chuckled despite herself, giving me a quick smile before turning back to her work. My interest in the TV had vanished and I instead watched Gloria as she stretched her borderline anorexic body up to wipe a cobweb from a corner. When she reached, her shirt lifted up to reveal the dainty ivy design tattooed on the small of her back. She looked even bonier than usual, giving the tattoo a slightly shrunken appearance. Then, when her hand started quivering at the top of her reach, I asked, "When did you eat last?"

Turning to look at me, she replied, "I dunno. Probably dinner yesterday. I had coffee this morning. That counts, right?" She was one of those women who could actually forget to eat.

Popping up from my chair, I started walking toward the kitchen. "Sandwich? I have turkey, and the Swiss might not be bad yet."

"Nah, it's all right. I'll be done soon."

I opened the fridge and pulled out a strawberry yogurt, popped it open, and dropped a spoon into it. "Here," was all I said as I set it on the coffee table near her spare dust rag.

Brushing away a strand of hair from over her left eye, she looked at the yogurt and frowned at me. "You don't need to do that, Riley." However, her eyes softened and she reached out, scooped it up, and spooned a pink glob into her mouth. "But thanks. I know I should take better care of myself."

Sitting back down, I said, "Yeah ya should. If you were mine, I'd treat ya well." The silence hung thick in the air like dust, so I asked, "How long you been comin' here?"

She put another spoonful in her mouth and swallowed it before answering. "Couple years by now, I'd guess."

"Have you ever wondered why I never asked you out?"

Setting the still nearly full yogurt cup back on the coffee table, she picked up her rag and started wiping around the knickknacks on the entertainment center. "Not really. You're my customer. It wouldn't be right."

"Whatdya mean it wouldn't be right?"

"Well, it wouldn't be smart, anyway. You're a good customer, a good guy. I'd hate to lose ya."

I already knew what she meant, but I felt like making her say it. "Why would you have to lose me? You don't think we could date and work together?"

Gloria did her best not to look at me, focusing on her cleaning. The Darth Vader bobble head had a healthy layer of dust embedded in its various crevices, and she had to work that cloth vehemently to get it in there. "Riley, you're a nice guy, but honestly, you're not really my type. I like riding on the backs of motorcycles and doing stuff like camping and sky diving. I'm not really into cartoons and wrestling and bric-a-bracs."

"Sure," I said softly, "I have too many toys for your taste. I get that. We're worlds apart, you and I. I could never fall for a woman who forgets to eat, or has a tattoo on her back."

As she spun around to give me what I assumed would be a glare of some sort, her bony elbow caught one of my more fragile items. It tumbled off the top of the entertainment center, hit the carpeted floor, and broke into several pieces. Her demeanor instantly changed, and she looked mortified. "Oh crap, I'm so sorry Riley! Geez, I'm sorry!" Bending down, she picked up the pieces and walked them over to me.

Pointing my finger at the coffee table, she turned and set the shards gently down. I kneeled at the edge of the table and tried to see if the pieces would go back together. "My ex-wife gave this to me, for my first birthday after our marriage. She knew how much I liked stuff like this. She understood me." Made of porcelain and painted light blue, it was a woman's hand holding onto a heart. The hand was missing a couple of fingers, and the heart was in three pieces. "You broke my heart, Gloria."

She apologized again and went back to cleaning.

~ Chapter Twenty-Six ~

I love when my wife comes to visit me at work. Because I'm such a hard worker, and because I'm cheap, I rarely go out for lunch, opting for a peanut butter and honey sandwich or a cup of mac and cheese at my desk. However, my wife is in town today, and I am meeting her at Culvers. She loves their cheese curds!

Driving into the restaurant's parking lot, I roll around until I spot her vehicle, backed into a spot on the corner of the lot. I pull in next to her, and offer her a smile through our windows.

We both vacate our cars, and after a quick embrace, I lead her into the restaurant, her arm in mine.

Once we've picked out our food orders (veggie burgers all around, with fries for me and cheese curds for her of course – though we will share each other's side dishes) we find a booth in the far corner. I take the seat with my back to the other patrons so my wife can sit where she prefers, facing everyone. If someone comes in wielding a machete, that deranged person can take me out first allowing my wife, who sees it coming, to get herself to safety. Chivalry – it's what's for lunch.

We chat about our various morning activities for a while, until a lull in the conversation brings her to say, "Tell me a story."

Grinning widely, I reply, "I was hoping you'd ask me that. I have a work-related one I know you'll enjoy."

~ First Day at the New Job ~

The thing I hate most about getting a new job is trying to remember the names of all these people. My supervisor Eric, at least I think that's his name, walks me around from office to office, introducing me to people in rapid-fire fashion. "And this is Ryan, our director of direction."

He probably didn't say that, but this is the 20th person I've met in the past 15 minutes, and I already forgot this guy's name, let alone what he directs. I hold out my hand, flash him my best fake smile, and say, "It's a pleasure to meet you... fella."

"Likewise, pal," he replies with barely a glance at my face. Maybe he's the director of looking in other directions. This place is big enough to have one.

My manager – geez I hope his name actually *is* Eric – points toward the end of the hall. "Down there is the break room. I'll give you a quick tour of the fridge and microwave."

As we enter the break room, I notice a heavyset, balding man sitting with his back to us at the round table in the center of the room. Fantastic, I think, another person. I'm hoping for a Napoleon or Reynaldo. Something memorable so I at least have a chance of retaining his name.

The boss man drops his hand on my shoulder and slowly pulls me out of the room. As my brow furrows in confusion, the man at the table turns to look up at us. "Oh hey Eric! I've been meaning to talk to you!" Cool, his name *is* Eric!

"Uh, now's not a good time, Tom." Tom. Of course, why the hell not? I still might call him Reynaldo. Eric adds, "I'm showing the new guy around."

Standing up, Tom shoves his meaty hand at me. "Hi there buddy, I'm Tom. I handle the accounts."

"Oh, um, hi. I'm Mark, and I too handle accounts around here."

Eric chimes in with, "He's taking over your job, Tom. You don't work here anymore. Still."

Releasing a huge, boisterous laugh, Tom says, "Oh Eric, such a kidder! I'll let you get back to showing the new guy here around, but we do need to talk later."

"Yes, Tom. Definitely." We turn and leave the break room as Eric continues, "You actually are taking his job."

I look over at him with wide eyes. "What? Are you serious?"

"That's the idea, anyway. In fact, I fired that guy weeks ago. I told him not to come back, but he just keeps showing up and doing his job."

"You're kidding?"

"No. We haven't paid him in a while, but that's not deterring him. I guess he thinks we're direct depositing his money, even though I've told him otherwise. No amount of conversation has helped to convince him that he no longer works here. It's so frustrating."

I have to assume this is a joke they play on the new guy, so I decide to go along with it. "I imagine it would be. So, security can't keep him out?"

Eric shakes his head slowly. "He keeps finding ways to get in here. We canceled his keycard, made sure all the windows and side doors are secured, but he's like a fat ninja. I swear he must be living here."

Having no idea what to say, I simply utter, "Huh."

Cracking the thinnest of smiles, Eric says, "The odd thing is, he's actually doing his job a lot better than he used to."

"It sounds to me like you have the perfect employee, frankly." As the words come out of my mouth, I realize I'm endorsing the man whose job they hired me to replace, so I quickly add, "But I'm here now, so I should probably get to work, huh?"

Eric looks at me and smirks. "Yes, I suppose so. Let me show you to your workspace."

As we wander through the maze of cubicles, we turn a corner and Eric gestures at one. "And this one is..."

He pauses when we both see Tom sitting in what is supposed to be my seat, hastily typing away at what is supposed to be my computer. Spinning around in my chair, Tom smiles up at us. "Oh hi Eric, and, um... I want to say... Margaret."

"No, this is Mark," Eric says as he reaches up and pinches the bridge of his nose. "Look Tom, let's try this one more time. You don't work here anymore. It's not a joke. I'm not pulling your leg, or feeding you some bull. You. Don't. Work. Here. Any. More. Go home, Tom, I fired you weeks ago!"

Standing up, he stares intently at his former boss. "Okay, I'll play along. Tell me why you fired me. Give me the reasons."

Eric releases a large sigh. "Okay, fine. Absenteeism is one reason. I fired you after you missed five days in six weeks."

"Okay. How many days have I missed since then? None. I've been here every day for the past month, even working weekends, so you can tell I'm serious about this job. What else?"

Holding up his left hand with two fingers outstretched, he says, "Number two is your quality of work. You've made several mistakes, losing this company a great deal of money."

"Have I made any mistakes lately?"

After a quick pause, Eric answers, "Well, no, actually you've done very well. In fact, you managed to reverse one of the mistakes and regained most of the money you cost us."

I suddenly feel like I'm on a first date, watching two recently broken up lovers realizing their mistake right in front of me. I say, "So, uh —" but Eric cuts me off.

"We could give you one more chance. But you'd have to keep up this work level."

Tom's smile widens. "Does that mean you'll start paying me again?"

Eric laughs. "Sure, Tom. I'll even make sure you get your back pay."

Then, they both glance over at me. As Eric's smile fades, he says, "Don't worry Mark. We'll find you something. I think."

As we leave my almost-cubicle, I glare back at Tom. He tosses me a wink. I guess that's one way to counteract being fired. I'll have to remember that… probably at my next job.

~ Chapter Twenty-Seven ~

After the Culver's meal with my wife concludes, we meander out to our respective vehicles, leftovers in hand. She opens her truck door, sets her food in, and turns back to give me a hug. It's a long embrace, held even longer by me. Finally, she pulls her head back and says, "You don't want to go back to work, do you?"

I give her a slow, tender kiss before replying, "Not so much, no. I don't want to leave you. Frankly, I don't ever want to leave you. And on top of that, it'll be a late work night for me." I pause for a moment before adding, "How about if I tell you one more story before you go?"

Now it's her turn to hold the embrace. "I hope you always have one more story for me."

"I will, sweetie. Count on it."

~ Poison Ivy? ~

Since the beginning of our civilization, people have been predicting the end of our civilization. From Nazis to zombies... to Nazi zombies, so many things were prophesized to be the apocalypse that would end our reign. Asteroid attack, viral attack... hell, Mars Attack! Some crazy ideas were bandied about.

But seriously, poison ivy? No one saw that coming. And no, I don't mean the Batman villain, though that would've been infinitely cooler than this itchy nonsense.

The sequence of events, turning a mildly annoying plant into the virulent, hyper-fast growing uber-weed that engulfed Cleveland in a weekend, caught everyone napping. Of course, no one really cared about Cleveland, but when it took out Vegas and the rest of the West Coast, people became concerned.

Even though only pockets of itch-free zones remain and anarchy rules the rest, some good did come from it. With most of the world dead or scratching, I have my pick of stuff. For instance, I love my red Stingray Corvette! I never thought I'd own this shapely beast, but now, I'm tooling up I-75 in the coolest car ever, trying to see if the rumors of an ivy-free Canada truly exist.

As I spot a figure lying in the middle of the highway, creeper weed closing in on all sides, I ease to a stop. My first reaction is to leave this woman to her fate, but hell, I've been alone for ages. I could stand the company. If she hasn't been ivied yet... Well, dating in this landscape is, shall we say challenging, at the very least. Red welts can really ruin the mood.

As she runs toward my Vette, I jump out and yell commandingly, "Stop! Stay right there!"

Pausing, she yells back, "Oh my God, thank you for stopping! You're my savior! I thought I was a goner for sure." Her bright, grateful smile beams at me like a beacon in the late afternoon sun.

I pop the trunk and reach in to remove my high-pressure power washer. I'm not letting her or anyone get that nasty Urushiol oil all over my nice interior. I proclaim, "I know how uncomfortable this is, and I apologize in advance. But you know how..."

Then I hear the unmistakable click of her partner's gun against my temple. "Shit!" I breathe.

I watch from the crumbling pavement as my shapely Corvette drives away. As the ivy creeps ever closer, I can't help but think if I had my druthers, I'd rather be killed by the comic book Poison Ivy. At least Batman's nemesis was hotter, more creative, and not nearly as itchy.

~ Chapter Twenty-Eight ~

"Twas the night before Christmas," I say as I walk into the living room while cradling two wrapped gifts in my arms.

"You mean the last day of Advent," my wife corrects.

"Hanukkah Eve, maybe?"

"No." She shakes her head slowly but authoritatively.

"Kwanzaa wrap-up?"

Cracking a grin, she replies, "Not even close, and if you add Festivus to this list I will take all of your presents back."

"Yikes," I say with a grimace. "Christmas slash Advent it is!"

The stockings are, in fact, hung by the chimney with care. They still hang empty, but I know she'll add some items to them before morning. I'll slip a few things in myself, but she keeps telling me it's her job to fill the stockings, so I have to be stealthy about it. "Y'know," I say, "I do have some Christmas stories I don't believe I've ever told you. Whatdya think?"

Her smile grows three sizes. "I think you should tell them to me."

~ Christmas Eve at Gouda's (Breaking Rule Number Seven of the Christmas Commandments) ~

As the manager of a restaurant called Gouda's – Where it's Not Merely Good-a, it's Great-a! – every day seemed to be full of emergencies to handle and fires to extinguish. I sat checking inventory levels on the computer in my office, wondering if today, being Christmas Eve, might be one of those rare, non-bizarre days. Could today possibly be free of drama and weirdness?

The moment that thought hit my brain, I heard shouting, then a sharp knock on my door. "Jerry," Belinda yelled, "you gotta get out here!" Cursing myself for even letting that thought surface, I stood up and walked out to the floor.

Three of my loveliest servers stood on our side of the counter, while an exceedingly angry man loomed large on the customer side. His head of unkempt black hair reminded me of a 70s rock star like Syd Barrett or maybe Jim Morrison, with wild, crazed eyes sticking out just underneath his swooping curls. He had on a fluffy, olive green jacket, a red t-shirt with a picture of... what is that, a Care Bear? In addition, he sported what I would categorize as pajama bottoms, shades of pink and red assaulting my sense of fashion. Jabbing a finger at Trudy, he said, "You can't treat me this way! You know the customer is always right!"

Oh geez, nothing good or intelligent ever came out after someone dropped that golden nugget of wisdom. "Hi sir," I said quickly, "I'm Jerry, the manager. What seems to be the problem?"

Eyes flaring, he said, "Breach of contract, that's what!" When I furrowed my brow, he pointed up. Dangling from our sign above the counter hung some mistletoe. "Your waitress is standing under the mistletoe, and yet she refuses to kiss me."

"Uh, sir –"

211

"Don't, 'Uh, sir' me! I know my rights!"

I really hoped this was some weird joke, but he sure did look legitimately angry. "Sir, mistletoe isn't a binding agreement. It's just supposed to be a silly tradition."

"No, you're wrong! She is breaking rule number seven of the Christmas Commandments. Mistletoe is a promise for a kiss, according to Kramer vs. Kringle. Failure to meet that promise can result in serious consequences!"

"I'm sorry. But if Trudy doesn't want to kiss you -" I turned to look at her, and she confirmed this by shaking her head vehemently. "Then I'm afraid that's the end of that."

When he reached into his pocket, I instinctively tightened up. I felt slightly better when he pulled out a cell phone. "I'm going to call my attorney." He kept his eyes glued on me as he hit a bunch of numbers on the phone. "Yes, is this the law firm of Clause, Noel, and Nicholas? Yes, I have a mistletoe infraction at Gouda's on Saginaw. How should I proceed?"

I started to say, "Look sir –" but he held up his index finger.

"Uh-huh. Yes, I tried that. That too, yes. Okay, if it must come to that, I'll tell him. Thanks." Slapping his phone shut and dropping it back into the pocket of his fuzzy PJ bottoms, he said, "Oh, you're in deep reindeer doo-doo now! You need to make this kiss happen right this second, or else my lawyers will slap a Christmas violation injunction on you. Your names will all be added to Santa's permanent Naughty List. No chance for parole! Coal for life!"

Wow. Okay. His smug smile, tinged with insanity, freaked me out. I could only think of one thing to say, one gambit to perform, though I didn't like it one bit. "All right, so be it. You want a mistletoe-mandated kiss? Fine. Look where we're both standing." I pointed up to illustrate. "Pucker up, dude!"

He glared at me for a good fifteen seconds. Man, I really hoped this fruit loop wouldn't call my bluff! Finally, he said, "That... that's not..."

212

He again pulled out his phone and made another call. "He just said... But he can't... Are you... Oh, c'mon... Dang it!"

He looked at me with fire in his eyes for a while longer, and then he sighed. "I officially release you from this contract. Darn you!" As he turned toward the door, he exclaimed, "That's it, I'm outta here. You're all a bunch of ho-ho-hos!" With that, he shoved the door open and dashed away.

Once the door slammed shut, the whole place burst into applause, customers and employees alike. Several patrons patted me on the back or shook my hand. I then turned to my three waitresses. "That was just too weird! I think we'd be wise to remove this mistletoe. So who hung it in the first place, anyway?"

All three raised their hands, each with a huge grin. "We actually did it for you, boss. You've been so good to us this year. None of us can afford to get you a gift, but we decided there is one thing we can afford."

One at a time, my lovely wait staff walked up and kissed me. Belinda and Loretta each gave me a sweet peck on the cheek. Then Trudy sauntered over. "My hero," she said as she planted a quick, delicate smooch on my lips.

Smiling, I replied, "Thanks, ladies." Then I grabbed a chair, jumped up on it, and removed the mistletoe. Several customers booed me. "Sorry folks, don't wanna break any more sacred Christmas edicts."

~ Chapter Twenty-Nine ~

"Y'know," my wife says as she walks down the hall, pausing under the light fixture, "your story and this light have something in common."

My puzzlement shows for a quick moment, until I look above her. The mistletoe hanging there beckons me closer, as does my wife's sly grin. "Works every time," she whispers.

~ Drowsy Trousers ~

I finish wedging the padding into the belly of my Santa suit, release a sigh, and trudge out into Santa's Kingdom. In my third year as the Mall Santa, I'm sure I've experienced it all: the beard pulling, the screaming, being whizzed on, dealing with angry kids and parents, and... well, there's really nothing worse than being whizzed on.

After yelling, "Ho Ho Ho, Merry Christmas, kids!" I take my place at Santa's throne. "Who's first to see Santa?"

A boy, I'd guess around seven or eight, came bounding up, goes airborne momentarily, and lands with an "Ooof!" in my lap. Glad I remembered my cup. "What is your name, little boy?"

"Jimmy," he says proudly.

"Well Jimmy, what can Santa bring you for Christmas this year?"

He takes a deep breath. I anticipate a long list. "I want a Hot Wheels Terrain Twister, the new Sonic Sizzler game for Xbox, and Itch the Witch!"

"What's Itch the Witch?"

"It's a new board game, silly!"

Do kids even play board games I had to wonder? I glance over at his dad, a 30-something man with the beginnings of wrinkles and grey hair. He gives me a short nod, so I say, "I think Santa can make that happen, Jimmy! Now off ya go!"

Lifting him off my lap, I set him gently on the ground. That was a good first one, I think. Looking up, I shout, "Ho Ho Ho, who's next?"

The father gives me a puzzled look. "Well, I am, Santa," and proceeds to plop his considerable weight on my left knee. I hear a distinct pop.

"You're kidding."

"No Santa," he utters with a joyous expression on his face, "I've been really good this year."

"Ohhh-kay. What can I get you, uh...?"

"Jerry! I want the new Drowsy Trousers CD, season two of Frisky Dingo – not season one, you got me that last year, as you recall – and a job. I really need a job."

Under my breath, I ask, "Ya want mine?" When he furrows his brow, I add, "Sure, Jerry. I'll see what I can do. Now please get up! You're killin' me here!"

"Oh, sorry Santa," he says as he leaps to his feet. "Thanks!"

After he and his son bound away, I say, "Who's next? Ho Ho..."

I pause in mid-ho when a gorgeous blonde woman saunters up and hops into my lap. She adds some extra wiggles to get comfy.

215

"Ho. I mean, hi."

"I've been naughty this year. Very naughty. What've ya got for me?"

"Okay everyone," I shout, "Santa has to, uh, water the elves. We'll be back in 15!"

~ Chapter Thirty ~

After completing the story, she crosses her arms and gives me a pout. "Do you have any Christmas stories where your lead character doesn't get kissed, or worse, by the women in the story?"

"Awww, are you getting jealous?"

Her pout turns slightly angry. "Do not make fun of me."

"But baby, I wrote these before I met you. They..." As the lines in her forehead deepen, I mentally yell at myself to shut up. I momentarily think about telling her how the character in that last story was her, but then I see a series of flashbacks in my mind where I said things I thought were either funny or brilliant, and how badly all those incidences turned out. After my Pepsi comment at the Coke plant jumps into my mind, I shudder and stuff my bad idea back into the recesses of my mind. Instead, I say, "Sorry, sweetie. Of course I have better stories for you. Here's one you'll like better, with no kissing!"

~ A Visitor on Christmas Eve ~

Rolling over to stare at his sleeping wife, Garrett whispers, "Audrey, honey, are you asleep?" When she doesn't respond, he says a bit louder, "Baby, how can you sleep? I'm way too excited."

Audrey groans, "Oh geez Garrett! How can you *not* sleep? You're 40 years old, for Cripes sake. How can Christmas Eve excite you this much? You're such an eternal boy, and that's –"

Interrupting, Garrett says, "Shhh! Hear that?"

"I didn't hear anything. Go to sleep already."

Garrett bolts upright for a moment, intently listening for the sound he thought he heard. "I'm gonna go check. Oh boy, I'll bet it's Santa!"

Audrey rolls her eyes, but knowing he can't see it in the dark, she releases a loud, exaggerated sigh. "Good gracious. Sure, fine, go down there." Rolling away from him, she continues, "Tell the fat bastard I said hi," then adding under her breath, "and tell him I want a gun."

Creeping carefully down a few steps, he peers over the railing. From the streetlights falling in from the windows, he sees nothing out of the ordinary. He sighs softly and trudges down the remainder of the stairs.

As Garrett walks past the front door, he hears a rattling sound. He turns just in time to see the front door slowly squeak open.

Kneeling on the other side of the door is an overweight man with a thick, plush beard. The man, dressed in black from wool cap to sneakers, quickly drops into his tool bag the screwdriver he used to jimmy the lock. It lands with a tink as metal hits metal. While the man rises to his feet, Garrett shouts, "Santa! You made it! Yay!"

The man barely has time to change his expression from shock at his discovery, to confusion when Garrett adds, "Well, don't just stand there. Come in, come in! I have your favorite: milk and cookies!"

Wasting no time, the man reaches into his pocket and pulls out a pistol, pointing it at Garrett.

Garrett's eyes widen and his mouth drops open. "Oh my goodness," he says slowly, "that's a sweet gun! My wife is gonna love it!"

As Garrett reaches for it, the man pulls the trigger.

The bullet whizzes past Garrett's left ear, coming to rest in the wall. Turning to examine the hole for a moment before spinning back, he exclaims, "Wow! That sucker's got some power to it!"

218

With a burst of speed that catches the criminal off guard, Garrett snatches the gun from his hand, quickly turning it on him. "Oh yes, this thing feels great in my hand. Nice and light. Audrey's hands are a bit smaller, but I'm sure this will do the trick. Thank you! She'll be thrilled!"

The man's eyes pop wide open. "Hey now dude, I don't want me no trouble, yo! I'm just tryin' ta make a livin'!"

"Well, of course you are, Santa! And you've got a lot more houses to hit tonight I'm sure, so I won't keep ya. Allow me," he says as he reaches down, grabs the man's bag of tools, and drags it in front of him. "Oh wow, tools! How did you know? Well duh! You obviously got my letter."

Peering longingly at his tools, the man says, "Hey now bub, I need those!"

Garrett casually gestures the pistol toward the man. "So where are the rest of the presents? You must have something for Uncle Russ and Aunt Marge, though perhaps not cousin Wallace. She's probably on your naughty list. Oh! They must still be in the sleigh. Well heck, what're we waiting for? Let's get 'em! You're a busy man, after all."

Using the handgun as a pointer, he marches the man out of the house, and over to his red pickup truck parked in the driveway. Garrett furrows his brow. "But... where's the sleigh? Why are you dressed in black? And why is your beard brown?" Staring at the man for a moment, a smile curls his lips. "Oh, I get it! You're incognito! Smart move, Santa. Keeps the children guessing, plus you don't want to brazenly advertise all these presents. This isn't the safest of neighborhoods. Lots of robberies in the middle of the night, from what I hear."

Staring into the bed of the pickup, he sees TVs, stereos, and computers, along with countless other small items like cell phones and tablets. "Why aren't all these presents wrapped? Looks like your elves are slacking this year. That's okay. You carry 'em in, and I'll wrap 'em. It's the least I can do." Gesturing with the gun, he adds, "Well Santa, you've got a schedule to keep, so let's get these inside!"

219

Garrett supervises the man as he carries all the merchandise from his night's escapades into the house, setting them delicately under the ornately decorated Christmas tree.

Once the job is complete, Garrett says with the widest smile, "Thank you Santa, thank you! This will be the best Christmas ever! Oh wait, before you go, hang on." He reaches over and grabs the plate of cookies from the end table. "By all means, grab a few. But not too many," he adds as he taps the barrel of the gun against the man's ample gut. "But the milk is skim, so have at it!"

As the bewildered robber leaves the house with a couple of chocolate-chip cookies and a plastic cup of milk, Garrett shuts and locks the door before heading up the stairs.

Climbing into bed, he says quietly, "Honey, are you up? Santa was really kind to us this year. He even brought you the g... Oh wait, sorry. I don't want to ruin the surprise!"

~ Chapter Thirty-One ~

Christmas day arrives, and we open our presents. Sweaters and space heaters, vacuum cleaners and CDs, we get what we wanted and needed.

She thinks we're done, but I have one final gift for her. Handing her a box wrapped with purple and silver paper, I can barely contain my joy. "One more thing, sweetie."

Giving me a momentary scowl, she says, "You've already given me plenty. I didn't want anything other than the vacuum cleaner."

"I know, but this one is exactly what you've been wanting as well, and it didn't cost us any money."

My wife shakes the box back and forth, and then side to side. She loves guessing at the contents of her presents, and to my annoyance, she's usually quite good at it. "It's paper, and fairly light. Is it a book?"

Kinda, I think, but I just reply, "Open it, love of my life."

When she rips the paper and pulls the box, her eyes light up. "Is this what I think it is?"

"Yup!"

She jumps up and gives me the biggest smooch. "Psychic Phil! I love your Psychic Phil stories!"

"I know. This collection has all three of his stories, including a never-before-seen adventure for Phillip Hammel. You'll get to learn about his past and meet some family, all wrapped around a mystery."

A squeal escapes as she hugs me again. "Will you read these to me?"

"Of course! That's part of the present!"

~ The Psychic Buddy ~

"Hello, friend," Phillip droned into the telephone, "you've reached the Psychic Buddies Network. What may I see for you today?"

Laughter exploded from the other end of the line, which made Phil's heart drop. *Oh great, another one*, he thought.

"Gee," the voice said, oozing sarcasm, "if you really were psychic, you'd know what I wanted. Huh, smart guy?"

Phil wanted to hang up, but one realization always made him feel better. *After all, this moron is paying $4.99 a minute to insult me. Who's the smart guy now?* "It only works that way sometimes, sir. There's no guarantee with a gift like this. I can't just turn it on like a faucet. Now, if you want to tell me the purpose of your call, I'll be happy to..."

It felt like a tidal wave hit Phillip directly in the brain. The psychic energy, that he himself did not have the power to evoke, could most certainly power up on its own and clobber him with a tremendous current. He had felt this torrent before, of course – Many times over the years. However, this one felt larger than life. It felt...death. Death waited around the corner for someone, but not this bozo on the phone.

He wanted, again, to hang up on the caller so he could help the one who really needed him. However, his job had to come first, so he needed to appease this fellow. Over his months as a Psychic Buddy, he learned that when he felt nothing for a caller, he could usually fudge his way through. Normally he needed to ask a few questions, to allow the caller to guide him subconsciously, but he had no time to play the usual games. "Sir, I'm going to save you some money on this call and make it quick. Tell her you love her. Tell her you are sorry and you realize she truly is the one for you. Trust me, it'll work."

Phil expected laughter but after a small pause, the man said, "Whoa... Um, okay, I will. Thanks, psychic dude."

Phil grinned. "Anytime. Call again, but next time, don't waste so much time and money being skeptical."

He then hung up and quickly started to dial. He had no idea how he knew the number, but when it came to his gift, he knew well enough not to question it.

Brannon Billsen stood in the upstairs bedroom of his new house, gazing out the window at his large backyard. His focus was so intense that when his wife came from behind and put her arms around his chest, he jumped. "Amy!" He exclaimed. "I didn't hear you come up!"

She smiled and rested her chin against his shoulder. "Sorry, Bran. What are you looking at out there?"

"Oh," he replied, "I'm still marveling at this place. We've been here a couple months now, but I'm still so tickled by it all. We actually have a huge, fenced-in yard. Sure beats that apartment, huh Aim?"

"Yes it does. But now that spring is here, we really need a mower."

He turned inside the circle of her arms to face her, laid his hands on her shoulders, and delicately kissed her. "Now Aim, don't be taking the magic out of this yet! It'll grow mundane soon enough, my dear."

They stayed in their embrace for a moment before Brannon turned back to the window. Looking beyond the edge of their property, he noticed someone standing in the middle of the adjacent restaurant parking lot. The man, clad in a beige jacket and blue jeans, appeared to be looking up at them. After a few seconds, the stranger turned as a dog trotted past him in a wide arc. From this distance, the guy appeared to be a few inches tall.

223

"Y'know, I wonder if he can see us up here," Bran wondered idly.

Amy laughed, "I highly doubt it. This window is what, three by five?"

"But look, honey, he's just standing there, staring up at us."

"Oh Bran, you can't even see his face from here, especially at this time of evening. Even in broad daylight, I doubt he'd see much more than a vague shadow. He's probably looking at the stars. I've seen a few people out there, walking their dogs. And besides, the light from our window is most likely obscuring us."

As the stranger led his dog out of the lot, Brannon turned again to face his wife. "It's the light that makes it so we can be seen, Aim." Brannon stared at her for a moment and then smiled devilishly. "Y'know, I think I can solve this little dilemma. I'm going out there. You stand right here, and put on the sexy black negligee. The one with the –"

"Yeah, yeah, I know which one!" Even though she joined in with her own version of a seductive grin, she could not hide the apprehension in her blue eyes. "But what if anybody else sees?"

"You'll know it's me. I'll have on my red jacket."

"Oh but Brannon," she protested, "it's late. Besides, we don't know the neighborhood yet. It seems safe enough, but how do we know for sure?"

He smiled a most confident grin. "I'm a manly man, remember? At least that's what you tell everybody. I'll be fine. Besides, I really want to see you in that negligee! Any excuse is a good one."

After tossing her a wink, he turned and vacated the bedroom, pausing to yell, "And try both ways, with the lights off and on, okay? This way, we'll know for sure what people can see out there."

As she removed her clothes, she let the arousal overcome her trepidation. *After all, I'll be flashing the man I love*, she thought as a sly smile crept upon her pretty face. *I suppose this isn't too weird. At least the man with the dog seems to be gone.* She found the nightgown, and quickly donned it. Being skin-tight, it accentuated her curves nicely, making her feel extremely desirable. Small wonder why Brannon liked this outfit so much.

She heard the outside door click shut. Knowing he would be in position within a couple minutes, she began to fantasize. She planned to give him the show of his life.

Then, the phone rang. "Oh great!" She yelled. "What lovely timing! This had better not be Mom!" She picked up the receiver and gave her greeting.

"Hi, this is Phillip Hammel, and I'm with the Psychic Buddies Network. I'm –"

"Hey look," she interrupted, "now's not the time. I'm not interested! Goodbye!"

She started to pull the receiver away from her ear when he screamed, "Wait! Your husband's life is in danger! Don't hang up!"

This stopped her in her tracks. "What the hell are you talking about? Who is this?!"

"Look," Phil said, trying to calm himself enough to avoid sounding like a crackpot, "I'm a psychic and I had a vision of your husband, Brandon, I think. He will be killed unless you act now! Don't let Brandon go into that parking lot!"

Although Phil's words concerned her, she found herself reacting with anger. "Ya got my husband's name wrong, idiot! Look, I don't know who you are, but this is one sick joke! I'm going to call the cops, you bastard!"

He began to say, "Look, I realize this sounds crazy–" but she slammed down the handset before he could tell her any more.

Phil wished he could jump in his car and drive to the scene, to stop this terrible vision from becoming reality. The problem was his psychic powers worked in unpredictable ways. Somehow, he knew the phone number, but had no idea where they lived. Unfortunately, he realized he probably had done all he could. Though Phil could call her back, he doubted she would answer. He just hoped his warning would be enough to forestall the situation.

Amy slammed down the phone with enough force to make it bounce slightly. *Great, we moved into a neighborhood with wackos in it!* She went to the window, to see if Brannon made it to his position yet. Though she certainly lost the mood, she did not want to ruin his enjoyment. The best thing, she decided, would be to put on the show and tell him about it afterward. Still, the call ate at the back of her mind. *Don't let Brandon go into that parking lot!* It troubled her that he knew Brannon's name, or close anyway. But what could she do? If she yelled for him, he would not hear it, and his cell phone rested on the end table next to the bed.

At that moment, she saw Brannon walk around the side of the building and into the parking lot. He waved up at her and she returned the gesture. She tried to force a smile, but then realized he could not see her face anyway. His head, from this distance, resembled a tiny peach-colored ball with dark hair. If he had not been wearing the red jacket, she would not have recognized him.

Amy began her striptease, moving seductively in front of the window. After coyly pulling at her right strap, she allowed it to drop off her shoulder.

After a couple minutes of her dance routine, she went over and turned off the bedroom light. Assuming no one would be able to see anything, she mustered enough confidence to drop the other shoulder strap, allowing her negligee to crumple to the floor. She got as close to the window as she could, striving to witness any sign of acknowledgment.

At that moment, she spotted another man out on the blacktop near Brannon, so she quickly pulled up her nightgown. It looked to be the same man from earlier, or at least he wore a similar beige jacket. However, even from this distance she could see the baseball bat in his hand. It glistened in the ambient lighting of the parking lot. He slowly crept up behind Brannon, bat poised above his head. Amy belted out a scream that Brannon could not hear.

Phillip stood with the phone still in his trembling hand, sweat beading on his brow. The image in his brain still haunted him; the man beaten to death with a baseball bat in a lonely parking lot. When he felt another flash hit him, he dropped the receiver. It loudly clunked upon the floor. The noise alerted several of his co-workers, who stared at him as if he had a screw loose. His supervisor, a nasty man with absolutely no psychic abilities or scruples, rapidly approached him with an angry snarl spread across his pudgy face.

At this moment, Phil cared nothing about his job. He bent over and retrieved the receiver. That last brain flash gave him a new number to call and he dialed frantically as his boss dropped a heavy hand on his shoulder. "Hey Phil," he yelled, his mouth wrapped around an unlit cigar, "You know the rules. No personal calls on the job!"

Phillip jerked his arm away from the cigar-chewer as the phone began ringing.

Staring up at his house, Brannon sighed. Amy was right. He could not see a darn thing from this distance. *She's probably naked*, he mused, *and here I am, standing in the cold –*

Suddenly, he heard a cell phone ring directly behind him. He spun around to see a man standing too close, an aluminum baseball bat raised over his head, ready to come crashing down. As the stranger paused, clearly startled by his ringing phone, Brannon shot his foot into the man's gut, sprinting away as quickly as his legs would carry him. He heard the bat clatter upon the ground as he continued to flee. He ran all the way to his front door, where his wife stood ready to greet him with a python-like hug.

Phillip's boss began to say, "You're –"

"Yeah yeah, I'm fired," Phil cut him off, his smile proud. "What do ya think, I didn't see that coming? I am psychic, y'know."

~ Fortune Cookies ~

Phillip Hammel's happiness faded slightly when he took a gulp of lukewarm coffee. Swallowing the mouthful, he tossed his gaze at the microwave. He had it down to a science – Exactly 51 seconds in the company microwave would warm his half-cup of coffee to perfection.

As Phil lifted himself off the chair, line number one of the multiline phone system rang, with its red light flashing insistently. Sitting back down, he stared intently at the blinking light, concentrating on it for a moment before answering the call. *Nope*, he thought, *no idea*. Picking it up, he proclaimed, "Citywide Alarm."

"Hello, this is Monica from Zazzy Shoes. We have an alarm going off and my code's not shutting this infernal thing up!"

Phil looked at the computer screen to his right. "Oh yes, there you are. The South Rear door is open."

"Yes," Monica yelled, "I know that! I can't get my code to work!"

"Hang on," he said as he keyed up the records for Zazzy Shoes. After hitting a few buttons on the keyboard, the light flickered off. Within the second, the alarm stopped screaming through the phone.

"Thank you," she breathed. "Jeez, I hate that sound. It's like a million birds attacking my brain."

"Well, I've never heard it put quite that way before. So, other than evil alarms, how are you today, Shoe Queen?"

"Oh, Phil, it's you! Sorry, I couldn't tell, what with that thing blaring at me. Anyway, hi. I'm fine, now. I won't be needing any coffee to perk me up, that's for sure. Nothing beats an adrenaline shot to start your day ... er, night, I mean!" She paused to laugh, then added, "And how about you, Phil?"

He took another slug of even cooler coffee and winced slightly. "I'm good but I need the coffee, that's for sure. So Monica, yet another late night at the ol' shoe store, eh?"

She let out an exaggerated sigh. "Oh, y'know. Owning a business can be downright revolting some days. I still have to reconcile AP and AR, finish up sales taxes, and... well, some other things I've already forgotten."

"Sounds like fun."

"Hardly. No time for a social life, that's for sure. So, how's the 'saving the world' business coming along?"

"Well, tonight's been utterly boring. But other than –"

Here we go again, Phil thought, as a series of images attacked his brain like... *like a million birds... not a bad analogy.* "Sorry Mon, gotta cut this short! I just got a vision!"

"Off to save another life, are you?"

"A psychic's work is never done! Bye," he said as he hung up.

He left his hand on the receiver, picking it up as the ringing started. "Get out of there, now!" he shouted.

"What?! I'm just having trouble setting –"

"No," he said forcefully, "there's someone breaking in through your East entrance. He has a knife and is high on something. You need to leave through the front door now. Understand?"

"Uh, wha –"

"Go! I'll call the police. Go now!"

"Okay," the caller agreed and hung up the phone.

Phil disconnected and quickly contacted the police. Then he sat back, breathed a huge sigh, and polished off his now-cold coffee. Even the shock of chilly coffee could not squelch his internal satisfaction.

Phillip Hammel liked this job at the alarm company infinitely more than his last gig, as the only true psychic at The Psychic Buddies Network. Being the only clairvoyant at a company full of alleged psychics always gave him a chuckle. He felt great satisfaction when the entire psychic telephone network phase fizzled out shortly after his departure. *Funny how they never saw it coming*, he thought with a grin.

Not long afterward, Phil landed a great job for someone with his unique abilities. Working the overnight shift at an alarm company, he enjoyed being the man on the front line, keeping the good people safe. About the only thing he would change, if he had the power, would be to see how everything worked out. Like an Emergency Room doctor, he only saw people at their worst, never receiving a return visit to witness a healthy patient. Did the man he just spoke with get out okay? Will the cops arrest the intruder? Just once, he wished he knew.

Over the years, he had tried to figure out exactly how his psychic ability worked. He was fairly accurate but totally random, with the one true constant of his powers being that he never saw anything of his own future.

Staring at the formerly blinking line, he thought about Monica, working another late night at the shoe store. He wondered if she ever thought about him, or was he just the guy who stopped her alarms? That south door sure gave her a lot of problems, but he thought it a blessing. It gave them a reason, over these past several months, to talk.

When the subject of his abilities came up, she was one of only a few people who did not think him a total nut job. Even though he had no idea what she looked like, Phil sure enjoyed the sound of her voice.

Lin Chen sat in the back room of her family restaurant, Chen China, staring at her computer screen. She had the *Fortune Cookie Wisdom* program running and had her finger on the key to print out a bunch of random, hokey, insultingly stereotypical messages to add to her father's freshly baked fortune cookies. Instead, a mischievous grin curled her lips. She switched away from the pre-created fortune screen, and entered the *Create Your Own* section. She typed, "This is the day everything changes! Seize this day or you will regret it forever!" and hit the save button.

Lin looked at that one fortune and kept grinning. Her fingers landed on the keys and she just started typing. "She is the one for you. You need to stop hesitating and call her now!"

Typing faster and faster, the words flowed through her, as if her ancestors were whispering them directly into her brain.

When she had a page completed, she hit the print button and out popped thirty of the most unique fortunes ever created. With the paper still warm, she grabbed the page and turned it over, sliding it back into the printer to begin the process again. Once completed, Lin snatched the double-sided fortune page and began detaching the small slips of paper and adding them to the cookies.

The next morning, Tu Chen glared at his daughter, catching Lin in the middle of a large yawn. "Look sharp, child. The lunch rush is about to begin." He accentuated the comment with a quick tap to the back of her head. It made the muscles in her shoulders and neck tighten up, just like it always did.

"Sorry, Father," she replied meekly, "I was up late with the fortunes."

"Bah," he spewed, "Americans and their fortune cookies! A sacred art turned into an after-dinner lottery number and a vague platitude."

Smiling a satisfied smile, Lin peered into the basket that held the cookies. She grabbed the container with yesterday's remaining cookies and dumped them into the new ones. Gently shaking the container, she mixed them around until she had no idea which ones were which. She attempted to stifle a chuckle, but her father heard her. He gave her a curt look but said nothing.

Lin sat looking across the mostly empty restaurant, her elbows on the counter while her hands cupped her cheeks. *Some lunch rush*, she thought as she observed a man wearing a downtrodden look that fit him as poorly as did his navy blue three-piece suit. He had only eaten part of his Peking Duck, stirring the remainder around his plate with a chopstick while staring at it, but clearly not seeing it.

Her mischievous smile crept back onto her face. *If anyone needed a fortune,* thought the young woman, *it was this guy.* She hoisted the basket and walked over to his table.

"As is our tradition here at Chen China," Lin lied, "we would like to offer you your choice of fortune cookies." With that, she placed the basket in front of him.

"Oh, well, I don't really eat sweets," he said softly.

Winking, she picked up the basket and shook it enough to make some noise. "It's not about the sweets. Trust me."

The customer stifled a sigh, smiled weakly, and pulled one from the edge of the basket. Setting the bill down on the table, Lin left with her fortune basket.

Cracking the cookie open, he pulled out the small piece of paper and read it as he nibbled on a shard of cookie.

The businessman looked up at Lin with a look of complete disbelief. In one quick motion, he yanked off his tie, stood up, wadded it into a tight ball, and threw it on the table. After tossing an extra couple bucks on top of the tie, he gave the young woman a quick glance and whispered, "Thank you." With a joyous smile, he dashed out the door. Lin heard him yell at the top of his lungs, "I'm opening a book store!"

After the door swung shut, Lin picked up the fortune he left on the table. It read: *You hate your job. You know this. So why are you torturing yourself? You know what you want to do with your life. Follow your bliss!*

She smiled as she cleaned up the table.

As people slowly filtered in for lunch, she gave out several more cookies. Having no idea which cookies had the special fortunes, she could only study the looks on their faces. The regular ones brought about the usual responses, ranging from mild entertainment to complete lack of interest. However, when customers happened upon one of her distinctive fortunes, the results were immediate and obvious. One woman openly wept. An older gentleman jumped up and bolted from the restaurant, the money for his meal tossed in the air behind him as an afterthought. Another man let loose with a primal scream, startling everyone.

Through the course of the day, Mr. Chen stood in the kitchen, looking out at the customers with pursed lips and a furrowed brow. "Bah! Crazy Americans."

At nearly two o'clock in the morning, Phil sat in front of the company computer, about to win yet another game of Spider Solitaire, when he felt another mental blast. It had an odd feeling of familiarity, and that bothered him. He saw as the robbers broke into the store, grabbed some jewelry, and quickly bolted. Looking up, he stared at the master control panel, trying to figure out which one would start to blink and how soon.

This was the third time Phil had felt this particular trio of thieves. The first time, he got the flash as it was happening, whereas the second time, he barely got the images in his brain before the alarms started going off. This time, he mused, perhaps he was more in-tune with the trio... *The Trio...* he thought, *is that what they call themselves?*

Phil grabbed the phone and hit the button marked POLICE. Maybe this time the cops could catch them. A woman with a strong voice answered. "Markay Police, Sargent Milner speaking."

"Yes, this is Phillip Hammel from Citywide Alarm. There's a break-in at a jewelry store in town."

"I understand, sir. Which store?"

Phil hesitated for a moment, started to say, "I'm not exactly –" then fortunately, an *Open Door* alarm light flashed on the screen. "It's Wissner's Jewelers, 12287 Elm."

The next afternoon, when Chen China opened for business, Tu looked at his daughter and said, "I believe I understand what went on here yesterday, child."

Her eyes expanded. "You do?" she asked nervously.

"There was a full moon last night. People act... unpredictably during the full moon."

"Oh," she sighed. "Sure, Father. That must be it." She wondered if she should tell him the truth. Though a deeply spiritual man, she doubted he would understand. Of course, Lin did not fathom it herself. Perhaps an all-knowing power briefly possessed her.

When the front door opened, she announced, "Oh, our first customers," partly to change the subject.

"I can see that." Tu swatted the back of her head. "Look sharp, child."

She tensed up, saying nothing.

"I hope everything was to your liking," Lin said to the young couple after they finished eating.

The man, a sharp dressed fellow with dark hair and a slightly nervous look, began to speak. "It was –"

His dining partner interrupted him. "Actually," the heavy-set woman with long, blonde hair said sharply, "the Moo Goo Gai Pan wasn't spicy enough for my taste and the Hot and Sour soup was too spicy. But still, it was adequate."

Smiling and nodding, the man added meekly, "Mine was good. Thank you."

Lin returned his smile and set the bill on the table, followed by two fortune cookies on a plate. Quickly, the woman snatched one and set it unopened on the table, so her dining partner carefully plucked the remaining cookie and cracked it open.

Upon reading his fortune, his eyes got wide and a puzzled smirk crept upon his face.

The portly woman, too busy eating the man's cookie pieces to open her own, noticed his bewildered countenance, and blurted, "What?!"

"Um..." He looked incredulously at Lin. Having no idea what the fortune said, she just smiled pleasantly and shrugged. "Well Charlene, this is our fourth date, right? I don't know much about your past. Tell me about...your last boyfriend."

She stared at him for a moment as her hand absent-mindedly began fondling the knife next to her. "Oh, that bastard! He had no right! We were together for five wonderful months, and then suddenly, without warning, he gets a restraining order against me! ME!!" As she continued, the knife became her pointer, accentuating the mounting tirade. "Oh, but he still got his, that's for sure!"

Lin, sensing trouble, came over to the man and said, "Excuse me sir, but there's a call for you, on the phone in the back. Come with me, please."

"What?! He has a cell phone, y'know," the woman yelled.

"Oh, um," the man said as he fumbled it out of his pocket, "it's off, see? I didn't want to disturb you... us, us I mean, during lunch. It... it must be very important, from the office, y'know. Hang on," he added as he held up one finger and forced a weak smile. "The phone's this way, you say?"

Once out of sight in the back, Lin pointed toward the back exit. "There's your way out. Hurry!"

"B...but," he stammered, "how could you –"

"No time... Hell, no idea, honestly. Just take your fortune, count your blessings, and bolt, man! Run from that crazy broad!"

"All right, thanks!" With that, he shot out the door. Exhaling heavily, he felt relieved at the fact he had never invited her back to his house. He realized that he just might be able to make a clean break.

By the time Lin got back to the counter, the woman had stood up, still breathing hard but beginning to calm down. Lin came around the counter and quickly cleaned up the table, making sure to grab the knife away as casually as possible. Using the knife as a pointer herself, she gestured at the woman's cookie. "Did you check your fortune yet?"

"What? No! Why would I? Stupid thing," she said as she drove her fist onto the cookie, shattering it. She pulled out the slip and read it aloud. *"You must seek professional help! People aren't meant to be unhappy all the time.* What the hell is this crap? Professional help?!"

"I think you should leave now," Mr. Chen said firmly. "Take your *bland* Moo Goo Gai Pan and go."

"I'm not leaving without Terrence! Where is he?"

"He's gone," Lin said quietly.

"He's what?!" She bolted up and started screaming, "Terrence! Terrence!"

Tu walked right up to her, putting his face inches from hers, and said very softly, "You leave. Now."

She pulled her head back, snorted, and stormed out.

Attempting to smile, Lin said, "Wow, that was very –"

Reaching down, Mr. Chen picked up the fortune that the scared man left behind, and read it aloud. *"She is not right for you. In fact, staying is extremely hazardous. Run for your life!"* He flipped the slip over and continued reading. *"Ask her about her last boyfriend.* Lin, where did this horrible fortune come from?"

"Oh, that? Well, funny story –"

The old man glowered at her. "You made these, didn't you? This is why everyone has been acting so strange, isn't it?"

Lin lowered her gaze to the floor. "Yes, Father. I don't know what came over me."

Walking toward the counter, he paused to smack her, a bit harder than usual, on the back of her head. Then, he took his fist and slammed it into the basket a few times, crushing the cookies. "Never do this again, child. You do not need to incite these people. Americans are crazy enough without your involvement."

Rubbing the back of her head she said, "Yes, Father."

After Tu went into the back, Lin walked over to the basket. Father had ground most of the cookies into jagged shards. However, two survived the onslaught. She quickly pocketed them and emptied the rest of the basket into the trash.

While at work the next night, Phil received a new flash about another robbery. *The Trio. They definitely called themselves that,* Phil realized. This time, he knew where they planned to hit and even had some time before it happened. However, Phil had a problem. This company was not a Citywide Alarm client. He had no button to hit, no name on file to call!

Frantically, he pulled out the local phone book and flipped through its pages until a name matched his vision. This time, it was a bar and restaurant called Buddy's on Pelson Street, the next block over from the street where they hit the jewelry store. Picking up the phone, Phil dialed the number.

"Buddy's," the harsh-sounding man said over the phone.

"Look, um, this is going to sound strange, but I'm Phil from Citywide Alarm. I know we don't service your business, but –"

"Oh, good lord," he shouted, "we're closed, you moron, and you're trying to sell me your services? Sheesh!"

"No! You're going to be robbed tonight."

"Excuse me? You threatenin' me, boy?"

"What? No, no. I'm… we've received reports of prowlers in the area, and –"

The man snorted into the phone, yelled, "Real funny, jerk!" and promptly hung up.

After that pleasant exchange, Phil dialed the police, figuring to report a tip regarding the robbery. "Markay Police, Sargent Milner speaking."

"Yes, this is Ph… Um, a concerned citizen. There's a break-in at Buddy's Pub in town," and quickly hung up.

Phil let out a heavy breath, said, "Well, I tried," to no one, and resumed his game of Spider Solitaire.

Hours after his shift ended, Phil lie sleeping in bed, dreaming of thieves. Someone started beating on his apartment door like it was a bass drum. Crawling out of bed, he tossed his robe on and trudged toward the door. "I hear ya already," he yelled sleepily at the closed door, "What?!"

"Phillip Hammel?"

"Yeah?"

"Markay Police."

"Oh," he said as he pulled the door open. "Come in."

The two officers, a man and woman in full Markay Police uniforms, quickly stepped inside the small, cluttered apartment. The man stood at least a full foot taller than Phil's five-foot-six frame and had that bald, clean-shaven look popular among men who have already lost most of their hair. The woman also had a couple-inch height advantage on Phil, but at least she did not tower over him, and she had a full head of espresso brown hair. They both had rigid looks on their faces, like people who assume the worst in everyone.

The man smoothed his hand across his cranium before saying, "Mr. Hammel, I am Detective Savage and this is Sargent Milner."

"We spoke last night," the female officer added, "when you called in the robbery."

"Oh, of course," Phil said as his eyes perked open a bit. "Did you catch them?"

"No," Savage said sharply, "and that's why we're here. According to the time of the report, Mr. Hammel, you phoned in twenty minutes before the break-in occurred. Now, how exactly is this possible?"

"Well... Okay, you'll probably want to sit down for this one," Phil said shyly as he gestured toward the couch.

"It's okay, Phil," replied Milner with a slightly friendlier tone than her counterpart, "just tell us what you're mixed up in."

"Um... mixed up in? No no, see, I'm... well, I'm kinda psychic. I get these flashes, see –"

"Psychic?!" The detective said with a snort. "So, what, you saw the crime in your mind and called us before it actually happened? Do you really expect us to believe this?"

Why should you? Phil thought. *No one ever does.* "Look officers, I don't pretend to understand any of this myself. It just happens. I see things, y'know?"

"Oh yeah, Mr. Psychic," Detective Savage said with a smirk, and Phil had been waiting for this, "so tell me, what am I thinking?"

"That I'm a lying sack of crap. That there's no such thing as psychics. And yes," he added, "that was a lucky guess, since my abilities or whatever you call them don't work that way. I get flashes in my head that warn me about the occasional circumstance before it happens. I wish I understood it or could control it, but I can't."

Sargent Milner sidled over to Phil and then began leading him toward the couch. "Phil, have a seat." Once he did so, she sat next to him and continued, "The way we see it, you were probably part of this group, but then they cut you loose for some reason. This is your way of exacting revenge." She smiled her best sympathetic smile and asked, "Isn't that right, Phil?"

"What?" Phil had barely sat down before he leapt to his feet. "No, that's nuts! I'm no thief!"

"You wouldn't need to be, Hammel," said Savage gruffly. "You'd be the guy at the alarm company with the fingers on the button, cutting the alarms and giving them access."

At that comment, Phil breathed a sigh of relief. "There's a problem with that theory, Officers. I've called in every one of the burglaries the moment they've happened, if not sooner. The last one wasn't even one of our companies. And the kicker? The alarms all went off! If I were doing as you'd suggested I would've turned off the alarms before the robberies took place. I wouldn't wait until they went off, now would I? I'd give my people as much time as I could."

At that, Milner stood up and walked back to where her partner stood. "Just understand that we're watching you, Phil."

"Uh-huh," Phil responded, adding, "Oh, and watch out for the rug," moments before Savage caught the edge of the area rug and nearly tumbled to the ground. He turned and stared daggers at Phil, who responded with a shrug and a smirk.

It was late afternoon, around an hour before Phil's workday began. He stood over the sink, eating a breakfast of Lucky Charms straight out of the box. Chewing on his third handful, another intense flash of insight smacked his brain. It hit him so hard that he chomped into his tongue.

He saw The Trio breaking into their latest victim's establishment. However, this time things go horribly wrong. While breaking in to a restaurant, the owner catches them but takes a crowbar to the head, killing him instantly. When his daughter comes down to investigate, one of The Trio shoots her through the heart.

This time, Phil recognized the business, having eaten there a few times. He also knew when it would happen. The only problem was he had no idea what to do about it. Instinctively he picked up the phone, but set it back down when he thought the calls through to their logical conclusion. He doubted the police would believe him and the old man would think him insane.

Therefore, he did the only thing he could think of, as foolish as he knew it would be.

Lin stood over a table, wiping up a small puddle of soy sauce and pocketing a measly tip, when Phil came bursting in to the restaurant. The man's wild-eyed look startled the young woman. Taking a couple fast steps inside, he then paused to compose himself.

Lin walked up to him and forced herself to smile pleasantly. "Hi, welcome to Chen China. Is it just you this evening?"

"What?" Phil, who still had no actual plan, took a deep breath and said, "Um, yeah, just me. How 'bout that table in the corner?" he asked with a jab of his finger.

"Yes, sir," she said politely but wearily, sitting him down and handing him a menu.

Phil glanced at it absent-mindedly, having no intention to order any food until he realized he barely ate any of those Lucky Charms. "The Cashew Chicken looks good," he said. As she turned to leave, he reached out and lightly touched her arm. "Um, can you hang on a sec?"

She pulled her arm away, but stood still. "Okay. You seem a bit… agitated. Is everything okay, sir?"

He sighed heavily, thinking, *God, how I hate having to do this!* "First off, my name is Phillip Hammel. I work for…" he paused to think. "That's right. I work for your alarm company, Citywide Alarm. I work the overnight shift."

She smiled amicably. "Well, it's nice to meet you, Phil. Shall I get your order going?"

"No, um…" he paused, and then simply decided to blurt it out. *Maybe she'll call the police on me. At least that'd get 'em here.* "Okay, I realize you won't believe me, since no one ever does, but I'm psychic. I've been seeing events before they happen since I was a child. I hate it. I wish I could turn it off. But it's not in my control. Bottom line is, have you been hearing about the robberies that have occurred around town the past few days?"

"No, I haven't. Robberies?"

"Yes," he replied as he picked up a napkin to wipe the sweat beading on his forehead. "Local establishments, a jewelry store, a bar. Yours is next. Tonight."

"Excuse me?" She took an instinctive step back.

"Tonight," he repeated louder. "And it gets worse. I saw... You and your father…"

"Me and my father what?"

"Your father … he surprises The Trio and … you're both killed. I saw it clearly. Your father was brandishing a medieval-looking sword, kinda like a Samurai sword but not. A curved blade, like … a pirate might carry. Ornate handle with jewels, but it's … orange … I'm seeing orange on the blade."

Moments before, anger had flowed through Lin with enough force for her to contemplate smashing a chair over Phil's head. However, after hearing his words, her shoulders slumped.

She knew the sword. It was an Arabian sword, not a Samurai as one might expect. As a child, she spilled orange paint on it. Her father was furious. He ordered her to clean it, but she stood defiant. After punishing her for her disobedience, he left the paint on the blade as a reminder of her shame. "The sword," she said slowly, "is locked away in a cabinet. I don't have the key and I haven't seen Father bring it out in years." She walked over to the table and sat down across from him. "How can you know this?" Even before she asked this, she somehow already knew the answer. Before her own fortune cookie incident, she never believed in this psychic nonsense. She had a different understanding now.

"I just do, Lin. And before you ask, I know your name because it's on your name badge."

A grin flickered briefly across her façade and faded as quickly. "Okay then, what shall we do? Have you alerted the police?"

"I've tried that. You can guess how that went down. Although I have an idea that might work, and would keep both of you out of danger."

Phil's watch chimed 2:00am, several hours after he called work, feigning illness. In about fifteen minutes, The Trio would arrive. Phil walked up to the rear entrance of Chen China and pulled out an aluminum baseball bat. Taking aim, he began beating on the steel garbage can in the alley. Then, he smacked the dumpster, the wall, the door, anything that made noise. To add to the cacophony, he yelled obscenities into the alley, echoing noise through the calm of the night.

Phil ran around the corner just as Mr. Chen opened the door, screaming, "You hooligans! I've called the police! They'll be here in…"

"…Fifteen minutes," Phil whispered in unison with the old man's rant.

The next evening, Phil sat in the same corner booth at Chen China, dining on Cashew Chicken and grinning happily. Lin stood at the head of the table, equally joyous. "The Trio showed up just moments before the police. They had their tools out and had just picked the lock. I did as you suggested, and took Father upstairs to our apartment above the store, so he wouldn't be down there when they broke in. You couldn't have planned it any better, Phil!"

244

"I'm glad it worked out so well," he replied through a bite of food. "It hasn't always."

Lin started to speak when she felt a rap on the back of her head. Flinching, she turned to see her father with his usual stern look. "Why you standing around gossiping? Table seven needs water!"

Reaching into her apron pocket, she removed the last two fortune cookies she had saved from her father's destructive hand. Without looking at them, she set one down in front of Phil, winked, then broke open the other one and handed the fortune to her father. *Tell your daughter you love her and are proud of her,* it read, *and for goodness sake, stop hitting her on the back of the head! She's a competent adult now, no longer your unruly child. Show her the respect she always shows you.*

He stared at it for a while before leveling his gaze on his daughter. A small tear formed in his eye as he said softly, "Oh child, I *am* proud of you. Surely you know this." With that, he walked over and gave her a hug, something he had rarely done before. Lin had a tear as well, until he reached up and lightly patted her head again. "But daughter," he said with a mischievous grin, "I will always do this. It's affection. Surely you knew that after all these years."

She chuckled. "Sure, Father. Affection."

Phil suppressed a smile as he looked at his own Fortune Cookie. Cracking it open, he read it aloud. "*She does feel the same way. Stop hiding your heart. You've been alone long enough. It's time to embrace love. Call her.*" He stared at it and said, "Huh. I wonder if it means who I think it means. Problem is I don't have her home number. It's programmed into the computer at work. And heck, I have no idea what she even looks like."

Turning the fortune slip over, it read: *Today's lucky number – 6, 9, 22, 39, 44, 57.* He noticed that it had *lucky number* not *numbers.* Something else caught his eye, as he stared at the numbers. The first three digits were this city's area code, 692. *The rest... could it be?* He shrugged, pulled out his cell phone, and dialed the numbers.

Within seconds, another cell phone rang at a table on the other side of the crowded restaurant. "Hello?" he heard, both on the phone and in the room.

"Um, hi," he said softly, "I don't suppose this is Monica, from Zazzy Shoes?"

"Yeah, who is…is this Phil? How did you –" She stopped when she turned to see a man in a crumpled overcoat standing at her table, with a cell phone in one hand and a fortune in the other.

"Always trust the fortune cookie, Monica," he said with a large grin, "Always."

~ Family Business ~

13-year-old Phillip Hammel stands in front of his 8th grade Literature class, reciting the poem he chose for his oral presentation, the Ernest Thayer classic *Casey at the Bat*. "Responding to the cheers, he lightly doffed his hat. No stranger in..."

Stopping in mid-sentence with a blank, faraway gaze, Phil appears to be staring at the far wall, but that is not what he sees.

His mind is no longer in the classroom, and he does not hear the chuckles of his classmates. Instead, he is watching a short, balding man in a standoff with police. Though he has not seen his father in many years, he instinctively recognizes him.

This vision encompasses and overwhelms all of his senses. Standing wide-eyed and helpless, he finds himself in a bank in some faraway city watching his dad as police enter the building.

Shifting the aim of his gun between a terrified teller and the stoic bank manager, Nelson Hammel has a powerful anger coursing through him. Phil feels this seething rage as if it is inside himself. The angry man spins toward the line of cops as he begins to speak.

As if reciting a new speech that suddenly formed in his head, Phil yells these words to his class. "This bank has wronged me! Everyone in this building will pay. And if you cops stand in my way, you too will pay the price."

Then, as if he's narrating a book on tape, Phil speaks as the cop. "Stand down. Drop your weapon or we will open fire. This is your last warning."

Again, Phillip utters the words of his father. "Get outta my way, cops! This doesn't concern you." Then Phil watches helplessly as his father lifts his revolver and shoots, aiming just over the policeman's right shoulder. The dust from the drywall flakes onto the officer's shoulder.

The bullets fly and Nelson Hammel crumples to the ground. Phil also falls to the tiled floor of his classroom, clutching his chest where the bullets struck his father's body. After a moment, as the hushed whispers and chuckles begin again, he looks up and sighs loudly. "He's dead."

The skinny, bearded teacher walks up to Phil, kneels down beside him, and rests his hand gently on his shoulder. Speaking softly he says, "Well, that was… dramatic. However, *Casey at the Bat* does not end that way. He didn't die; he only stuck out. The next time you forget the words, don't wing it. Go sit down, Phil."

Though Phil wants to head directly to the principal's office, to save them the trouble of coming to him, he does as instructed.

After several other students recite their poems to the class, the door to the classroom creaks open. Principal George, a pudgy man in a suit one size too small, pops his head in. "Sorry for the interruption, Mr. Skipinson. Phil Hammel, could you come with me, please?"

Before the students in the room can react, Phil says softly, "My dad's dead, right?"

"Uh… son, let's talk about this outside."

"Just say it!" Phil screams.

The principal lowers his head. "Yes, Phil. He is."

The students gasp as one.

Phil jolted awake. Sweat poured down his forehead as he sat up in bed.

"Honey," whispered Monica, "did you dream about your dad again?"

Nodding slowly, Phil waited for his breathing to calm before he could answer her verbally. "I don't understand why I keep reliving that moment. It happened so long ago."

Monica reached up and clicked on the bedroom lamp, causing them both to squint at the intrusion of light. "Have you been thinking about him lately?"

"No, not at all. I haven't thought about him… in a long time. Years."

Resting her hand on Phil's shoulder she said, "You've never told me anything about him. I don't even know his name, what he did, where he lived. All I know is what you've told me about his last moments of life."

Phil released a heavy sigh. "His name was Nelson. He was shot dead in a bank when I was 13. Now you know pretty much everything I know." He slumped back onto his pillow.

"Oh Phil. Why don't you want to talk about him?"

Rolling over to face her, he spoke more loudly than he intended. "I didn't know the man! He left my mom when I was in kindergarten. I have practically zero memories of him. He abandoned me before I had the chance to form any lasting impressions. That horrible image of him being gunned down by cops is pretty much the extent of it." He paused as he sat up, shoving the pillow behind his lower back. "You don't understand what that vision did to me, Monica. That moment ruined my life for years afterward."

Monica crinkled her forehead. "What do you mean?"

"After I had the vision in my class, everyone thought I was either a nutcase or a messiah. And I mean everyone – students, teachers, the principal, even the custodians. Kids would either avoid me like I had the Black Death, or they would hound me for the answers to an upcoming test. The security guard once pulled me aside and insisted I tell him the next day's lottery numbers. I got beat up all the time, and not just by the kids."

"My goodness Phil, that's so horrible!" Monica reached over and gently caressed his arm.

"Tell me about it. So when it comes to my dear old dad, I know nothing about him, and I want to know even less." Tossing his feet off the bed, Phil stood up and grabbed his yellow robe off the hook.

Monica climbed out of bed as well and faced Phil. "But the question remains, why have you been having this recurring vision, or dream, or whatever? Clearly there's something in your psyche or something… I dunno, otherworldly I suppose, that is trying to get your attention. I really think you need to find out more about your dad." When she saw the angered look on his face, she smiled sympathetically. "Or don't, and keep reliving that afternoon each night. It's your choice."

Phil glowered at her. He loved Monica, though he hadn't found the courage to express it to her in so many words. So often, her wisdom had helped him through some trying times, and she had done an amazing job at assisting him in understanding some of his more esoteric visions. Still, he wanted so badly to remain adamant in his resolve. Even though that man was half the reason for Phil's being born, he abandoned him and his mom. Nelson Hammel did not deserve his understanding.

However, he really needed this vision to go away so he could enjoy sleeping again. Phil let out a long, exaggerated sigh when he realized his next move. "Well then my dear, I guess you get to meet my mother."

In the morning, Phil gave Lois Hammel a call and set up a long-overdue road trip to visit her, and for her to meet his beloved. They headed out just after sunrise.

Monica looked radiant in her pink dress, and she acted giddy, like a child heading to Cedar Point. "So, give me some pointers on what to say and what not to say to her. Do I call her Mom or Mother?" She chuckled loudly.

Phil tried to stifle his sigh, but a small amount slipped out so she added, "What's wrong? I know you haven't seen her in a while, but it's your mom! Aren't you excited to see her?"

"Monica," he started, but trailed off. He wanted to express this in a much nicer way, but better words eluded him. "You can probably already guess I didn't have the most normal of childhoods. When I was around seven, or maybe even younger, I started having these... little snippets of events, like memories, but things I hadn't experienced."

Removing a breakfast bar from her pocket, Monica unwrapped it but before taking a bite, she replied, "That must've been fascinating."

Phil shook his head vehemently. "Not in the least. It ranged from scary to creepy to bizarre. Back then, I would sometimes have visions of my own life. Before my daddy vision in Lit class, I'd already seen the A+ I would receive in that class, just as I saw Marcus Widmore beat the crap outta me at recess weeks before he did it. I had no idea why I'd be having these memories of events that hadn't occurred yet, and I had no one I could talk to about them. So I spent a lot of my early life confused and frightened."

Swallowing the bite, Monica asked, "Did you tell your mom about your visions?"

"At first I did, but she vacillated between not believing me, like with what happened during my eleventh birthday, and thinking of me as a possessed devil child. That vision of my father's death, for instance, was a devil-child moment. I learned pretty quickly not to talk about what I saw, with her or anybody."

Monica looked at Phil with sadness. "That's awful." Pausing for a moment to take another bite of the bar, she added, "So, I have to ask, what happened at on your birthday?"

"I had a vision, of course. I clearly saw the present she had bought me, except it was weeks before my birthday, and she apparently hadn't even purchased it yet. I kept seeing myself playing with the Atari video game system, laughing as I shot the space invaders out of the sky. When the big day came, I pointed at the wrapped package and said,

'Thanks for the Atari!' Oh, she got so mad at me because she assumed I snuck into her bedroom and found it. To punish me, she took the present away and never gave it to me. I tried to explain it to her, but that was one of the times she assumed I was lying."

"Oh my!" Monica wrapped up the rest of the bar and put it in her purse. "I'm so sorry."

"It was a turning point for me. I stopped confiding in her. I withdrew from her, into my own shell. That was when I stopped having prophecies of my own life, and I didn't tell people about my other visions." After a pause he added quietly, "In fact, I've never told anyone that story about my father, other than my mom."

"And me," Monica said softly.

Offering her a slight smile he replied, "And you. Well, the entire school found out about it because my classmates started blabbing."

She reached over and gave him a quick kiss on the cheek. "I'm honored that you told me. Truly I am."

"Thank you." Pointing to a white ranch-style house with faded black shutters and overgrown weeds filling the yard, he added, "We're here. And don't call her Mom. Lois will suffice."

Phil pulled up in front of the house, parking a few feet behind the mailbox. Though Monica wanted to ask why he didn't pull into the driveway, she kept the question internal.

After he shut off the engine, Phil sat there for a minute, staring blankly out the window with both hands tightly gripping the steering wheel. While he had so many questions he needed to ask, and so many pent-up comments he wanted to say or even scream, he wanted no part of this. Had Monica not been seated next to him, with her worried yet supportive expression and hopeful eyes, he would've slammed the car into drive and sped away.

Instead, he turned to her, offered his best fake smile, nodded faintly, and opened the car door.

Those several feet from the car to the front door took forever, yet were over before he realized it. Phil took a deep breath, exhaled it slowly, and rang the doorbell.

After a pause that lasted long enough for Phil to contemplate turning around and leaving, the door opened a crack. "Hello?" asked the woman from the inside, her blue eye framed by deep wrinkles.

"Hi Mom. It's Phil. Your son." As he uttered the last two words, he felt foolish even thinking he'd have to say it.

"Phil? Oh my God! Phil!" And then she slammed the door.

Turning to Monica, he said, "Well. Should we –"

The sound of jingling metal and the swinging open of the door made him realize she had to remove the safety chain first. Once Lois pulled the door open, she stood there with a puzzled yet intrigued look on her face, as if she was not sure what to do next.

The last time Phil saw her, she wore her blonde hair long, past her shoulders. Now, it sat tightly cropped on her head like a greying platinum bowl. He thought about complimenting her hairstyle but before he had a chance, she reached out and gave him a tentative, stiff hug, which he did not reciprocate. "Come in, come in!" she said as she turned and walked into her house. Phil stepped in, reached back, and grabbed Monica's hand to guide her inside.

Lois Hammel's home was a dichotomy of order and chaos. While the house had a neat and tidy appearance, even the most cursory glance pointed out the layers of dust that covered the plethora of knick-knacks placed on every flat surface.

Sitting in a wooden rocking chair, Lois pointed to the well-worn love seat. "Sit, sit." While they did as instructed, she added, "So, are you going to introduce me to this gorgeous woman?"

Phil formed the slightest blush to his cheeks. "This is Monica."

"Hi Mrs. Hammel," Monica said as she offered her hand, "it's nice to meet you. You have a lovely home." Glancing around, she added, "I like your figurines."

"I've been collecting them since Phil was a boy." Reaching out, she picked up a ceramic duck. "Phil, do you remember getting me this for Christmas? I so cherish it."

"No, but I do remember not getting that Atari for my birthday."

Mrs. Hammel's face formed a scowl. "We both know why that happened. I would not reward your snooping in my room."

"Mom, we've been over this. I wasn't snooping! I had a... vision."

Instead of responding to Phil's comment, she said, "So when's the big day?"

Phil's brow formed a beep furrow. "What?"

"I haven't seen you in nearly seven years. You call out of the blue, then show up holding hands with a beautiful woman. So she's either pregnant or you're getting married. Either way, when's the big day?"

Turning to Phil, Monica said, "At least I see where you get it from," adding a nudge to the ribcage.

"What? What are you... what are you both... no! No married, no pregnant, no... whatever you just said to me, Monica. Mom, look. The reason we're here is I need to know about Dad."

Lois's face twisted into a scowl. "Oh. I see. You cut me out of your life years ago and you come back for the sole purpose of asking about that deadbeat son of a bitch. He was a horrible man who left me in my prime and you at your most vulnerable. He did Lord knows what in that time and then was killed while robbing a bank. What more do you need to know?"

"Mom, he wasn't robbing that bank."

"Oh, and how do you know, Mr. Smarty pants? Were you there?"

His gaze dropped to the carpet. "In a manner of speaking, yes."

Standing up, Lois took a couple steps toward them. "You are not going to come here and talk about those damn daydreams of yours. I will not have it."

At this moment, Monica felt the need to interject. "Mrs. Hammel, I've seen firsthand how often your son's visions come true. He saved my life and the lives of many other people. There are scores of people who would happily come forward to sing Phil's virtues."

Lois's scowl etched deeper into her forehead. "I don't care how many of your friends believe his parlor tricks and lies. And if he actually does see things it's the devil's work, pure and simple."

As Monica opened her mouth to speak, Phil lightly touched her arm. "Okay fine, Mom. Parlor tricks and lies. Whatever helps you to sleep at night. I'm only here to get any information you can tell me about your former husband. Where he grew up, went to school, his last known address, relatives. Give me anything you've got and we'll take my devil's work and vacate your life. I'll even take the name of the bank he was... robbing. Whatever you got."

Exhaling heavily, she replied, "I don't have any of that stuff. Why don't you just ask your grandfather? He probably knows, if he's still lucid."

Unable to speak, Phil's mouth literally hung open. Monica looked over at him and couldn't suppress a breathy, tiny chuckle. In her mind, he resembled a cartoon character. "Are you okay?" she asked.

"My... grandfather? My grandfather!?" He bolted to his feet. "I have a grandfather?"

Lois replied with a snort, "Well yes, of course you do. Everybody has grandfathers."

"You've never, *never* mentioned I had a grandfather," Phil said through gritted teeth.

Shaking her head vehemently, she replied, "I'm sure I did at some point."

"No," Phil shouted, "you never told me about any grandfather! I just assumed he died. Or did you actually tell me he died? I wouldn't be surprised."

"Oh now, why would I do that?" Lois folded her arms tightly across her chest.

"Why do you do anything? So what is his name? Where does he live? Is this your dad or Nelson's dad?"

Mrs. Hammel sighed. "His name is Christopher Hammel. He's on your father's side. I haven't really kept in touch with him. Last I knew he was in an assisted living facility up state somewhere. Happy something. Acres, I think. Hold on," she said tersely as she left the room.

Standing and facing Phil, whose face held firm with shock and anger, Monica placed her hand gently on his upper back. "Well this is good news, honey. You have a grand pappy!"

Phil could only nod. How could his mom have kept this information from him? She clearly hated Nelson, for everything he did and didn't do, but to withhold family from her only son? It made no sense to him.

When Lois returned, she held a small bundle of envelopes. "He used to write me from time to time. I haven't heard from him in a few months, but he's probably still there." She handed Phil the envelopes.

Too angry to say much other than a curt, "Thanks," he turned and marched out of the house.

Monica offered her a quick smile. "It was nice meeting you Lois," and turned to catch up with Phil, who had already reached the car.

Hopping into the passenger seat, Monica looked over at Phil, who already had the car started and was beginning to pull away from the house. "Phil honey, I know you're upset with your mom, but –"

"She had no right to withhold this information!" He yelled at the windshield. "I've lived for twenty eight years and I just now found out I have family I never knew existed!"

"That's true," she replied evenly, "but on the plus side, you have family that you never knew existed." Reaching down, she picked up the pack of letters, studied the address for a moment, and then started typing on the GPS.

"What are you doing?"

"Pleasant Acres is only a couple hours from here. We have all afternoon."

The female GPS voiced stated, "In 2.3 miles, turn left."

"We should do what she says," said Monica.

Phil scowled. "No. Not now."

"Why not?"

"I need to process this information."

"Okay," Monica replied while tucking a strand of her brunette hair back behind her left ear. "We have a little over two hours before we get there. Get to processing."

"In 1.1 miles, turn left."

"Shut up, Garmin!" Phil said, and then chuckled at the absurdity of that comment.

"It's a lovely day for a drive," Monica said with a mischievous smile. "I say we head that direction. If we get there and you're not done processing, we turn back around. I'll even pay for the gas, so you don't have to worry about the cost."

Before that moment, Phil didn't realize a heart could sink and soar simultaneously. Though they had yet to exchange the words, he felt compelled to say, while staring straight ahead, "I love you, Monica."

257

"Oh my," she breathed. Leaning over, she kissed him lightly on the cheek. "I love you too, Phil."

"In 500 feet, turn left."

"I don't love you, Lady Garmin," Phil uttered, but obeyed her instruction and turned.

They had driven for over an hour, mostly in silence, before Phil made his decision. "Yeah, I gotta meet him. He's the only other family I have, and the only one who can tell me anything about my dad. I have a feeling I'll just keep replaying that day until I do this. Oh, and see that couple in the Buick next to us? The wife is cheating on him with her tennis instructor."

"Oh my God," Monica shouted.

"I know, right? Who even has a tennis instructor? Actually, she doesn't have one either. That's just what she's telling Ivan over there."

"Wait, you know his name is Ivan?"

"Yeah I do. That's weird, huh? I don't think I've ever had a vision of another driver before. Oh, and that lady there," he said as he pointed his thumb at the Ford Expedition passing them, "she's thinking seriously about having an affair with the gardener. I see the two of them having way too much fun in the backyard gazebo. It's a really lovely gazebo, with those little ornamental bushes all cut attractively. He does good work! But she's still contemplating the affair. She loves her husband but is super bored with him."

"Wow! You got all that as she drove by?"

"Yeah. Oh, that that family there will go to Cedar Point later this summer. The youngest, Kirk, will get a wicked sunburn."

Monica looked over at Phil. The expression on his face worried her. He seemed far away, deeply ensconced in the lives of those around them. "Phil honey, why don't you pull over and let me drive?"

Turning, he offered her a smile. "No, it's fine, honey."

After another half hour of driving, with his mind reeling, Phil pulled over at a rest stop. As the afternoon progressed, he saw more of the peoples' lives as they passed by. At first he found it comical and more than a little voyeuristic, but it was starting to get a bit much. "If you don't mind driving the rest of the way there," he said softly, "I'm going to try to get some rest."

"That's a good idea," she replied. "I'll wake you when we get there."

Curling up in the back seat, Phil fell into a restless slumber. Though he saw many random lives flutter in and out of his brain, the image his father's final moments kept intruding. The blood ran from several bullet holes, flowing off his chest to pool under him. Nelson tried to speak, but only gurgling emanated from his mouth. However, Phil could hear his dad's final words clearly, as he spoke them directly into his mind. *I can't die now! I'll never get to see my son grow up. Oh God, I should never have let Lois convince me that Phil was better off without me. I'm so sorry, son!*

Phil awoke with a jolt. "Wha?"

Turning to face the back seat, Monica replied, "We're here, Phil. My goodness, are you okay? You look a bit pale."

He took a deep breath and exhaled it violently. "Yeah, I'm okay. I didn't sleep well. Lots of dreams." Opening the car door, he stepped out into the abundant sunshine. "Let's go meet Grandpa Christopher."

As the facility's automatic door slid open, several images struck Phil simultaneously. A woman in scrubs walked by, and he paused to drop his hand upon her shoulder. She turned to glare at him as she uttered, "Excuse me?"

"When you go home tonight, there will be a large mouse in your bathtub. Knowing how much you hate mice, do yourself a favor and call the landlord to meet you at the apartment."

"What?" She said as she pulled her arm out from under his grasp and marched away.

They approached the front desk and Monica said, "Excuse me. We're here to see –"

Leaning in and looking intently at the receptionist, Phil blurted out, "In three weeks, you'll develop skin cancer on your lower back. Get it taken care of now, or you'll be dead inside of a year."

"Excuse me?" shouted the receptionist.

"It's that mole you've been trying to see in the mirror. You were right to question it, but you keep putting off the doctor visit. Please don't."

Placing her arm in front of Phil, Monica gently but firmly shoved him back. "Anyway, we're here to see Christopher Hammel. Is that possible?"

She hadn't finished the last sentence when Phil turned and started telling a male caregiver to avoid the highway on the way home tonight. Monica leaned in and whispered, "I'm sorry about that. I may need to check him in here myself."

"No no no," she said while shaking her head vehemently. "We don't do crazy here. We already have one nutjob in this place." Then her face flushed a bright pink. "Oh, I'm so sorry! I shouldn't have said that about your... anyway, yes, you can see Christopher. He's in room 209. Down the hall, last door on the right."

"Thanks," Monica replied as she grabbed Phil by the hand and gave him a yank.

"Remember," he yelled at the caregiver, "Take surface streets tonight! You can thank me later."

Pulling him close, she whispered, "What's going on with you? You're acting like a…" she paused, but couldn't think of a better word than what the receptionist used, "nutjob."

"I know, I know," he said in his own hushed tone, "I'm sorry. I can't seem to control it. It's like I'm getting flashes of everyone I come in contact with." As if to prove the point, he turned to a young couple who were passing by, pushing an elderly, frail-looking woman with curly silver hair. "I know you both are worried, but she'll be around for at least another year. She's a lot stronger than she looks."

"Uh, thanks?" said the woman hesitantly.

Dragging him along, Monica and Phil arrived at room 209. As she reached for the handle, the door swung open and a clearly agitated woman came rushing out, muttering to herself, "Who does that old son of a bitch think he is, telling me −" Then she saw the two of them standing there and cleared her throat. "Sorry. That guy… Anyway, are you here to see Chris?" When they both nodded she added, "Wonderful! He never gets visitors. Just take what he says with a grain of salt. He's in rare form today." She left without awaiting a response.

Looking intently at the door, Phil took a deep breath, reached out, and pulled it open.

The room, though small, had a nice look and feel to it. Complete with table and chairs, a mini-fridge, and a tiny stove, it somewhat reminded him of his first apartment, fresh out of high school.

In an easy chair facing the window sat a white-haired man. "Um," said Phil tentatively, "hello? Mr. Hammel, may we come in?"

The man slowly turned his head. Deep groves had long formed into his leathery, gaunt face. To Phil, this man looked like a skeleton wearing loose fitting skin.

When he spotted Phil and Monica, his eyes lit up. "Phil? Grandson? Is that you?"

Phil's eyes opened wide. "Grandpa? You actually recognize me? Or..." He had a brief hope that perhaps this man had the same types of visions. His smile expanded as the thought formed.

Bursting into a wheezy laugh, accentuated by a brief coughing spell, he replied, "I'd hoped to keep that up longer. No, your mom called and told me that you might be stopping by. She didn't want you to surprise me and give me another heart attack, I guess. Though personally, I think she's just a party pooper."

His heart sinking, he forced a smile. "Oh, sure, that makes sense. But it is nice to finally meet you." Phil walked over and stuck out his hand.

Christopher took Phil's hand in his and applied a light amount of pressure to it. While Phil's hand had some warmth to it, Christopher's hand felt cold to the touch. "Likewise," Christopher said. "You look like a strapping young man. So who's this lovely lady?"

"This is Monica, my girlfriend." As the word girlfriend came out of his mouth, his face flushed a light shade of pink, realizing they had never formalized their relationship. *So many firsts in one day*, Phil thought.

For her part, Monica didn't even flinch at the comment. Smiling pleasantly, she took her turn in shaking hands, surrounding his hand with both of hers. "It's a pleasure to meet you, sir."

"Oh now, none of that sir stuff. Call me Christopher, or Chris, or Grandpa if you'd like."

As Monica smiled at the thought of calling him Grandpa, the door opened. When the young nurse walked in she said, "Hello Christopher, it's..." When she saw his company, she added, "Oh, you have visitors. How wonderful! I have your pills. Once you take these, I'll leave you to your guests."

Phil stared at the skinny blonde-haired woman. Flashes of her sitting at a desk, surrounding by books and papers, pounded his brain. "Don't worry," he said to her, "You'll pass that test just fine. Just keep in mind that there are 27 bones in the human hand."

"Remember, that's five metacarpals and eight carpal bones," added Christopher, "not the other way around the way you keep doing it. Oh, and your Chemistry book is under your couch."

"Jeez," the nurse said as she turned to leave, "now I'm getting it in stereo." She then spun back and offered a practiced smile. "But thanks, to both of you."

Once the door swung shut, Phil and his grandfather turned and pointed at one another. Simultaneously, they shouted, "You see things too?"

Grandfather and grandson spent the next few minutes attempting to talk about their abilities. However, every time one of them began to speak, someone would walk by in the hallway, and one or both of them would get a flash of that person's life.

"I don't understand this," said Phil. "My visions are usually few and far between."

"Mine too," replied Christopher. "I've never had this many all at once. I swear I can see the lives of half the staff!"

After a few more lives interfered with their conversation, Christopher suggested, "There's a garden area out back. Hopefully, it's far enough away from people so we can actually talk."

"And also think," added Phil. "I can't even begin to form relevant questions with all these people in my brain."

Pointing at his wheelchair, the grandfather said, "If you can help me into that contraption, we'll get out of this room all the quicker."

Fortunately for Phil, Christopher didn't require much assistance. The 85-year-old man could still get around with the use of a walker, so he only needed Phil's stiff arm as a brace to help him stand, pivot, and sit in the chair. Once he was situated properly, Phil grabbed hold of the handles on the back of the wheelchair and rolled him toward the door.

As they entered the hallway, a large, dark-skinned orderly came bounding up. "Where are you two off to? I'm not really supposed to let other people wheel you around. You know that, Chris."

Jabbing his finger at the orderly, Christopher said, "You need to get home as soon as you can, Trey. Trouble's brewing at your house."

"Yeah," said Phil, "the pipe under the kitchen sink is going to burst in the next 20 minutes."

"More like 15," added Christopher. "Your lower level will completely flood if you stay here."

"You'll lose your entire comic book collection. All seventeen boxes."

Trey's eye shot wide open. "What the hell you talkin' about? How could you possibly –"

"I see your couch floating around the room," said Phil with sadness in his eyes.

Christopher shook his head. "Well, only until it gets saturated. Then it sinks. It's a horrible mess."

"If I were you, I'd leave right now."

He turned to look at Monica, who retuned his panicked and disbelieving stare with a stilted shrug.

Trey's right hand clenched into a fist and started shaking. "I love them comics. Got me some super valuable ones."

"Uh-huh. The one with Superman holding up a bus, is that an expensive one? I specifically see that one soaking up with water."

"No!" he yelled as he spun and ran off.

264

Turning to his grandfather, Phil said, "We gotta get outside now. I can't take much more of this!"

Christopher pointed toward a set of glass doors. "It's right there."

Phil rolled his grandfather out the door, pushing him down a winding cement pathway, past ornately trimmed shrubs and small trees. The flowers were still in bloom and gave off a pleasant aroma. Moving them as far from the building as possible, Phil vacated the path, forcing the chair through the short, immaculate green grass.

Finally, both men sighed and smiled. Then they turned to look at Monica. Holding up her hands, she said, "Whoa fellas, don't you start seeing my life! I'll just leave you two to talk. I'll be... somewhere." She gave Phil a quick smooch, then waved and strolled off.

As Phil took a seat on a bench next to his grandpa's chair, Christopher opened his mouth to say something, but decided against starting that conversation now. Instead he said, "So Phil, how long have you had these visions?"

Staring up at the nearly cloudless blue sky, he said, "Well, I was around 7 or 8 when they started, I guess. At that time, they were mostly images of my own life or those around me. Nothing too exciting, just things like what we were going to have for dinner that night, or where Mom misplaced her car keys. Only rarely would I see someone else's life.

"But when I was 13, I saw Dad's death as it was happening."

Christopher's eyes opened up wide. "That's amazing! I too saw it as it happened. I was at work, on the factory floor. I started acting out the scene, like I was in a play or something. Nearly got fired over it."

"That's exactly what happened to me! Well, not the firing part. I was doing a presentation in Lit class when it hit me. And the weird thing is, I've been reliving that vision in my dreams for the last several nights."

"Holy moly! Me too! That's intriguing."

265

"Something, some higher power I guess, clearly wanted us to finally meet," said Phil.

Chris stared at him for a moment. "So Phil, why have you never come to see me before now?"

Anger began to seethe and bubble under the surface. "That's because Lois failed to mention your existence until I asked her about Dad earlier today." Leaping to his feet, he continued, "She kept you from me! She hated my dad so much that she wanted us to have nothing to do with each other. How dare she?"

Christopher motioned with his right hand. "Sit back down, son." When Phil did as instructed, his grandfather placed his hand on Phil's shoulder. "I think we saw exactly why she kept us apart." When Phil gave him a puzzled look, he continued, "You were really young, like two or three, so you wouldn't remember this, but the last time I came to visit, my visions kicked into overdrive. You were getting really fussy too, fidgety, like you had ants in your britches. I didn't think anything of it at the time, or of my increased visions for that matter, but I suspect we were being affected by our proximity to one another. Lois never said anything to me, but I wouldn't be surprised if she knew, on some level, what was happening, and kept us apart for our own wellbeing."

Phil jumped up again and began pacing. "No! That makes no sense! She never believed my visions were real. Though... she sometimes acted like she thought I was possessed, like I was evil. Oh! So she did believe me! She was just scared of me."

"And she often felt the same way about me. She did everything she could to keep me away. It's one of the reasons why she and Nelson split up, truth be told."

Turning, Phil walked back to the bench and sat down. Placing his hand on top of Grandpa's hand he said, "You mean I was one of the reasons why Dad left?"

Moving his hand to be on top, Christopher replied, "No no Phil, not at all. It was never about you. Lois and Nelson should never have gotten married in the first place. They had a fiery passion, but not a true love.

He told me that just after he filed for divorce. He said Lois was scared of me, of my visions, and that made Nelson angry."

"Wait – did Dad have these abilities too?"

"No, nothing. Not even a little bit of intuition. It must've skipped a generation."

"I see. So why did he die?"

Christopher sighed. "Unfortunately, I only know what I learned from the vision. The bank wronged him, or he perceived it as a wronging, but that's all I know. I'm sorry I can't be of more help."

After a pause, Christopher said, "Let's talk about your abilities for a moment. What do you normally see?"

"Oh, it's weird and random. Sometimes I can get a sensation through the telephone, sometimes it's in person, even occasionally it's due to a touch, but that's rare."

"Do you see much of your own life?"

Shaking his head, Phil replied, "No, never. Well, I used to, when I was young, but they pretty much stopped after Dad died. No, that's not quite right. It was after my 11th birthday."

After he told Grandpa the Atari birthday incident, Christopher said, "How did that make you feel?"

He stared at his granddad. "How do you think it made me feel? I was hurt, confused, angry. I hated what seeing things could lead to. I just hated it."

"So, after that, you stopped seeing things from your own life?"

It was as if a light bulb brightened in Phil's head. "Oh my God! That's right. I suppressed my visions. I couldn't stop all of them, but anytime I saw something of my own life, I would shut it down, ignore it, cram it deep inside. I wouldn't allow myself to think about it, even for a moment. I essentially trained myself not to see my own future!"

"It does sound like it," replied Christopher.

"So you see stuff from your life?"

"All the time. In fact, I know when I'm going to die."

That statement, said so casually, completely floored Phil. "Holy crap! You know when you're going to die?"

"Yup," Chris said with a nod of his head.

"When?"

"Tonight."

That simple word nearly made Phil pass out. "You're… tonight? When? What time? Oh my God! How much time do we have?"

He shrugged softly. "I don't know exactly. I assume when I fall asleep tonight, I won't wake up. It looks peaceful enough, my death."

Phil stood up, walked in front of his newly found grandfather, and kneeled. "But…no! We just met! We finally found each other! I have so many questions!"

Patting Phil gently on the top of his head, he replied, "I know you do, son. I know. I wish we had more time, too. But an orderly is about to come and get me."

As if she heard her cue, the glass door opened up and a black-haired woman in nurse's scrubs came out. "Well there you are Christopher! We've been looking all over for you!" Turning her attention to Phil she said, "I'm sorry sir, but I really have to get Mr. Hammel back to his room. He needs his evening medication, a sponge bath, and it's off to dream land."

Phil wanted to scream *NO*, shove the woman to the ground, and wheel his grandfather off to safety. But he knew there was nothing he could do to stave off the death his grandfather already saw happen. Christopher looked up at him and gave him a reassuring smile. This was their first and last meeting. "I understand," he said, both to the nurse and to Christopher, trying not to sound defeated, but failing miserably. "I'll help you wheel him back to his room."

"Okay, thanks," she replied. "Don't look so bummed, sir. You'll be able to visit again, real soon. Isn't that right, Christopher?"

Grandpa nodded softly. "Definitely. This is my grandson Phil, and he's always welcome."

As they returned to the room, Monica was sitting on a high backed, cushioned chair. "Yay, you're back!" She walked up to Phil and placed a hand on the small of his back, kissing his cheek.

"Before you go," said Christopher as he pointed a shaky finger at the nightstand, "there's something in that drawer I'd like you to have."

Pulling open the drawer, he saw a small, thick book. He removed the rubber band holding it together, and saw some scribbled handwriting. "That," said Christopher with a wistful smile, "is my diary. I think people call them journals now, but regardless of what you call it, I want you to have it."

A small tear formed in Phil's left eye. "Wow. Thanks... Grandpa."

"Okay Christopher," said the nurse, "we have to get started now."

"Sally," Christopher said to the nurse "Could you possibly give us just a few more minutes? I think Mr. Hawthorne is about to push his call button."

"It won't be serious," added Phil, "but he'll keep hitting it until you go investigate."

"Best to get it over with now. I'll keep," said Christopher with a sly grin.

Sally pointed at one, then the other. "You two really are related, aren't you? All right, I'll go check on Mr. Hawthorne. I'll be back in five."

"Three actually, but who's counting," said Phil with a smile.

269

She shook her finger at him. "You're both trouble!" Then she left the room.

Christopher said, "Actually Monica, I'm sorry, but do you mind giving us a minute as well?"

"Oh. Of course." She walked over to Chris, and put out her hand. "It was nice meeting you, sir."

Christopher made a 'come here' gesture with both hands, saying, "No no, we're a hugging family, and you're part of this family now."

Now it was her turn to form a tear as she leaned down and embraced him. "Thank you," she whispered.

Once she left, Christopher said, "Oh my. Did you see?"

Phil's brow furrowed. "Did I see what?"

"Concentrate on Monica. Picture her in your mind. Focus on her and her alone."

"But we don't have much--"

"This is important. Do it. Concentrate on her, only her."

Doing as instructed, Phil cleared his mind of everyone and everything except Monica. He could feel her love radiating toward him from the other side of the closed door. He sensed her glowing, beautiful face, smiling at him, caressing his mind.

Then, he saw it.

"Oh my God! It's... I see... our baby! Our little baby girl! She's so perfect!" Phil started to weep. "I never thought I'd be a father, have a family. But there she is, our little, delicate... Crystal! Crystal, named in honor of the grandfather she will never know, but will hear all about."

Christopher's eyes formed a tear as well. "Thank you for naming her after me. I'm honored!"

"So wait," Phil asked, "When is this, exactly? How many months or years down the road is this?"

Grandpa shrugged. "Sorry, I don't know. It's in your future, and that's all I can see."

The two men embraced for a long, tearful hug. "I'm so glad I got this small amount of time with you. I want more, but I'll take this, at least."

On the drive home, Phil kept smiling at Monica. Finally, Monica said, "What? Why do you keep looking at me like that?"

"Oh, I'm just so happy. You look positively radiant tonight. Thanks for coming with me." Though he wanted to tell her, he thought it prudent to wait, at least a little while. First, he had to decide when and how to propose. After all, in that vision, he saw the ring on her finger.

The next morning, after the first peaceful night's sleep Phil had had in over a week, the phone rang. Monica rolled over and said jokingly, "Do you know who it is?"

Nodding, Phil replied, "Yes. It's about Grandpa."

~ Epilogue ~

Before we got married and bought our beautiful house in the country, I lived in South Lansing. For nearly 20 years, I fell asleep to the sounds of traffic, sirens, bingo (seriously – who knew how annoying it would be living near a bingo hall?) and neighbors speaking far too loudly on the sidewalk out front. With the streetlights, as well as floodlights from the parking lots of the surrounding businesses, I learned to sleep without the need for all that much darkness. Even the blinds that covered the windows didn't remove much of the light that filtered inside.

Now, as I lie inches away from my wife, the darkness envelopes us and I cannot see her beautiful face.

From the black I hear a whispered, "Tell me a story."

"Okay, sweetie. I'll tell you my favorite bedtime story."

Though I can't see her at all, I can practically sense her radiant, sleepy smile. "Okay!"

"Once upon a time, there was a king. He ruled his small kingdom with velvet gloves. His people adored him, since he kept them safe and secure. Because his kingdom was poor, he asked very little from them. He only collected enough taxes to keep the streets clean and the perimeter secure.

"However, this king was lonely. He had spent his life in search of a woman to be his queen, and help him rule. Members of his court offered their assistance, as did the townsfolk. He even used carrier pigeons to communicate with maidens from far across the neighboring lands.

"When he acted like he normally did, as a friendly, silly, soft-spoken man, the women would reject him. They would ridicule his choice of clothing, the food he ate, the way he spoke. He didn't have enough money to buy them the lavish gifts they expected from a king. Though he had the power to order their beheadings, he did not do this because it was not his style.

"The older he grew, the more difficult it became. People would gossip behind his back about his lack of a spouse. Was there something wrong with him, they wondered? How could a king not have a queen?

"In order to attract and keep a mate, he started changing who he was. He dyed his hair, wore the trendiest fashions, and even had the sorcerer fix his eyes so he could see without spectacles. He lied about his height, and the net worth of his kingdom. He read parchments that told him to treat women poorly, to lie to them and say cruel things, to lower their self-worth so as to make him seem more desirable.

"He found it wasn't in his nature to be unkind like that, and none of those other things worked the way he wanted. The women he met were after his money, or wanted to mold him into something different. They were vapid and two-dimensional. They were not ladies with which to share his life.

"Then, one day, while strolling through his kingdom, he stopped at his favorite store. At this store, they sold the finest scrolls and parchments. Sitting and reading a tome, the proprietor walked over and said, 'Sire, I would like to introduce you to one of my most loyal customers.' A lovely lady was she, with long, chestnut hair and a sincere, buoyant smile. It only took those few moments of discussion to intrigue him enough to exchange carrier pigeons for further conversation.

"Night after night and day after day, the two swapped notes and sonnets, stories and musings. All that back and forth exhausted those poor pigeons, which made the maiden unhappy because she loved animals, so they prepared plans to meet the next day at the local tavern.

"Normally, the king would've spent the day summoning the tailor for fresh clothing, the blacksmith to create a bauble with which to impress, and perhaps the sorcerer for a potion or spell. However, he felt he needed none of these things. He believed he could truly be himself around her, and would not have to put on airs.

"At the tavern, the king spent the day chatting with the maiden about the latest parchments, the state of the kingdom, and even spoke of the jousting tourney. They both agreed they didn't enjoy the barbarity of such a sport, but understood the appeal of such entertainment to others.

"When the king noticed the time, he walked the maiden back to her hovel. It being a chilly evening, she invited him in, to warm himself by the fire before making the journey back to the castle. She introduced him to her daughter, a lovely girl indeed. The king and the maiden spent several more hours watching the fire and talking.

"Noticing the time, the king excused himself. Taking the maiden's hand in hers, he kissed it gently before departing.

"In the days and weeks to follow, the king and the maiden regularly communicated and visited one another. It didn't take him long to realize he had found the one woman in all the lands with which he truly meshed. He loved how she talked and acted, as well as how she cared for others, both human and animal alike. Her beauty, while considerable, was not the determining factor. Long before his eyes fell for her, his heart had already spoken.

"He saw it in her eyes that she liked him for him, not for who he was or what he could do for her. He found he could be himself—silly, forgetful, sweet, authentic. He did not have to pretend. He could simply be whom God had intended him to be.

"When they met the next day, he said to her, 'With you, maiden fair, I have found the missing piece of my heart. You are the other half of my soul. I love you!'

"Her smile grew ever sunnier as she replied, 'And I love you!'

"Not long after, the king went down on bent knee and asked for her hand in marriage. She gave it gladly, and they were married in the church on a beautiful spring day.

"And they lived happily ever after."

A long pause fills the darkness, and I initially wonder if she has fallen asleep. Then I feel the gentle caress of her fingers on my cheek and a softly spoken, "I love you!"

"And I love you!"

After moment of silence she adds, "I didn't live in a hovel."

"I know."

Acknowledgments:

I'd like to thank:

All of my friends and colleagues at Writing at the Ledges. Without your encouragement and guidance, I would still be writing stories that no one ever reads.

Colleen Nye, for being an awesome friend and, once upon a time, being my awesome publisher.

Pam Bollier and Lori Hudson, for helping me to make this story (and my life) so much better.

My friends and family, for always being there for me.

Wendy, for loving me, being my inspiration, and for lending me your critical eye. You make everything better, and I do mean everything.

About the author:

Randy D Pearson has been displaying his creativity for as long as he can remember. Starting at an early age drawing comic strips and cartoon books, he quickly realized he enjoyed writing stories more than he did sketching.

When he discovered his other childhood passion, the Atari computer, everything came together. He spent many late nights typing stories, winning several writing contests in the process.

His writing kicked into high gear in 2007 when he became a member of Writing at the Ledges. This Grand Ledge, Michigan based writing group helped him to turn his interesting ideas into well-crafted works of fiction.

Since then, Randy's writing has been featured in several publications, including the Washington Square Review, Pets Across America: Volume 3, Small Towns: A Map in Words, Seasons of Life, Voices from the Ledges, Fiction 440: Volume 1, and Retrocade Magazine.

His debut novel, Driving Crazy, was published nationally in 2015. It received rave reviews, both locally and internationally.

In 2018, his latest novel, Trac Brothers, was released to rave reviews.

Visit Randy online: www.RandyPearson.org

Facebook: www.facebook.com/author.randypearson

~ Did You Enjoy These Stories? ~

If so, please help this author by giving him a review!

Go to Amazon

Or to Barnes and Noble's website

Or perhaps Goodreads

Tell your friends

Ask your local library to carry it

Visit him at an event and tell him in person

Thanks for reading Tell Me a Story!

.